Miracle
in the Mist

Elizabeth Sinclair

Gold Imprint
Medallion Press, Inc.
Printed in the USA

DEDICATION:

In loving memory of my dear friend Karen, who now resides somewhere in the mist of time.

Published 2005 by Medallion Press, Inc.
225 Seabreeze Ave.
Palm Beach, FL 33480

The MEDALLION PRESS LOGO
is a registered tradmark of Medallion Press, Inc.

Printed in the United States of America

Library of Congress Cataloging-in-Publication Data

Sinclair, Elizabeth.
  Miracle in the mist / Elizabeth Sinclair.
    p. cm.
  ISBN 1-932815-65-1
  1. Oncologists--Fiction. 2. Hudson Highlands (N.Y.)--Fiction. 3. Vacation homes--Fiction. 4. Women healers--Fiction. I. Title.
  PS3619.I5677M57 2005
  813'.6--dc22

                              2005025284

ACKNOWLEDGEMENTS:

MIRACLE IN THE MIST would never have seen
the light of day without the love, support, guidance
and faith of some very special people in my life:

The Plot Queens: Dolores Wilson,
Heather Waters, Vickie King, and Laura Barone,
guardians of my muse and critique group extraordinaire.

My agent, Pattie Steele-Perkins, who
never gave up, never lost faith.

Vicki Hinze, for her unwavering
support and deep, abiding love of Miracles.

And last, but most importantly, my husband Bob, who
taught me the meaning of faith, trust and love everlasting.

Welcome to Renaissance!

Step into the mist.
Draw up a chair to the fireside
and bask in the healing powers of love.
Whatever your troubles,
you'll find the answers here in the
enchanted, mist-shrouded glen of
the Hudson Highlands.

Renaissance lives in your heart . . .

always near . . .

always waiting . . .

on the edge of a misty miracle.

PROLOGUE

December—Tarrytown, NY

As Anna Hobbs maneuvered her walker to the front of the Tarrytown Library's main room, then lowered herself into the brown leather chair, Durward Hobbs' gaze followed the sure-footed movements of his wife. No longer did she baby herself and spend her days closed up in their small apartment because of her increasingly acute rheumatism. Since they'd come back from the village, she'd reverted to that emotionally strong, gregarious woman he'd fallen in love with over a half a century ago.

Nowadays, Anna Hobbs had a special glow about her that drew people to her. With her snow-white hair encircling her head like a halo, her blue eyes shining, her cheeks rosy with anticipation, and her smile so friendly, she reminded him of one of the angels in the stained glass windows at church. Her always cheery voice warmed him inside, just like a rainbow after a surprise summer shower.

He studied the children gathered around his wife's feet, waiting expectantly for the weekly story hour to begin. With a smile, he settled into the hard wooden chair at the back of the room and waited for Miss Anna, as the children called her, to start her tale. For a while, she thumbed through the worn volume in her lap, trying to decide where to start. As she studied the table of contents, she spoke to prevent the children from becoming restless while they waited.

"In the early 1800's, a boy named Washington Irving lived here in the Hudson Highlands. When he became a man, he wrote stories about his birthplace, which were published in a book called *The Sketch Book of Geoffrey Crayon, Gentleman*." She held the book aloft. The cover showed loving wear, but endured, as did the tales it held. "Some of them make us laugh. Some make us shudder." She shook, as though frightened. The children followed suit and giggled. "It's nearly Christmas and Mr. Irving's stories are more for Halloween. But I'm afraid there are so many wonderful Christmas stories that it'll be hard for me to choose. Do any of you have a favorite?"

"Miss Anna, please tell us the story of Emanuel." The request came from Elethia Stanton, a young girl with a quiet voice and the face of an angel. She cradled a worn teddy bear in her thin arms.

Though her smile seemed genuine to an observer, Durward knew her cheerful mask hid a deep and profound sorrow.

3

Anna glanced at the child, then looked at Durward and nodded almost imperceptibly, confirming what he already knew. This was the child they'd been waiting for.

Anna turned back to the gathering of young expectant faces. As always, when requested to tell the tale of Michiah Biddle and the mist, Anna's face broke into a beautiful smile. But Durward paid little attention to his wife at that point. He sat up straighter, stretching to see the girl better.

"That's the best tale of all," Anna said, laying the book aside, then leaning forward, warming to her subject.

Durward knew his wife loved telling this tale above all the rest.

She scanned the faces in the room. "Do any of you know who Michiah Biddle was?"

A unified "no" came from the children. The young girl listened intently to Anna's every word. Her grandparents stood beside her, her grandfather's hand resting protectively on the girl's slim shoulder. A bright red bandana concealed her hairless head, but nothing could hide the sadness that filled the old man's eyes.

Durward took comfort in the fact that the sadness would soon be a thing of the past. He and Anna would see to that just as soon as the story hour ended.

"Michiah came to the New World a long time ago, when the United States still belonged to England, before New York became a state. He brought with him his wife Rachel, whom he loved more than anything else in the whole world. Together, they built a cabin out near the river."

Half listening to his wife's soothing voice, Durward concentrated all his attention on the girl and her grandparents. The girl smiled, but her grandmother and grandfather exchanged apprehensive looks above the girl's head. Clearly they doubted. Durward smiled to himself. He and Anna had doubted, too, but no more.

Anna continued with her story.

"Michiah and Rachel lived very happily in their little house. After a few years, Rachel had a baby. They named him Emanuel for Michiah's great grandfather. From the very first, Michiah adored his small, inquisitive son. Emanuel had a serious nature and asked questions Michiah, a man of little book learning, found difficult to answer. Where did the robins go when the snow came? Why did the river flow down and not up? Where did the clouds come from?

"When Emanuel reached the age of twelve, Rachel became very sick. Michiah was beside himself with worry that his beloved wife would die. What would he do without her? How would he go on? Searching for solitude to pray, Michiah went into the woods to the top of a hill, a hill where he often sat to think while he watched the Hudson River flow lazily to the sea.

"On this day, a mist had gathered in the glen, blocking Michiah's view. An odd mist, thick and white, it glowed softly from the inside. He stared at it for a long time until his curiosity got the better of him, then, descending the hill, he walked into the fog.

"Later, when Michiah came out of the heavy mist, then climbed back up the hill, the mist had disappeared, but something wondrous had happened to him inside that white cloud. He knew in his heart things would be better. When he arrived home to tell his wife and son of his strange adventure, he found Rachel fixing dinner for the first time in weeks. In his joy of Rachel's recovery, he forgot to tell his little family what had happened in the glen.

"Michiah went back to the hill many times after that, but the mist never reappeared. One day he took Emanuel with him, and while they sat side by side on the top of the hill, Michiah told his teenaged son the story of the mist.

"The young boy questioned his father about what he'd seen in the mist. Michiah said he'd seen nothing, but he'd felt such overwhelming peace and love that, if it hadn't been for Emanuel and his mother, he would have been content to remain there forever.

"Emanuel, captivated by the story, returned time after time to the hilltop, waiting for the mist to reappear, but it never did."

The group began to stir, as if ready to leave. Anna put up a hand. "Wait. That's just the beginning of the story. The best is yet to be told."

Durward turned his attention from the child back to

Anna. His heartbeat quickened in his chest. He slid a little farther forward on the chair. She smiled. Not outwardly. Her face didn't change, but Durward could feel Anna's smile inside him, as if he'd just walked into an open meadow filled with sunshine.

"Two days after his fourteenth birthday, Emanuel's parents died of a fever that swept the valley. Emanuel was very sad, and no matter what anyone said or did, they couldn't cheer him up. He buried his parents together on the hilltop overlooking the glen where his father had seen the mist.

"That same day, some said, the mist reappeared, and Emanuel walked into it. Others said he just ran away into the woods, unable to bear the sorrow of losing both parents, and the Indians got him. Whatever happened, no one ever saw Emanuel again." She paused. "Except for—"

"Except for who?" a young boy called out.

"Shh," his mother admonished. She sent Anna an apologetic smile.

Anna went on, undisturbed by the interruption. "Except for Josiah Reeve."

"Who's he?" asked a little girl in the front row.

"Josiah Reeve ran the local livery stable. A stingy man, he'd hoarded all his money and kept it stashed in a secret hiding place, refusing to give anything to the poor. 'If they can't earn an honest dollar, then let them die an honest death instead,' he'd say.

"Two years after Emanuel disappeared, one of Josiah's horses ran off, and he chased it into the woods. Josiah saw a glowing mist in the glen." The children gasped. "Yes, it was the same mist Michiah had seen. He went into the mist, thinking his horse might have wandered into it and couldn't find its way out.

"When he came out, finding that he'd only been gone for a few minutes astonished him. He thought it had been days. When the town's people didn't believe him, he tried to convince them by telling stories of what he'd seen in the mist. Wondrous tales of an entire village. He told of local people who had disappeared from their little settlement and who now lived inside the white cloud and had strange powers. *And* he had seen Emanuel, not as the boy who had vanished, but as a full-grown man." Anna's voice took on a wispy quality Durward knew well. "But, what he remembered most was the love he'd found there, a love so powerful that no man could resist its pull."

Durward smiled and glanced at the young girl. He knew about love. Love happened when Anna touched him, and he felt a peace beyond description. Love happened every time he looked into her face. Love happened in the heart of every child who listened to her stories.

"When asked to give the name of this village he claimed to have seen," Anna went on, "he said the people called it Renaissance, which means rebirth."

A collective "oh" rose from the children and adults

alike. No one remained aloof for long from the drama Anna put into her tales.

"His stories made the people of the settlement laugh. No such village existed near the river. Nothing could be found there except wild animals, trees, and grass. 'How, when Emanuel was only gone for two years, could he have grown to manhood?' they questioned, laughing harder still.

"But the laughter died when Josiah began to give the poor all the money he'd hoarded all those years. To their amazement, by the week's end, he didn't have a cent, and he was blind. Then they knew something *had* happened to him in the mist. They thought about it and discussed it amongst themselves. They could find but one answer. Something evil lived in the mist and had stolen Josiah's mind. The old man had gone crazy."

She paused and gazed expectantly around the room. "After that, fearing Michiah's glen to be an evil place inhabited by witches and demons, no one went near it. Those that did were never heard from nor seen again. Back then when people couldn't explain something, they always said that evil spirits were to blame. So, when other townspeople disappeared, everyone believed witches in the glen lured them into the fog, then pushed them over the cliff into the river."

"Why didn't they just ask Josiah what happened to the people?" ask a small girl, who had sidled up to Anna and rested her cheek against Anna's knee.

"Because, child, Josiah not only went blind, he also never spoke another word after he told his story and gave away his fortune." Anna patted the child's head gently. "Some say a curse had been put upon him by the mist demons as punishment for telling their secrets. After a while, Josiah also disappeared. Everyone said his craziness had driven him back to the woods and that he'd grown confused and died out there somewhere in the wilderness.

"The cabin that Emanuel and his parents lived in still stands in the woods, but, sadly, their graves are no longer visible. Some say that the woodland flowers grow brightest on the hilltop, and even in the dead of winter, when the weather is bad, the creatures come to Michiah's and Rachel's cabin for shelter, knowing they'll find food, love and protection from harm. Since they loved the woodland creatures, I like to think that would please Rachel and Michiah."

Happy tears rolled down Anna's rosy cheeks. Durward nodded knowingly. Telling Michiah's story always exposed Anna's emotions. It brought back to her the secrets they'd discovered together in the mist.

Story time had ended, and Durward moved to his wife's side, then laid a tender hand on Anna's shoulder. She patted his hand, telling him in her own silent way not to be alarmed. Drawing from her pocket a white, lace-edged handkerchief, embroidered with a small, fancy "A" on one corner, she dabbed at the tears collected on her lashes. He recognized the handkerchief; he carried one much like it.

The young girl and her grandparents came forward. "Is the cabin ready?" the grandfather asked Durward in a low voice.

Touching her heart with the hand clutching the handkerchief, Anna whispered, "The cabin is *always* ready."

The girl pivoted toward her grandmother. "Nana, I'm tired. Can we go now?" Fatigue colored her voice. Her eyes, which should have sparkled with the excitement of life that all children had, were lifeless and sad. Her cheeks were pale and dark circles rimmed them. Her arms, embracing the teddy bear, had grown limp.

"Would you like me to take you to Michiah's cabin now?" Durward waited for the child to respond.

She stared thoughtfully at the teddy bear. Finally, she turned her face up to his. "Yes." Her voice betrayed her fatigue.

The girl's grandfather pulled Durward aside. "I'm not sure I believe all this gibberish about the mist, but if it'll help our little girl, I'll walk barefoot over hot coals." He glanced at his granddaughter. "She's all we have, and we love her dearly." He frowned, blinked back tears, and turned to Durward. "I pray you're right, but I think we need a miracle."

Anna, overhearing the end of the conversation, sidled closer with the aid of her retrieved walker. "If it's a miracle you want, sir, you must believe." She stroked the young girl's thin hand resting on the arm of the chair. "Only faith and trust can make a miracle."

The small group left the library and climbed into Durward's mini van. He steered the car carefully over the ice-encrusted streets and soon they were going down the main highway. Not far down the road, Durward turned into a narrow side road. They bumped over ruts and blown snow piles until they came to a half-hidden driveway.

At the end of the driveway stood a cabin, small and old, but spouting a welcoming curl of gray smoke from its chimney. In the front window a Christmas tree's lights scattered dollops of color on the snow that had collected on the porch.

For the first time that night, the girl smiled a genuine, from-the-heart smile. Durward thought he heard her whisper "I'm home," but it had been so soft that it could have been a bit of breeze blowing through the trees.

> *One word frees us all from the weight and pain of life.*
> *That word is love.*
> — Sophocles

CHAPTER 1

December three days earlier — New York City

Pediatric oncologist, Dr. Steve Cameron, hurried toward the children's wing of St. Francis Memorial Hospital. One hand held a clipboard; the other was shoved deep in the pocket of his white smock. The squeak of his rubber-soled shoes on the waxed floor echoed softly in the deserted corridor. Disinfectants, alcohol, and various other hospital odors familiar to him weighted the air.

In the last five years, he'd made this trip to the bedside of a terminally-ill child more times than he could count; he'd tried to forget these children by assigning them blank faces, while storing memories of them in the far reaches of his mind. Most of the time it worked, but there was always that one child, the child who reached out and wrapped themselves around his heart, who looked at him with eyes filled with trust despite his best efforts to remain distanced. These children were different.

Thirteen-year-old Ellie Stanton, was different. She'd

given re-birth to old doubts, doubts that left him personally defenseless and professionally floundering for stable
footing. Doubts he hadn't experienced since childhood.
Doubts expressed by his stern father more times than Steve
could count. He pushed them back into the darkness they'd
come from and thought instead of Ellie.

The first time he'd seen Ellie was in his uptown office.
If a human replica of an angel existed, she was it. Her
golden curls had hung past her waist, and her big, blue eyes
had looked at him with an inherent trust. She'd stepped
into his soul as no other child had. And no matter what
he'd done, he could not shake her loose.

Since then, her hair had surrendered to the side effects of chemo, but her eyes had never lost the trust. On
more than one occasion, that trust had caused Steve to look
away, feeling less the doctor and more the patient.

Through the years of administering to terminally-
ill children, he'd kept himself aloof, separate from their
emotional pull—a lesson he'd learned his first year of med-
school. But something about Ellie prohibited distance.
Keeping his heart free of the effects of her sunny nature
had been a constant uphill battle for Steve. One he feared
he was losing.

Already, as he stood outside her door, he could feel her
pull, the pull that threatened to suck him into an emotional
vortex he couldn't afford. He took a deep breath, steeled
himself, and pushed open the door to her room.

"Hi, Ellie. How's my favorite girl today?"

To his ear, the brightness lacing his words sounded as fake as the tiny plastic Christmas tree on Ellie's bedside table. Intentionally, he avoided looking at Ellie and focused on the vase of pink sweetheart roses her grandmother had arranged on the dresser that morning. Their light scent filled the room, dispelling the smell of death that only he seemed to detect.

Normally her grandparents hovered over her bed like a pair of guardian angels, but today they'd gone to lunch in the cafeteria, leaving him free to visit Ellie without their presence intensifying his guilt. Their placid masks would have taken a heavy toll on him today. Like their little granddaughter, they seemed to have surrendered to the inevitability of the cancer.

In his heart, he knew Ellie could take full credit for their acceptance. Busy fighting his own emotional demons, he'd certainly done little to help them through this. He envied Ellie her strength and understanding of her fate and found it nothing short of remarkable. She'd already faced more than her share of tragedy, losing her parents in a fire. Her attitude came as close to a miracle as he'd ever seen, though he'd stopped believing in miracles a long time ago—about the same time his mother had died and left him with a father who cared little for, but demanded too much of, a five-year-old boy.

But somehow, Ellie still believed in miracles. He'd

found that out one day after she'd been particularly sick from a chemo treatment.

She'd touched his cheek gently. "Dr. S, do you believe in miracles?"

Words had deserted him. How could he tell a child there are no miracles where cancer is concerned? "What kind of miracles?" he'd asked.

"A Christmas miracle. I prayed for one so I won't die." She'd puckered her brow. "I know that's a hard one, and I probably won't get it, so, just in case, I also prayed that, when I die, Grandma and Grandpa won't miss me too much. I don't want them to be sad. Do you think I'll get my miracle?"

"I'm not sure." Steve had hesitated, chosen his words carefully. "I don't know much about miracles."

"Well, when Mr. Hobbs came to visit me, he said all you have to do to get a miracle is have faith and trust. I believe in God, and Mr. Hobbs says that's faith. And I trust you. So, I have all the stuff I need, right?"

He hadn't answered her. Anger had flooded his throat. Anger at this perennial optimist, Mr. Hobbs. Anger at death for snatching away this child's life. And, God help Steve, anger that Ellie believed in miracles when he couldn't.

He'd started to tell her she'd be better off believing in Santa, but stopped himself. Ellie trusted him. Who was he to destroy her hope, just because he'd been unable to save her life? All those other lives? Hope was all they had left. Death gobbled them up like a hot meal on a cold day, and he could do nothing, nothing except dull their pain and sign their death certificates. He could at least leave them their hope, their belief in miracles—no matter how futile he personally believed them to be.

He roused from his thoughts, then looked at her, clutching her constant companion, Rags, a bald-headed, brown teddy bear missing an eye, her skin pale against its dark brown fur, her hairless head resembling that of her stuffed friend. She looked tired, drained. Deep purple circles ringed her eyes and stood out starkly against her milky skin. Irony played with his mind. Mending the tattered teddy bear would be easier than mending this little girl. The tiny, artificial Christmas tree's cheerful lights taunted him.

"Dr. S?"

Had there been another sound in the quiet room, Steve would not have heard Ellie.

Slowly, he made his way to the bedside. "Yes, Ellie?" He took her wrist and pressed his forefinger on the faint throb of her thready pulse.

"May I go home for Christmas?"

Steve forced a smile to his cold lips and then laid her hand back across the teddy bear's legs. "If that's what you want, I don't see why not." What difference did it make where the end came?

Ellie's face came alive. "My grandpa said Mr. Hobbs will let us use his cabin, and we can have a real old-fashioned Christmas with candy canes and popcorn. He even said we could build a snowman."

Steve's heart twisted. She barely had the strength to lift her hand, much less build a snowman. Why did these people insist on giving her hope where there was none? He straightened, forcing the pain to subside under the sheer power of his refusal to accept it. When she spoke again, he'd already taken two steps toward the door and his escape.

"Don't go yet."

Despite the fact that all he wanted right now was to escape this room, escape Ellie's eyes, he turned back. "Yes, Ellie?"

Ellie slipped her hand under her pillow and pulled out a small box wrapped in shiny gold paper and tied up with a slightly crushed, red bow. She extended it to him. "Merry Christmas, Dr. Steve."

Stunned, Steve took it from her. "I don't know what to say. I'm afraid I don't have anything for you."

"That's okay. You've already given me the best present ever."

Steve stared down at her smiling face. "I have?"

"You gave me love. Mr. Hobbs says that's more important than anything else in the whole wide world."

Her words slammed into Steve's middle like a balled

fist. Had he really given her love? He wouldn't know. He hadn't had much experience with the emotion. Then again, a child could interpret a doctor's care as love. He fingered the smooth paper, and forced a smile to his lips. "My pleasure, sweetie."

She didn't reply. Instead, she yawned, shifted the teddy bear closer in her arms, and then rubbed her pale cheek against its threadbare head. "Please, open it. Mr. Hobbs made it for me to give you."

Fatigue colored her wispy voice. Her eyelids dipped against her pale cheeks, then lifted again. She sought to keep them open, to see his reaction to her gift.

Steve removed the ribbon and peeled back the paper, revealing a small, white box. After lifting the lid, he removed a slab of cotton. A rectangular piece of clear plastic with a string of silver beads threaded through a hole at one end lay in the bottom of the box. A keychain. Inside the plastic, several golden strands of hair curled in a tight circle. He read the words engraved in the plastic. "Faith and trust make miracles."

"The hair's . . . mine," she said. "So you won't . . . forget me." Her eyes drifted closed.

Tears clogged Steve's throat. He swallowed hard and blinked several times to keep them from reaching his eyes. Laying his hand lightly on hers, he bent, then placed a kiss on Ellie's cheek.

"That's not likely, little one," he whispered to the

sleeping child. "I could never forget you."

Outside the room, Steve clutched the keychain and leaned against the cool, green wall. To keep from thinking about Ellie, he concentrated on his heart's slow, steady beat. The plastic edges of her gift dug into his skin. Using his own pain as a shield, he tightened his grip and tried not to think of Ellie's pain. Tried not to think of her disappointment when her Christmas miracle failed to become a reality. And tried not to think of all the other kids who'd waited for the miracles that never came.

Steve classed miracles right up there with UFOs and guardian angels. People reported having seen all three, but until he witnessed one personally, in his mind they'd remain a possibility with a slim-to-zero likelihood.

"You okay, Steve?"

Blinking, Steve met the gaze of his old friend, pediatric cardiologist, Dr. Frank Donovan. A worried expression creased Frank's face; the swarthy face most of the O.R. nurses went to sleep dreaming about.

"I'm fine."

"Sure could have fooled me. You look like hell. Have you given any thought to taking that vacation we talked about last week?"

Pulling himself erect, Steve threw a castigating glare at his friend. They'd talked about vacations many times in the past, and Steve tired of it. "I don't need a vacation." He turned away, and then strode down the hall, aiming his steps in the direction of his office and privacy.

"Right. And the Sahara doesn't need water, either." Frank fell into step beside Steve. "Exactly how long do you think you can keep up this pace before you snap?"

A derisive chuckle burst from Steve. "Have you thought about a stage career? You're getting damn good at this routine of yours."

Frank adroitly sidestepped a gurney being wheeled down the hall by two nurses, who paid more attention to the handsome doctor than where they were going. Frank didn't appear to notice their admiration.

"Hey! This is no joke." Frank's seized Steve's arm. "We're discussing a man's life here. A man I care about."

Looking down at his friend's giant hand, Steve wondered how such paws could perform some of the most delicate open-heart surgery known to man. This burly bundle of laughter and concern saved children every day. Frank gave them back their lives. Why couldn't Steve?

He sobered. "Okay, buddy. No jokes. I'm fine. I just had to stop and catch my breath for a minute. It's been a long day." *Let it go, Frank. Just let it go.* But his excuse went unheeded.

"You don't know how to put in anything *but* long days. When was the last time you had a short day?"

"Look who's talking about long days. When was the last time you went home before the sun peeked over the horizon?" Steve walked faster, trying in vain to lose his friend. Right now, he needed time alone, not a lecture on how hard he'd been working.

Frank waved off the question, and sent Steve an impatient glare. "We aren't talking about me. Dammit, Steve. You won't do these kids a bit of good if you're sharing a room with one of them."

How much good do I do them anyway? Steve wanted to yell back but held his tongue. Frank only wanted to help. To appease him, Steve told Frank what he wanted to hear. "Okay. You win. As soon as Ellie Stanton goes home, I'll take some time off. Are you satisfied now?"

They'd reached Steve's office door. He grasped the knob and felt Frank's strong grip encircling his upper arm.

"Promise?"

Forcing a smile, Steve slapped Frank's arm good-naturedly. "Promise."

Frank studied him for a moment, then, releasing his grip, started to walk away down the hall. Steve watched him go, suddenly feeling like a real louse for being so short with Frank when all he was doing was trying to help.

"Hey." Steve called out. Frank turned but kept walking backwards. "Thanks for caring."

"No problem, buddy." Frank pointed a threatening finger at him. "You better not be feeding me a line of shit just to appease me. If you are, I'll nag you 'til your last breath and if that doesn't work, I'll personally pack your bags and put you on the first boat to the Fijian Islands."

Shaking his head, Steve shoved his hand in his coat pocket. Ellie's keychain scraped his knuckles. He ignored it. "You'll make some lucky lady a wonderful wife, old boy."

Steve's sarcasm rolled off Frank like rain on a greased goose. "Damn straight, but she's gotta catch me first." He flashed Steve a rakish grin, followed with a salute, twisted around, and then sauntered off down the deserted corridor.

For a time, Steve's gaze followed the green-garbed heart surgeon. How much pain did Frank's happy-go-lucky attitude cover up? Frank had lost a wife and an unborn child several years earlier, but how it affected him remained a mystery. He never talked about it, not even to his friends. On occasion, when Frank thought no one was looking, Steve had caught him staring off into space, his face sad and brooding. But as soon as he'd seen Steve the look was wiped away and he was his usual grinning self.

He continued to stare after Frank, then shook his head. He had enough of his own problems right now and he certainly didn't need to buy into someone else's.

Turning the knob, Steve entered his silent office and then flung himself down in his desk chair, wishing Frank would lay off. Steve had enough on his mind without worrying about how to get his well-meaning buddy off his back. Oh sure, he knew Frank had only his best interests at heart. Nevertheless . . .

※ ※ ※

That evening, after supper, Steve signed Ellie's release papers, then watched her grandparents' car disappear down the snow-covered hospital drive, headed for that old-fashioned Christmas in a mountain cabin. He hoped Ellie lasted that long. She blew him goodbye kisses through the back window.

Quite suddenly he felt more tired than he ever had in his life, even when he'd been studying for finals and putting in back-to-back shifts as an intern. He leaned against the stone wall edging the drive and looked around.

Every bush and shrub on the lawn of the city's newest medical facility glowed with colored lights. Colorfully decorated Christmas trees peeked at him through the windows of the apartment complex across the street. In the distance, he could just make out the strains of *Joy To The World* being sung by a disembodied voice.

Joy! What joy came in knowing you'd just sent a child home to die? What joy existed in coming to understand that, despite all his years of training, despite all the money spent on his college degree, despite his unquenchable desire to heal, the children died anyway? None of it mattered. None of it changed anything.

Maybe his father had been right all along. Maybe he just didn't have what it took. Maybe he should have gone into banking where the worst he could do was deny some poor schmuck a loan.

He'd been so sure he could make a difference, save lives, become the great healer. Guess Father really might have known best.

❋ ❋ ❋

Back in his office, Steve took off his coat and hung it on the clothes tree in the corner. He switched on the desk lamp. The golden circle of light fell on the plastic keychain Ellie had given him. He scooped it up, then sank into the desk chair and stared out at the flakes of snow falling past his window.

Maybe Frank had a point, Steve concluded. Maybe, if he rested, he could get back on track, and all these doubts he'd been having lately about his profession and himself would evaporate. Perhaps some time off would expel the demons once and for all—or at least put them in perspective and help him forget his father's dire predictions that he'd never make it in the field of pediatrics.

His mind made up, he checked his appointment calendar. Due to the holidays, he had a light week coming up. He made a quick call to a colleague and then buzzed his secretary.

"Miss Holsted?"

"Yes, Doctor."

"Clear my calendar through next week. I'm going to

be out of my office for a while."

Her pause told him just how much he'd caught her off-guard. "I'll need to know how to reach you in case something comes up."

"As far as you know, I'm out of the city visiting relatives for the holidays. Dr. Andrews has agreed to take my patients until I get back."

"And exactly when will that be, Doctor?" she asked.

For a long moment, he stared down at the beige plastic intercom. He thought for the thousandth time of Ellie and her smiling face, her long blond curls and her Christmas miracle. His fingers curled tighter around the keychain clutched in his free hand.

"As soon as I find a miracle, Miss Holsted." He cut off their connection. His gaze drifted back to the falling snow. "Just one lousy miracle."

❄ ❄ ❄

December — Somewhere in the mist of time
"Am I late?" Meghan Peese flashed an excited grin at the tall, white-haired man hovering in the doorway of her small cottage. "Is the Assignment here already?" The arrival of a child in the village always stirred her blood with anticipation, especially a motherless child.

Meghan never knew her own mother, and the lack of parents was something that resonated strongly with her.

Emanuel returned her smile, a gentle twinkle lighting his gray eyes. With familiar ease and astonishing grace, considering his size, he strolled into the cozy living room. Tucking the folds of his long, off-white robe around him, he seated himself in one of the wingback chairs near the blazing hearth and patted his long, white beard down against his chest. "No, child. I'm early. The Transition hasn't started yet. We need to talk before the village begins the transformation to the material state."

"Oh?"

"This Assignment is a little different from the others you've counseled."

Meghan poured coffee into the two porcelain cups she'd placed on a tray, and then carried the tray to the living room. She pushed aside a small lantern and placed the tray on the low table between the chairs. Returning to the kitchen, she retrieved a plate of sugar cookies, then sank into the chair across from Emanuel.

Lifting one of the cups from the tray, she settled back. "Different? How so?"

"She's prepared to go over."

She placed her cup and saucer on the table at her side, and then picked up her embroidery basket. From its depths, she extracted a lace-trimmed, white handkerchief with a partially completed letter "E" embroidered in one corner.

Odd. Assignments only came to Renaissance to heal. Then they went back into the world to fulfill their lives.

She, as well as everyone else in the little village, knew that Assignments never entered into a new state of being. "A prepared Assignment always goes straight to the celestial level. If the Assignment is prepared, then why—"

"Why come here?" Emanuel sipped from the delicate cup, which looked so incongruous in his large hand, and enjoyed a thoughtful pause. "Ah. Nothing like hot coffee at the end of a long day." He smiled. "Perhaps *prepared* was a bad choice of words. *Resigned* might have covered it more aptly."

Meghan nodded. That made more sense. "Resigned is an entirely different matter. I see why you think this one needs special attention." She paused, her needle hovering above her crewelwork. She was confused. The people of Renaissance never interfered with humans who were ready to pass on to the celestial level. Their job was to counsel the living and help them toward their destinies. "Then again, if the Assignment is resigned . . ."

"*Resigned* not *scheduled.*" He looked around the room at the boughs of evergreens strung from doorways and across the mantel. "You always make Christmas such a festive occasion, Meghan. This room makes a fellow want to put up his feet and stay forever. But then forever is such a nebulous term, isn't it?" His casual observation made, one she'd heard many times before, he breathed deeply of the rich pine odor saturating the air and then helped himself to a frosted star cookie. He sighed contentedly.

Meghan hid her grin and slid the needle carrying a tail of pink embroidery floss through the snowy linen. His appeared to be totally absorbed in the contents of his coffee cup. She knew better and waited. Emanuel would make his point—eventually.

His gaze slid back to her. "This particular Assignment has a special mission, very special." He bit into the cookie and chewed thoughtfully.

She glanced at Emanuel. "Special?"

"Mm. You must make it abundantly clear that her journey through life is not over, my dear," he went on, putting the last of the cookie in his mouth and brushing the crumbs from his beard.

Meghan laid her needlework in her lap. She had no idea what she would do to "make that abundantly clear," but she'd find a way. The amazing thing about working with a human heart and soul was that, when it seemed as if she'd never find her way through the tangle her Assignments made of their earthly emotions, the solution always made itself known to her.

"I shall do my best."

"I'm sure you will, my dear. I'm sure you will."

For a long time, the two enjoyed the companionable silence. Meghan picked up her embroidery and continued to work steadily on the small handkerchief. However, when Emanuel helped himself to two more cookies and a second cup of coffee, it did not escape her notice. Nor did she miss that at one point, he selected an angel cookie gowned in white frosting, studied it for a long time, then with a slight shake of his head, returned it to the plate.

Meghan smiled. As much as Emanuel loved her sugar cookies, he could not bring himself to eat the angels. She mentally put them aside for the new Assignment. Little girls, she'd been told by Clara, the village weaver, loved cookies, especially angels.

As Meghan snuggled up a perfectly executed French knot, then secured the thread beneath it, Emanuel picked up the small, green lantern from the table.

Meghan's attention left her embroidery and centered on the globe, where the lantern's wick would normally have resided. Inside the clear glass ball, a mist gathered and began to swirl, imitating the twin mist she knew had begun to form outside the cottage. Inside the mist a pinpoint of light began to grow and expand until its luminescence reflected off Emanuel's face.

The village elder nodded, replaced the lantern on the table and then announced, "The Transition is beginning."

Meghan gazed outside and saw the thickening, iridescent mist that would soon encase the village. Her heart sped up with the happy expectation of having a child in her house.

"It's time, Meghan."

Smoothing the handkerchief on her knee, Meghan folded it neatly, then tucked it into the pocket of her full red skirt. She straightened the billowing sleeves of her snowy white blouse and stood. "I'm ready."

CHAPTER 2

Central Park, New York City, Six Years Later

Winter's icy breath attacked the few leaves clinging tenaciously to the trees in Central Park. Some gave up the fight and fluttered down around the bench where Steve sat. At his feet, several pigeons clustered, cooing softly and gobbling up the crumbs he'd scattered over the frozen ground.

He hiked his jacket collar around his neck with one hand, fingered an object in his pocket with the other, and then pulled out the keychain Ellie had given him almost six years ago. He'd kept it, not totally as a reminder of Ellie, as she'd wanted, but also as a reminder of all the children who had passed through his care. The words, almost worn off from him stroking it and trying to believe in its message, continued to haunt him.

Faith and trust make miracles.

How much Ellie had believed in those words, and how much Steve wished he could. God knew, he'd spent long enough trying. What had started out to be a week to appease Frank had turned into two, then into a month. The vacation hadn't helped. The doubts about himself and his skills as a healer still haunted him.

Ellie had died anyway. Oh, he hadn't signed the death certificate—Dr. Andrews had probably taken care of that—but Steve knew. Deep in his heart, he knew she was gone. She had to be. That was the way cancer worked. Once it had selected a victim, it rarely changed its mind.

Torn and shattered, he knew, if he went back and watched one more child die, his helplessness to stop it would drive him mad. So, six months after the night Ellie left, Steve had returned to the hospital to work in the geriatric wing. The conclusions there were easier to rationalize. People saw death and the elderly as synonymous. But children . . .

Ellie's death had marked a turning point in Steve's life. Over the last six years, he had recalled all their faces: the Tommys, Patties, Susies and Davids—all of them. All the lost lives. All the children who would never marry, never have their own children, never know the joy of living to old age. One by one, he'd gone through their treatment looking for mistakes, for flaws in his judgment. He'd found nothing. He'd done everything humanly possible and, in the end, his best hadn't been good enough.

He came to the park every day. Sat on the same bench. Mulled over the same thoughts, trying to understand why such things happened. But no answers came. And until he found some, he couldn't go back to the children's wing.

The pigeons scattered, heralding the arrival of Steve's daily companion and halting Steve's thoughts, for the time being.

"Hey there, Mr. C."

Steve looked up into the rheumy eyes of the bag lady whose noisy approach he'd missed. "Hi, Irma. What's new?"

Irma parked her overflowing grocery cart near the bench and took a seat, fastidiously brushing at her grime-encrusted skirt. "Not a damn thing." She flashed him a gap-toothed grin. "Unless you take into account the god-awful orange paint the city slopped on the trash can at 42nd and Madison. It's been run over a few times. I 'spect drivers will find it easier to hit now."

Despite his sour mood, Steve chuckled. A few minutes with Irma always lifted Steve's flagging spirits. He wasn't sure how he would have gotten through the last few months without these daily meetings.

He picked up a small brown bag at his side, opened it, and extracted two containers of coffee. He handed one to Irma. Since he'd met her here almost a year ago, this open-air coffee klatch had become their daily ritual. He felt at ease with Irma. She knew nothing about him, nor did she ask. With Irma, he could be Steve Cameron, any man. He could forget he was a doctor who carried the souls of so many kids on his shoulders.

Irma pried the lid off with fingers gnarled by time and covered to the knuckle with gloves missing the fingertips. She brushed at wisps of her gray hair that had poked through the holes in her ski cap, lifted the cup, took a sip, and stared off across the open park. The icy wind picked up, slamming them in the face. The frozen breath of the north brought moisture to her blue eyes.

Quickly, she hauled a bright yellow handkerchief from her sweater pocket, then dabbed at the wind-induced tears escaping down her reddened cheeks.

Steve had seen the handkerchief before and still found it odd that it was the one thing about Irma that was always fresh and clean. From the "I" embroidered in the corner, he assumed it was also the only personal thing she still retained from her life before she had taken to the streets. She never talked about that time of her life, and Steve didn't ask. He respected her privacy, just as she respected his. Still he couldn't help but wonder silently what had driven her to this life. Had she lost all her money in the stock market, gambled it away, been robbed? There were so many possibilities, but none Steve cared to explore by asking her.

She tucked the handkerchief back in her pocket, then eyed him speculatively. "You're looking poorly today, Mr. C."

No more so than any other day. "I think it's the weather," he explained, glancing at the overcast sky. "Puts a person in a brooding mood. Begs for deep thinking."

"Hmm. Thinkin' 'bout how ugly life can be, I 'spect."

Steve started, unnerved by her intrusion into his thoughts and stunned by her accuracy. She knew nothing of him. How could she know that he saw the world as an ugly, unforgiving place that held little hope for anything but more of the same?

She sniffed loudly, swiped at her nose with the back of her glove, and looked out across the park lawn. "Ah, it ain't all ugly. Take those kids over there, building that snowman." She pointed a shaky finger toward a group of noisy children constructing their version of Frosty. "Now, that's beautiful. Ain't no two ways about it. Children are beautiful."

Ellie's face floated before Steve. "Beautiful," he murmured, not immune to the hint of sadness in Irma's voice.

Irma cleared her throat, straightened her spine, and went on. "Now, just take a gander at that ugly, old maple tree. Looks dead, don't it? But that tree knows it has a purpose, and, come spring, it'll bust wide with buds. Before you know it, it'll be covered in leaves, shading all those youngsters. Rebirth. That's the answer. Sometimes things just need time to come alive again. Time to learn why the good Lord put us on this miserable planet. Time to see the light and forget the darkness."

She turned to Steve. A touch of sadness still lurked in her eyes, but her face held that determined quality that forecasted what she called a new "project." He didn't know too much else about this lady, but he did know Irma loved a good challenge. Steve very much feared, from the look on her face, that, this time, he would be her victim.

He didn't have long to wait until she confirmed his suspicions.

She frowned, the folds of skin nearly hiding the star-shaped scar between her eyebrows. "You need a vacation, Mr. C."

A vacation! Lord, save him from well-meaning friends.

"No. No vacation. I've got too much to do. Besides, I've tried that and running off to the beach is not the answer to what ails me."

She slammed her hands on her hips and glared at him. "Who in hell said anything about the beach? Getting sand in your eyes and salt water in your mouth is hardly what I'd call having fun. I'm talking mountains, Mr. C. Mountains. Fresh air. Sunshine. Endless forests. Mountains. That's the ticket!" She punched the air. "A body needs to take a rest from life sometimes, just like that old maple tree. You need to get your second wind, give your soul an airing-out, and look for the reason you're on this old planet. Whaddaya say?"

Sometimes, he found it difficult, if not impossible, to follow Irma's train of thought. Steve glanced at her in total confusion. "About what?"

"Why, taking a trip to the mountains. What else? It's

just what you need. Get you away from the city and give you a whole new perspective on life. I guarantee it." She leaned closer. "You're stagnating, Mr. C. That's what's wrong with you. Pure and simple. Stagnating. You got yourself in a mental rut, lost track of who you are."

That she had hit so close to what ailed Steve and uncovered the raw wounds, totally unnerved him. For a long time he was speechless. He thought about just leaving, but he knew Irma well enough to know that this would not be the end of it.

He'd seen Irma sink her teeth into one of her "projects" before. Tenacious didn't come even close to describing her persistence. He'd also seen the outcome of her endeavors.

Just last month he'd heard her advise a young girl to try out for the star role in a new Broadway play. The girl not only took Irma's suggestion, she came back a few days later to say she hadn't gotten the role, but she had gotten the part of understudy. Three days later, the star got a plumb offer from Hollywood and broke her contract, leaving the play without a leading lady. The young girl went on in her place. Irma greeted the young woman's news with a knowing smile and "The Lord works in mysterious ways."

But this was different. "No. I don't think so. A vacation is out of the question right now." Still, despite his words to the contrary, Irma's suggestion brought a prickle of intrigue, the first real emotion Steve had felt in months. Against his better judgment, he listened.

"When I was a young girl, a terrible thing happened to me." She sliced the air like a knife with her hand, cutting short any idea he had of asking what it had been. "I didn't think I'd ever get over it. I tried, Lord knows I tried, but it stuck to me like toilet paper on your shoe. No matter what I did, I couldn't shake it off. It just kept getting worse until I felt like it was dragging me down to the very depths of hell." She glanced at him as if to make sure he was still listening. "Then a friend sent me to this cabin in the mountains. I swam in the river, walked in the woods, and discovered who I was and what I want to do with my life. Came back feeling new and shiny." She placed her hand over his, then squeezed. "It was truly a miracle cure. I found myself and my reason for living while I was there. Why don'tcha go there and see what happens? What have you got to lose?"

Steve started. He and Irma had enjoyed an unspoken agreement to let their pasts remain a mystery. He didn't pry into her reasons for taking to the streets, and she didn't ask questions he didn't want to answer. Like what he did for a living. Irma's reference to her past came as a shock. Despite her hands being icy cold, her touch left him strangely unsettled, anticipating more, compelling him to listen to her every word.

An odd warmth invaded him, but despite its calming qualities, he continued to doubt the effectiveness of Irma's miracle.

"I don't know. I really can't afford the time to go running around in the woods."

"Time." Irma scoffed. "Everybody is so concerned with wasting something they can't even hold in their hand. Time is relative." She drained her coffee, recapped the container with the plastic lid, then tucked it into the side of the grocery cart with her other treasures. Before she turned back to face him, she took something from a brown paper bag in the seat of the cart. "The cabin's north of Tarrytown, not far from the river. There's acres of woods and no one around for miles to bother you." She nudged him with her bony elbow. "If nothing else, you can brag to your buddies that you slept where Rip Van Winkle slept and walked where the Headless Horseman rode." Her grin widened, displaying the gaps in her front teeth, making her smile resemble that of a jack-o-lantern. "Trust me. Those mountains are pure magic."

"*The* cabin? You mean the one you went to?" He had never been able to assess Irma's age. But she certainly wasn't a young woman anymore. One day she looked eighty, the next she looked fifty. He'd willingly bet that the cabin had long since turned to fertilizer for the housing development flowerbeds that probably had taken its place. "What makes you think that cabin is still there?"

With a crooked forefinger, she pointed at her chest in the region of her heart. "I know in here. That cabin will *always* be there."

A protest at the absurdity of her belief hovered on his lips but never found a voice. Something sparkled in her suddenly clear blue eyes. Something mystical. Something that convinced him she *did* know.

Without conscious thought, he took the pencil stub and the old envelope she handed him and began, as she drew them one by one from her memory, writing down her disjointed directions.

"To my recollection, there's a caretaker. Name's Howell or Howe or Hobbs. Nice old guy."

This was rapidly becoming more than Steve could swallow. *"Old guy*? The caretaker when you were there?" She nodded. "I strongly suspect the man will have gone to meet his Maker long ago. In fact, my guess would be that they've probably gone through several caretakers since then—*if* this cabin is even there."

"It's still there." Irma extracted the yellow handkerchief from her pocket, lifted it to her cheek, and then smiled. The residue of sadness he'd seen earlier intensified for a moment then disappeared. Replacing it was a magical light that kept intensifying. "I'd know if it wasn't. I'd just know."

Moments later, Steve watched Irma maneuver her grocery cart down the path, the right front wheel trembling like a nervous old maid on her first date. Then she rounded a large, leafless bush beside a high stone wall and disappeared from sight.

If anyone deserved a miracle, it was Irma, and, if there weren't any to spare for her, it must be because miracles were about as real as Irma's cabin.

Glancing down at the envelope, he shook his head. "Nonsense. Pure and utter nonsense." A cabin that should have turned to dust years ago and a caretaker old enough to be Irma's grandfather? Absurd.

As fond as he'd grown of Irma, this cabin of hers—probably born of nothing more than a fragment of her clouded memory—was a pipe dream. He crumpled the envelope. Rising from the bench, he walked to a nearby trashcan, and tossed the wadded paper down the chute.

Resolutely, he made his way down the path in the opposite direction, away from Irma. As he walked, he slipped his hand in his pocket to finger the ever-present keychain. This time, however, it was not the only item in his pocket. Stopping, he pulled out the foreign object. In his hand, neatly folded, lay the envelope he'd just thrown away.

CHAPTER 3

Somewhere in the mist of time

Meghan."

Meghan looked up from her embroidery. She hadn't heard Emanuel enter her cottage, but that hardly surprised her. She'd gotten quite used to his soundless comings and goings.

Almost imperceptibly, she nodded, then went back to pushing the sharp needle through the soft, blue material of the handkerchief. Normally, his sudden appearances gave her reason to smile. Normally, when she sensed he would come, she had his favorite sugar cookies and hot coffee ready. And normally, she welcomed his visits.

But she didn't feel like she did every other time. From the moment she'd awoken that morning, she'd felt like she had a cloud of doom hanging over her. Worst of all, she had no rational explanation for it, nothing that made sense at all. At first, she'd thought she might be sickening with something, but she'd never been sick. In fact, she could not recall anyone in Renaissance ever being sick. Then she decided she might have just slept too long and was feeling groggy. But then she looked at her bedside clock and saw that she'd only slept four hours.

She had no desire for Emanuel to see the telltale emotions she knew lurked in her eyes, or, when she finally voiced her unusual request, for him to ask the inevitable questions. How would she answer them? She didn't have any idea what fostered the dread that had been with her since that morning.

Her head bent farther than necessary to oversee her movements, some of her white-gold hair fell forward across the material caught up in her embroidery hoop. She brushed the strands away from her face, then went back to her crewelwork.

"Are you ready for your new Assignment? It's going to be a difficult one."

Again she nodded, but kept her head down, her gaze fastened on the intricate stitches. His announcement itself didn't disturb her. After all this time, she knew what to expect, and this wouldn't be the first difficult Assignment she'd had to contend with, nor would it be the last. What did disturb her was that even before Emanuel made this pre-Transition visit, every corner of her being had been filled with a horrible sense of dread. Why? Were they somehow linked?

She stabbed the needle through the cloth, as if by the

sheer power of her action, she could pierce the wall hiding the answers to her dilemma. Then, without raising her gaze to his, she voiced the question niggling at her. "Can someone else take this Assignment?"

Emanuel placed a gentle hand on her shoulder. "You know that isn't an option. Once you're charged with the duty, it can't be changed."

Meghan didn't respond. She heard Emanuel take his usual seat in the wingback chair. She glanced at him from beneath her lashes and could almost see the questions forming in his mind. What would she tell him?

Her deeply drawn breath brought to her the orange pomander's spicy scent, reminding her that Christmas was not far off. Christmas. A time for giving of oneself.

In the past, Christmas made her heart light, her spirits soar. Not this year. With each tick of the mahogany grandfather clock, the time for the Transition crept closer and closer, and her heartbeat grew heavier and heavier. She was glad the clock had no hands to count off the passing minutes. A small blessing.

The fire's crackle echoed that of her brittle nerves. Tense silence saturated the cozy room. She studied Emanuel. He leaned back, placed his elbow on the chair's arms, then rested his chin on his curled fingers and centered all his attention on her. Even after she'd moved her gaze back to her crewelwork, she could still feel his probing study of her.

"Will you tell me what prompted this request?"

She'd expected his curiosity. After all, she usually anticipated an Assignment with enthusiasm. But how she dearly wished this one time he would not ask and would rely on his ability to read her mind. She scrambled for an answer that didn't sound ridiculous. None came.

"A feeling . . ." She dropped her hands to her lap. ". . . that this Assignment will alter things." She toyed with the edge of the handkerchief, tracing, and then retracing the tiny stitches with her fingernail.

"A feeling? What kind of feeling?"

She frowned. "I don't know. I feel as if something is going to happen, something terrible." She looked at him with a plea coming from her heart. "Are you sure someone else can't take this Assignment?"

Emanuel nodded solemnly. "I'm sure." He took her hands in his. "What we do here is much like the fabrics Clara weaves for the village. To be strong, all the threads must work together, each doing its job. If one thread breaks, the design changes radically, as does the fabric's strength. Now, Clara can leave the thread that way and hope that the flaw won't weaken the finished product, or she can replace the broken thread and insure that this fabric will be as strong as the last. In the end, for the good of the fabric, each thread must do its assigned job." He gazed at her with understanding eyes. "It is not for the threads to question the wisdom of the weaver."

She sighed. Where were the reassuring words that her premonition had no basis in fact? She'd expected his help, and he offered only riddles. "But I—"

Emanuel held up his hand to stop her words. "You know as well as I that we cannot alter Fate to suit our whims. We can only show the way. If the showing leaves a lasting effect on us, or on those we love, then we must accept that as part of Fate's design. We must live out our destinies. Even if I could appoint someone else, I wouldn't. Aside from being difficult, this Assignment requires special attention. No one else can handle it."

She tore her hands from his grasp. "Fate! Weavers! Threads! You speak in riddles, old man!" Meghan spat the words as if the very presence of them on her tongue left a bad taste in her mouth. No sooner had they passed her lips than she regretted her outburst. She tucked her unfinished embroidery into the wicker basket on her lap, then cast a repentant glance at Emanuel. "I'm sorry."

He said nothing, but smiled tenderly, then patted her hand.

What had come over her? She never lost her temper or asked for special consideration, but then, she'd never before felt this uneasiness about an Assignment. When she turned to Emanuel with one more plea, desperation colored her voice. "Are you absolutely sure *nothing* that can be done to delegate this Assignment to someone else? The rules can't be altered just this once?"

In response to the shake of his head, a thick wave of snowy hair fell across his forehead, then swung back and forth. "Nothing." He stood. His robe settled in soft folds around him. "I'm sorry, Meghan." He walked slowly toward the front door. With his hand poised on the latch, he looked back at her. "The Assignment will be here, as always, shortly after the Transition. Despite your misgivings, you will do well. I have faith in you." He paused still longer, then asked, "The boy is well?"

She glanced at Emanuel. "You know he is. Why do you ask?"

"I sense that he worries you."

She frowned, and looked back at her embroidery. Timothy did worry her. He'd been brought to the village some time ago and still hadn't spoken a word. He should be with his parents for Christmas, but until he disclosed their identities, the village would remain his refuge.

"You worry without reason." Emanuel's deep voice cut into her thoughts.

"I try not to, but he's so young to be lost in the woods and separated from his parents. Since the Guide brought him here, he's cried himself to sleep every night. If only he would speak . . ." Reaching into her basket, she extracted a wad of dark blue thread, then began untangling the snarls as if in doing so she could bring the same order to her thoughts.

"He will speak again." The door latch clicked loudly,

and a gust of spring-like air invaded the warm cottage. "When the time is right and there is good reason for his voice to be heard." The door closed behind Emanuel.

Meghan rested her head against the back of her chair, exhaled a long sigh, and gazed around the living room.

Large and open, the room glowed softly, the age-darkened wood paneling mellowed in the firelight. In the daytime, the four mullioned windows allowed the rays of the sun to bring life to the brilliant reds, greens and oranges she'd used to decorate. A happy home, it came to life with the sound of her voice humming softly off key. The touch of her loving hand was evident everywhere.

Down through the timeless years she'd spent here, it had become a reflection of her. The cottage *was* her. Was her home in danger? Was that what this strange feeling meant? Why couldn't Emanuel have broken his silence just this once and told her what to expect? But she knew he wouldn't. Concerned that the Healer might make a pre-judgment, he always kept all the details about the Assignments to himself.

Her gaze drifted to the glass cabinet where she kept special mementos of other Assignments. The faded beauty of a dried, yellow carnation; a scrap of old lace from a wedding gown; and a bald, one-eyed teddy bear. She'd kept herself separate from all of them, and she could do it again.

Fate could not be altered. She knew that. Still she made

a vow to the silence. *This Assignment will be no different than the many others I've successfully completed. I'll give what is expected of me—nothing more. Nothing will change. Nothing.*

Meghan slipped back into the loving embrace of her favorite chair and picked up her embroidery. With grim determination, she put the finishing touches on the monogrammed "S" she'd worked into the intricate design on the blue linen, man's handkerchief, and tried not to think about how she no longer felt a part of the village. She tried not the think about one day losing all this, one day being an outcast from the life she'd always known here.

❄ ❄ ❄

Hudson Highlands, Upstate New York, just before Christmas

For the thousandth time that day, Steve told himself he had embarked on a fool's journey. Trying to find Irma's cabin, in his book, made him certifiable. If she and Frank hadn't ganged up on him and talked him into this hair-brained adventure, he'd be home in front of the TV watching reruns of some sitcom.

He steered the car around a sharp curve in the unpaved road the Tarrytown mechanic had said led toward the river. He'd heard of the cabin Steve had described, he'd assured Steve, and it was off this road somewhere.

Somewhere. A key word in this little treasure hunt. He recalled the mysterious appearance of the envelope in his pocket. Now, as then, he had no rational explanation as to how, in a matter of seconds, and with no help from anyone, the envelope had gotten from the trash into his pocket. More than anything, that incident had prompted him to see if Irma's cabin did, indeed, exist beyond the fringes of her tired imagination.

He was going to ask Irma about the envelope, but he hadn't seen her again since that day. It was almost as if she'd done what she'd planned to do and had no further need for their meetings in the park. Odd. But then, Irma was not your normal run-of-the mill bag lady either. He sighed and tried not to think about how she'd made this seem like a life or death decision to come up here.

If nothing else, the drive had made the trip worthwhile. The winter sky, cloudless and bright blue, made an artistic backdrop for the skeletal trees lining the snow-covered road. Despite it being mid-December, an intermittent breeze held the faint promise of spring.

Steve daydreamed about what the landscape would look like green, and dotted with wildflowers. Too late, he noticed the mound of snow in the middle of the road. He slammed his foot down hard on the brake pedal. The car skidded sideways. The steering wheel snapped from his grip. He snatched it back, and then jerked the wheel. As the car careened over what had looked like harmless snow, the sound of crunching metal filled the wintry silence. The car came to a stop with the front end teetering on the edge of the ditch bordering the road.

Cursing softly, Steve climbed from the car. No need to check for damage to the undercarriage. The large rock that had been hidden in the mound of snow and that now jutted out from the roadbed behind the bumper said it all. Between the sound of ripping metal and the heavy stream of oil turning the white snow an ugly black; he knew trouble had found him. He slammed the door. The car quivered, pitched forward, and, with a metallic groan, ended up with the front bumper buried in the ditch.

Great!

He looked around for a house. Not a building in sight. Nothing but trees and more trees. Resigned, he started walking. Just as he started up the road to town, the glimmer of something red caught his eye. At first, he thought it was a bird, but a closer look revealed the eave of a roof.

A house!

Pushing through the bushes, he started toward it. He skirted rocks and downed trees, weaving and winding his way blindly through the snow. Oddly, the farther he walked, the farther away the house seemed to be. He trudged on. After a few minutes of walking, he looked behind him. The car was lost to sight. Although he hadn't come far, the trees seemed to have closed in on him, cutting him off from everything.

He said a silent prayer that he hadn't been wrong about the house. A born and bred city boy, if he had to retrace his steps, he wasn't at all sure he'd find his way back. And if he didn't find his way back, he'd end up freezing to death out here and not be found until spring.

A few minutes later, the trees thinned into a clearing surrounding a small, log cabin. Could it be? No. His luck didn't run that good. Yet, there it stood exactly as Irma had described it—made of logs, a wide front porch stretching from one corner to the other, smoke curling from the fieldstone chimney and a roof covered with shingles the dark green color of a pine tree.

He *had* to be mistaken. There had to be hundreds of cabins in this remote area. What were the chances of him stumbling, quite by accident, onto the very cabin he sought? Zero to nothing, he figured. He'd be better off hoping that someone was at home and that they had a telephone to call the Tarrytown garage.

The thought had barely crossed his mind when the door opened and an old gentleman in a blue parka, looking oddly as if he'd expected him, stepped onto the porch.

"Hello, there." He descended the steps, and headed in Steve's direction. "You must be Mr. C."

About to extend his hand, Steve paused, his mouth gaping open in surprise. "Excuse me? How—"

"How did I know who you were?" The old man chuckled, his green eyes sparkling with some hidden merriment. "Irma told me to expect you."

"Irma? But she—"

The man held up his hand. Work calluses encrusted the upper part of his palm and fingers and a plain gold ring encircled the third finger. "Irma has her ways, my boy. And crotchety as she can be, it's best we don't pry into them."

That was the fist thing the old man had said that Steve didn't question. Irma could get downright unpleasant about having to explain herself. She had her own means of communicating around the city, and they didn't include modern conveniences like the telephone, the US Mail, or telegrams. What they did include, he didn't know. Nor did he want to know. Once, he'd made the mistake of asking, and she'd gotten so testy, he'd never mentioned it again. The old man was right. Best they leave Irma's secrets to Irma. One thing was not a secret. The more he learned of her, the more questions he had.

"Name's Hobbs. Durward Hobbs." The old man extended an arthritic hand to Steve. "I'm the caretaker here, like my father and his father before him."

Well, that explained Irma knowing the caretaker. It had probably been his grandfather that Irma remembered from her childhood. Steve felt a little reassured. Maybe he hadn't stepped into the Twilight Zone after all. However, the envelope incident still needed explaining, and Steve planned on asking Irma about it just as soon as he got back to the city. Right now, more important things had to take precedence—like his car. "My car is—"

"Wrecked." The old man smiled at Steve's slack-jawed

expression. "Heard it hit bottom. Nasty rock, that. I been after the county to get it out of there for months. All they need is to bring in a road-grader to push the rock into the ditch. You're about the fifth person this winter to lose an oil pan on it." He clicked his tongue and shook his balding head. "Makes a body wonder where our tax dollars go." He clasped Steve's arm, then guided him toward the porch. "Don't you worry about the car. I'll call the garage and have it towed in."

Dazed, Steve allowed himself to be guided up the steps. He might as well go along with Hobbs. Obviously, he had about as much control over this situation as a snowball rolling hell-bent-for-leather downhill. "I'm afraid it's wedged with the front end in the ditch. If they can get in there to tow it out, it'll be a miracle."

They ascended the stairs together. Mr. Hobbs reached for the door, stopped, then turned, his gaze mesmerizing Steve. Hobbs' eyes held the identical sparkle that Irma's had that day in the park. And like that day, Steve knew if he looked away for a split second, he'd miss something very important.

"Now, miracles ain't all that hard to come by," the old man said. "Faith and trust. That's all you need, my boy. Faith and trust."

* * *

An hour later, after having given him the twenty-five cent tour of the cabin, Mr. Hobbs disappeared into the woods, leaving Steve to wonder if he'd just had the screwiest dream ever. He backed into the cabin, then closed the door. It couldn't have been a dream. If Hobbs had been a figment of his imagination, then who had prepared the cabin for his arrival? Who had started the fire in the hearth? Who had filled the cupboards with provisions? Who had made up the bed in the little room off the kitchenette?

He pulled the keychain from his pocket, and looked at the nearly illegible words carved into the plastic. *Faith and trust.*

Steve shook his head. The old man had a real attachment to that phrase. First, he'd carved it in the keychain Ellie had given him. Now, the old fella had repeated the words three times in the space of a few minutes, as if by sheer repetition, he could bring Steve to believe in them.

"Ain't gonna happen," Steve muttered.

The keychain still clutched in his hand, he glanced around the cabin. Not palatial by any means, but very cozy, despite needing the touch of a good decorator. The furnishings were eclectic, to say the least—a couple of well-worn but serviceable couches flanked the fireplace, a table and two mismatched chairs were tucked away in a corner, a hand-braided oval rug covered the worn pine board flooring and over the mantel was a mounted moose head. A cobweb hung between two of the antler points and a bald spot had begun to emerge on the neck.

Steve moved and could have sworn the animal's eyes followed him around the room. He shook his head. His imagination was working overtime. Maybe he needed this vacation more than he thought he did.

A little fresh air might bring some order to his crazy thoughts. Maybe he'd take that walk toward the river that Hobbs had recommended. The old man had assured Steve he wouldn't get lost on the well-marked path. Steve stuffed the keychain back into his pants pocket, grabbed his red plaid, wool jacket, and headed out the door.

The afternoon had just begun to wane. The cloudless sky showed faint signs of evening approaching. Purple and red streaks painted the horizon just below the setting sun. If he didn't want to end up wandering around in the dark, he'd have to make this a short walk.

A few minutes later, Steve paused at the foot of a hill, then glanced at his watch. About a half an hour before sunset. He should start back. But the fresh air had him feeling better about life in general, and he loathed returning to the cabin before he had to. Maybe he'd just walk a bit farther. He trudged forward, to the top of the hill.

It overlooked a small glen and, just beyond, he could make out part of the frozen Hudson River. The deep blue and orange sky reflected off the snow, turning everything to a soft, dusky salmon. He breathed deeply of the unpolluted air.

A man of medical science, who didn't pay much attention to anything that didn't come from a lab or a prescription bottle, he could never recall being this aware of nature before. Trees had always been somewhere to shelter during a sudden shower or to provide shade on his visits to Central Park on a hot day. Snow had been an encumbrance that had to be tolerated each winter and which, at best, gave the school kids an unexpected holiday and, at worst, made a snarl of city traffic until it either was removed or melted.

Today, everything seemed to have taken on a magical quality that took his breath away. The trees appeared to have been ripped off a Christmas card and plopped down here. The snow lay like a blanket of sparkling diamonds waiting to be harvested. Steve was loath to even step on the unmarred surface. If the cold hadn't started to seep into his bones, he could have stayed here forever, just drinking in the winter beauty of his surroundings.

Ready to turn toward the cabin, a shifting fog in the glen captured his attention. He studied it closely for a moment. An odd glow emanated from inside the misty cloud. Even as he watched, the glow intensified, growing brighter and brighter by the minute. He'd never seen anything like this in his life. Driven by his naturally inquisitive nature, he hurried down the hill.

At the bottom, the glow appeared even more brilliant. Incandescent. What could be inside the mist that gave off such a light? Thinking it would be safer to just ignore it and get back to the cabin, he turned away. Then, as if it were magnetized, he found himself being drawn around to face it again. Although his brain told him this was probably a very foolish thing to do, his body moved forward, seemingly controlled by something or someone outside himself.

Cautiously, he stuck his hand into the mist and then quickly pulled it back. He looked it over. Nothing different. Once more he slid his hand into the fog and left it there. When nothing happened, he stepped through the wall of white. Warmth overwhelmed him, stealing the chill of the cooling day's air from his body. Oddly, the warmth seemed to come not from anything in the mist, but from within him. He walked deeper.

Trails of foggy mist swirled around him, enveloping him. Breathing became difficult. Nearly impossible. His lungs labored for his next wisp of air. But no discomfort accompanied it. He could barely feel the ground beneath his hiking boots. He pushed deeper into the mist, unable to turn back, but at the same time searching for a way out.

Gradually, the cloud thinned. Steve found himself standing before a gently arched, narrow footbridge leading to a small cluster of cottages. A village? Neither Hobbs nor the mechanic had said anything about a village by the river. He crossed the bridge slowly, taking in his surroundings.

A thatched roof capped each of a half dozen stone dwellings. Long fingers of gray smoke curled from the chimneys with the promise of warmth inside. Bright flowers spilled from crudely made window boxes beneath mullioned windows. More flowers hugged the cottage's foundations. Then it suddenly hit him. Flowers? In December? How very odd.

Almost simultaneously, he became aware of the smell of spring in the air. Curiously, although at least six inches of snow had covered the woods he'd trekked through, none lay on the ground here. Almost as if some unseen finger had drawn a line of demarcation and not allowed winter to pass beyond the wooden footbridge marking the threshold to the settlement. Strange. A shiver ran down his spine.

Steve shook himself. A logical explanation could justify the absence of snow and the blooming flowers. Probably the warmth of the mist or an underground hot spring. Nothing strange about that. After all, if Maine could have a desert, why couldn't this garden spot exist in the middle of a winter landscape?

Satisfied with his logic, he looked around him. No shops lined the narrow, dirt street. An occasional wooden sign swayed in the breeze, proclaiming it to be the house of a weaver, a teacher and a storekeeper.

What an odd little place. Where were the people? The square in the center of the village appeared deserted. Oddly, inside him, he could feel the throbbing pulse of life going on here and a sudden, inexplicable need to be part of it.

He backed away, denying his feelings. A village meant

people, somewhere, and he'd been enjoying the solitude of the deserted woods. He had no desire to make idle talk. Besides, this place gave him the creeps.

Quickly, before someone discovered his presence, and before his hallucinations went into overdrive, he strode back across the bridge toward the wall of fog. He'd go back to the cabin, have a stiff shot of Scotch and get a good night's sleep and all this would begin to make sense, he told himself.

Just as he felt the warm mist close around him, he heard a voice, a woman's voice.

"You can't go back, Dr. Cameron."

CHAPTER 4

Meghan stood in her cozy living room, calmly studying the swirling mist in the lantern's globe, waiting. Dr. Cameron would reappear quickly enough. After all, he couldn't go anywhere else. The first of many lessons he'd have to learn before leaving Renaissance. Rarely did it take an Assignment long to understand that the village, a law unto itself, ignored scientific facts and logic as the outside world perceived them. The fact that he was a doctor might make this a little harder to accept. But all that would come in time.

Placing the lantern back on the table, she walked outside and slowly made her way toward the small footbridge. A soft breeze whipped her hair around her face, blocking her view for a time. She swept it back impatiently and moved to the edge of the footbridge, then stopped, her gaze fastened on the swirling mist.

Moments later, Dr. Cameron stepped through the mist and back inside the perimeter of the village. He strode purposefully toward her, his gate transmitting his displeasure with being herded back.

At one glance, she could tell he was not only very handsome, but also he was a man to be reckoned with. He had the build of an athlete, lean, muscular, made for movement. Far from what she'd been expecting. The last doctor to enter the mist had been soft and slow, a product of his sedentary life style. Not so Dr. Cameron. His dark hair was mussed from the wind and his cheeks were red, perhaps more from anger than the cold. His dark-eyed gaze locked on her.

He approached her, quickly, with all the deliberation and grace of a stalking cat. Meghan concentrated all her senses on him. Slowly, the aura of awareness began to form inside her. Precisely, she analyzed each emotion emanating from her new Assignment. Frustration. Despair. Indecision. Guilt and a lack of self-esteem. No. Not self-esteem. Confidence.

Meghan continued to mentally monitor his approach. She sensed more. A dark part of this man that needed illumination to heal. She targeted her mind on this place he kept hidden. Scars. Each scar had a name. Billy. Mary. Sheri. David. They went on in a never-ending list of the souls he carried on his conscience.

But she detected something else, something she couldn't identify. It seeped into her on a very personal level. For the first time ever, Meghan was aware of the man and not just his soul. She took a step back, not in fear of him, but the feelings generated by his presence.

He stopped a few feet from her, fisted hands resting on his hips. "What in hell is this all about? How did you do that? How do you know my name?"

These questions he hurled at her didn't surprise her. She'd heard them all before, maybe not this forcibly, but definitely in similar words. She tried to ignore her earthy reaction to him and zero in on his emotions.

Despite her efforts to push aside the strange sensations his nearness brought on, under the glaze of anger, the defeat, the scars of the children's deaths, lay shadows of things she couldn't clearly make out in him. Things that made her pulse pump and her breath catch in her throat. Her soul seemed to blossom forth, reaching for his.

Meghan sucked in her breath. Another totally foreign sensation bombarded her senses. Her heart contracted. The dread she'd experienced earlier, but had been unable to explain adequately to Emanuel, came rushing back—a hundred times stronger. Instinctively she knew that this man represented more than an Assignment. Somehow, she was unequivocally bound to him by a link that had nothing to do with being his Healer.

Normally, Meghan went to extra measures to ease the confusions and frustration each Assignment felt initially, to see that they were put at ease as quickly as possible. In Dr. Cameron's case, and considering how her senses pulsated just standing near him, throwing her arm around his shoulder for comfort didn't seem to be a safe answer. She averted her gaze, giving herself time to regroup her emotions, to fight off the foreign sensations he'd brought to life in her. Marginally successful, she turned away, then, speaking to him over her shoulder, she began walking slowly toward her cottage.

"I'll answer all your questions. But since you're not going anywhere for sometime, let's do it in comfort, shall we. Please, come with me, Dr. Cameron." She fought to keep her voice soft and even.

A strong hand ensnared her upper arm. He spun her toward him. "What do you mean I'm not going anywhere? I want some answers now. What the hell is happening?" Then he smiled knowingly. "I know. I fell asleep under a tree in the woods, and I'm dreaming. Right? I'll wake up, and you'll be gone and everything will be normal again." When she didn't answer, his expression darkened again. "Answer me, dammit!"

Men of science are always the hardest to convince, Meghan thought.

She avoided his glittering, dark-brown gaze and instead looked pointedly at where his hand gripped her arm. Fighting to ignore the sudden surge of heat that emanated from his hand, then chased through her body with the speed of a lightning strike, she looked at him. "I've already told you I'll answer any questions to your satisfaction . . . inside the house." His gaze followed hers to one of the small, thatched cottages to the left of the footbridge. He held onto her for a moment more, then seeming to have come to a decision, released her.

They walked the few paces to her house. After ushering him inside, she took his thick, red plaid jacket and hung it on the pine-doweled coat rack. Leaving him to wander around the cozy room, one hand stuffed in his jeans pockets, she hurried to the kitchen to get the coffee and try not to think about how, when he stepped inside, her house seemed to shrink in proportion to his overwhelming presence.

She noted, while stealing covetous glances at him, his firm step and his proud carriage. Who was this man? Why did her soul reach out to him in a way that caused her such alarm? What did he conceal within that small, dark corner of his being that she couldn't penetrate? And what had caused her to react to him as she had? She'd had male Assignments before, some more handsome than the young doctor. What made him different?

"This is a strange collection you have here," he called from the living room. "A piece of material, a dead flower and a bear with one eye. Aside from luring unsuspecting strangers into the village, is this your hobby?" Sarcasm dripped from his words like sap from a sugar maple.

She peered through the opening beneath the cabinets that provided her with a clear view of him. She gave no answers. Far too soon for him to learn the stories behind her keepsakes. In time. All in good time. After he'd accepted. After she could look him in the eye and think coherently at the same time.

He stared at the bear. Reaching out a finger, he ran it over the stuffed animal's threadbare head. Another moment passed. He shrugged. She carried the tray into the living room. He turned toward her, his gaze asking a myriad of questions.

Once seated, Meghan poured coffee for both of them, leaving him to add sugar and cream to his. He took neither. A purist, she thought. He didn't believe in wading through the trivia to get to the heart of the matter. Emanuel was right. This one isn't going to be easy—in more ways than one. A soft sigh escaped her lips, drawing his attention.

Whatever scars he carried on his soul, he was strong, healthy, and had a look of unbendable determination. Her unruly mind immediately began assessing his broad shoulders and how his Irish-knit sweater and jeans molded to his body just right.

She blinked and then dragged her attention to her cup of coffee. Nonsense thoughts, she told herself, but the lingering sensations her appraisal of him had produced testified differently.

"Well? I'm waiting."

At the sound of his deep voice, she lifted her gaze to meet his. Again that connection to him assaulted her. "Waiting?"

"For an explanation. You said you'd supply one after we had coffee." He elevated the porcelain cup, as though she hadn't noticed it residing in his strong, finely boned hands. The hands of a doctor. Perhaps hands of a lover?

She took a deep cleansing breath. She had no idea what had prompted such an outrageous thought, but this had to stop. Resolutely, she directed her thinking back to the questions Steve had wanted answered.

"I said I'd answer your questions. You haven't asked any yet," she reminded him.

The corner of his mouth quirked slightly, giving her the impression he might smile, but then it straightened and any hope of a smile disappeared. While the mixed odor of orange potpourri, cinnamon and freshly brewed coffee wound around them, she waited. The silence filled with the sound of the blaze in the hearth devouring the logs. "Let's start with who you are"

"I'm Meghan."

"Just Meghan?"

"Meghan is all that is necessary." Somehow, despite her writhing emotions, she managed to keep her voice even and controlled.

He shrugged, as if her reasons didn't matter, and he refused to waste time pursuing them. "Where am I?"

"Renaissance."

"Why couldn't I go back through the mist?"

"The mist is the village's protection from the outside world. A city wall, if you will. Once you've come inside it, leaving for good is impossible until after."

"After what? That doesn't tell me a damn thing." He leaned forward and deposited his cup and saucer on the tray. "What is that mist?"

"I'm sorry, but all I can tell you about the mist is that it comes and goes. No one knows why. No one asks." She thought for a moment. "If it's of great importance to you, then perhaps Emanuel can tell you."

"Emanuel?"

"The village elder. He oversees all the Assignments and their progress."

"What's an Assignment?"

"You are, Dr. Cameron."

His jaw dropped. Snapping his gaping mouth closed, he stood and began wandering restlessly around the room, while raking his fingers through his thick, dark brown, wavy hair. "I don't understand any of this. What do you mean by *after*? What exactly is an Assignment? And how did I get to be one?"

"One of the guides saw to it."

"Guides?"

"The guides find people in the outside world with troubled souls and send them to the village. We call them Assignments. Each arrival is assigned to a villager. You've been assigned to me. I'll be your Healer while you're here. My job is to help you."

He stopped pacing, then glared down at her. "I don't need help."

"Don't you?"

Meghan could read rebellion in every feature on his handsome face. That he would not be an easy student was becoming more and more apparent to her with each passing minute and each word he spoke. "Steve." Intentionally, she softened her voice, hoping to calm him, hoping he'd listen more with his heart than his head. "Everyone needs help sometime. It's a wonderful gift to find someone willing to give that help. You should know that. You've given more of yourself to your children than most people give to anyone in a lifetime."

He swung toward her, his eyes large and bright with the surprise her words had fostered. Then the brightness dimmed. "I gave them nothing." His tone emerged in a monotone, neither angry nor emphatic—just very resigned and heartbreakingly sad. He turned away.

"Ah, but you did. That's why you're here, Steve, to learn that, and that no matter how much you give to others, you must remember to save something for yourself."

"I—"

The door opened. A small, blond boy of about six or seven stood hesitantly inside the threshold, casting questioning glances from Steve to Meghan.

"Hello, Timothy," she said softly, then opened her arms to the child.

He ran into them, snuggled his cheek against her, then stared at Steve with large blue eyes framed by skin pale and translucent enough to put all Steve's medical senses on alert. He forced himself to push them away.

"Timothy, this is Steve. He'll be staying with us for a while."

The boy smiled tentatively and then waved.

Steve opened his mouth to deny what she said, but knew instinctively it would do little good. He decided to wait until everyone had gone to bed, then he'd slip away before they could stop him. He wasn't going to spend one more minute in this . . . this loony bin than he had to.

Steve acknowledged the boy with a curt nod and swallowed hard. Timothy's blond hair reminded him of Ellie. The keychain in his pocket seemed to burn into his leg.

The child smiled and then hid his face in the folds of Meghan's voluminous, multicolored skirt.

"He doesn't speak." Her gaze held an anguish that told Steve without words how the child's disability upset her. "I don't know that he ever has. When Mr. Hobbs—"

"Hobbs? Hobbs from the cabin?"

She nodded. "When Mr. Hobbs brought Timothy to us, he couldn't speak." As she explained, she stroked his hair, then bent and deposited a kiss to the top of his head.

Steve smiled. Now he had her. "If the boy can't speak, how do you know his name?"

She smiled, while caressing the boy's head absently. "It was written in the label of his sweater. Unfortunately, only his first name and last initial–Timothy K." She glanced lovingly at the boy. "We want to send him back to his parents, but until he tells us what the K stands for, he has a home here, and we'll watch over him for them."

Steve noticed for the first time, the boy had snow on his shoes. He must have been outside the village. "What's the difference between him and me? Why can he leave and I can't?" Not that he believed for a moment that she could keep him here against his will, despite having been unable to get out of the mist and return to the cabin earlier. It had been some kind of trick. Maybe a smoke machine hidden under that bridge. Certainly nothing that couldn't be logically explained.

Meghan bent toward the child, then whispered something in his ear. He glanced at Steve. Timothy's face brightened, and he grinned and nodded at Meghan. A moment later he raced off through the kitchen, then toward the back of the house.

"Timothy is a child," she said, coming back to her chair near the hearth. "He's here by accident. You aren't. In any case, you both can leave as long as you do so with the intent of returning." She sighed. "You are an Assignment. Assignments can't leave permanently until the time is right."

"When is that?" His lack of control over his circumstances, not to mention her evasions, began to grate on his nerves.

"When the time comes, you'll know."

She didn't know it, but the time had come. He didn't

plan on being here a minute longer than necessary. The first time she turned her back, he'd be long gone. And he had no intentions of returning.

Deal with that, Miss Meghan Whoever-You-Are.

"You can try," she said softly.

Had she read his thoughts?

"And just who's going to stop me?" He looked her slight body up and down, then laughed. "You?"

"No need. You're your own keeper, Steve. We don't tamper with free will."

"Then what do you call not allowing me to go back to the cabin?"

She smiled. "A beginning."

Frustration exploded in him like lava shooting from a volcano. He couldn't go until he'd learned whatever the hell it was she thought she could teach him. Yet she was now telling him he still had free will. It couldn't be both ways. This made about as much sense as anything else that had happened to him in the last few days, and he was rapidly running out of logic to explain anything and the patience to understand it

Steve stared at the lovely woman sitting before him. The serenity reflecting from her eyes drained his anger as efficiently as a plug pulled from a bathtub drain. Beautiful weakened in the face of trying to find a word to adequately describe her. Ethereal came closer, but still didn't do her white-blond hair and her strange blue eyes justice. She had the delicate features of a China doll and a slight body that looked breakable, until he looked into her eyes. They held a strength he'd never seen in another human being before.

But he also saw vulnerability, and that fostered an urge to protect her. Oddly enough, that scared him. He had no desire to be responsible for anyone but Steve Cameron and most certainly not a young woman who gave birth to emotions in him that would complicate his life even more.

"What about you? Why do you stay here?"

Meghan tilted her head as though she could hear something he couldn't, then rose abruptly and began fussing with the items on the tray. She poured more coffee for both of them, then got another cup and saucer from the kitchen and placed it on the table beside theirs. She filled it with coffee and laid two sugar cookies on the edge of the saucer. "Because this is my home," she finally said.

Before Steve could ask about the extra cup, the boy reappeared, his face wreathed in a wide grin.

Wordlessly, Timothy came to Steve. He felt the child's small hand slip into his. The sensation of the boy's soft skin on Steve's brought memories flooding back of other times he'd held the hand of a child and whispered soft reassuring words he neither felt nor believed. With them came other emotions, emotions he'd been effectively blocking out for years. Steve pushed them away. He tried to remove his hand from the boy's grasp, but the youngster held on like a vise. Tugging on Steve's arm, Timothy tried to pull him from the chair.

"What does he want?"

Meghan smiled. For a moment, Steve thought the room got brighter, warmer, more welcoming. "He wants to show you your room."

"My room? But I already told you that I'm not staying."

"Ah, but I'm afraid you are, my boy."

Steve jumped. He hadn't heard anyone enter.

The strangely accented voice came from a white-haired man standing near the door. His white beard nearly reached his waist. A light-colored robe of coarse material belted at the waist with a rope-like sash concealed his robust torso from neck to toe. His face bore the ravages of time, yet he looked to have the health of a man four times his junior, making his age impossible to estimate. His gray eyes held a kindness and a depth of wisdom Steve could not even contemplate. His voice was soft, yet commanding attention and dispensing kindness and understanding all at once.

Steve glanced at Meghan. She seemed neither alarmed nor surprised at her unexpected guest's appearance. "This is Emanuel." She made the introductions as though they'd been standing in the lobby of the Hilton before enjoying a leisurely lunch together.

"As Meghan has explained, you cannot leave until your time," the man added.

Timothy dropped Steve's hand and raced to the older

man. He bent and scooped the boy up in his arms. An arrow of jealousy knifed through Steve. How he missed holding a child and seeing one smile up at him. How long had it been?

"Too long."

Had Steve thought that, or had Emanuel said it?

The older man had set the child down on the floor and taken a seat in Meghan's empty chair. In his hand rested the cup of coffee Meghan had just poured. No wonder she hadn't shown surprise, Steve thought. She'd sensed his appearance.

Sure, Cameron. How can she tell someone is coming before they get here? You're getting as batty as the rest of them.

Only one thing in this crazy place was for certain— it got weirder by the moment. When had his life taken a sharp left turn into Never Never Land? One minute he'd been a perfectly rational individual, the next, envelopes showed up in his pockets that should have been in the trash. On top of that, he'd found himself engaged in a wild-goose chase through the mountains on the word of a deranged bag lady—

He abruptly interrupted his round of angry thoughts to temper his description of Irma. A dear, sweet lady who worried about him, she didn't deserve that. Irma may be many things, but crazy wasn't one of them. Compassionate. Wise. Never crazy.

With Irma off his conscience, Steve went back to

assessing the happenings of the last few hours. As if all of his other adventures hadn't been enough, he'd stumbled onto a cabin that he didn't even believe existed, walked through a mist, and then gotten trapped in this—whatever this place was.

A thought crossed his mind. Hobbs? Irma? All conspiring? It appeared as though everyone who'd crossed his path lately had done so with one objective in mind—to get him here. Could it be possible that Meghan had been straight with him? That he couldn't leave here until he learned . . . whatever she had to teach him?

He looked at Meghan. She was, perhaps, the most beautiful woman he'd ever seen. She was gentle with the boy, soft spoken—even when Steve had been less than cordial. Maybe hanging around here for a while and getting to know her better would be worth it.

Self-conscious about his train of thought, Steve's gaze darted to the man seated opposite him. He smiled—knowingly.

Steve tore his gaze away from the stranger devouring his third cookie and centered it on the orange flames leaping in the hearth. What was happening to him? He'd just met Meghan. He knew nothing about her, and what he did know was, at the very least, a bit unnerving. Had he finally gone over the edge that Frank had warned him about? Would he wake up to find himself in his wrecked car with a large knot on his head and in the throes of a nervous breakdown?

* * *

Supper had been consumed in silence with Meghan watching Timothy pick at his food, Timothy eyeing Steve suspiciously and Steve trying to ignore both of them. Now, with Timothy tucked in for the night that left Steve and Meghan sitting at the table over coffee. Though he drank his coffee black, Steve occupied himself by swirling the spoon around in the liquid and staring thoughtfully into the eddy in the center of the cup.

"Acceptance will come soon enough."

Meghan's words roused Steve from his contemplation of the behavior of his coffee. "Excuse me?"

"Acceptance of your situation. Isn't that what you're so deep in thought about?"

He didn't reply. Instead, he propped his forearms on the table and looked her in the eye. "Shouldn't I be?"

She laughed aloud, a very bright, musical sound that transformed her features, making her even lovelier, if that were possible. "I would seriously worry about you if you weren't." She shifted in her chair. "It would be easier if you could forget your training to believe only that which can be proven in a research lab or on paper with complicated equations or explanations."

"I've found that life is much simpler if you believe only

what can be proven beyond a shadow of a doubt."

"Then I feel sorry for you."

"Sorry? For me? Why?"

She sipped from her cup. He had to turn away from the sight of her lips caressing the edge of it. But his gaze rested instead on her throat as she swallowed and the muscles undulated. His fingers itched to touch her right where her collarbone indented.

"For all the wonders you've missed that defy *logical* explanation."

He dragged his gaze back to her face. "Such as?"

"Such as the simpler things in life. Clouds that look like dragons or dogs or castles. Flowers that pop up where none have ever grown before. Snowflakes that look like tiny lace doilies, each perfect, each different. Babies who hold our hearts in the palms of their tiny hands from the very second they enter the world."

Steve snorted. "Don't be ridiculous. I've seen all those things."

She studied him for moment. "Have you? Have you *really* seen them, Steve?" She rose and went to the sink and began washing their supper dishes.

He thought about her question. When was the last time he'd really looked around him until today in the woods? When had he actually seen a flower, let alone where it grew? When had he turned himself off to the beauty of life and instead concentrated on nothing but death?

"Is that what I have to learn here?"

Meghan's movements stopped. "Among other things."

"Such as?"

Turning, she leaned her back against the edge of the counter. "Such as who you are and why you've turned your back on the things in life that always used to matter to you. Things like love, happiness, and fulfillment."

He stood abruptly. "I haven't turned my back on any of that."

"Ah, but you have. When you gave up on the children, you gave up on yourself. You forgot how to dream, how to imagine, how to accept anything that wasn't based in scientific fact. And when you gave up on yourself, you surrendered your right to love, happiness, and fulfillment. You became so preoccupied with death that you forgot to celebrate the living." She turned back to the sink, washed the last few dishes and then dried her hands. "I'm going to bed now. See you in the morning." She walked from the room, leaving Steve to stare after her.

That was nothing more than a load of crap. How was finding himself in a snowflake going to save a kid dying of leukemia or bring back a life snatched away by the ravages of lung cancer?

If this was her idea of teaching him to cope with the state of his life, then she might as well save her breath. He left the kitchen and flopped into the chair near the hearth. He'd give her an hour or so to fall asleep and then he'd make for the cabin.

Behind him, the grandfather clock ticked away the minutes until silence blanketed the tiny cottage. Steve listened intently for signs that the other two occupants were stirring from their sleep. None came. He crept into his bedroom and grabbed his coat.

Cautiously, he tiptoed from his room, eased through the darkness into the kitchen, then into the living room, his jacket tucked beneath his arm. Illuminated only by the dying embers in the fireplace and the moonlight slanting through the window, the room still retained its homey feel. He glanced toward the grandfather clock ticking monotonously against the far wall.

"What the . . ."

He blinked, then moved closer to the clock, forgetting, for the moment, his plan for escape. At close range, he examined its silver face. It made all the sounds of a working timepiece, but to no avail. The hands that would have recorded its movements were missing.

Time is relative.

Irma's words came from nowhere, as if she whispered them into his ear, leaving behind the tingling sensation of her breath having caressed his skin as she did so.

This was too much. His imagination was becoming infected. He had to get out of here before he became as loony as the rest of them. Shrugging into his jacket, he hurried toward the door. On his way, he passed the memento case he'd been looking at earlier. The firelight bouncing off the bear's face and catching in its one remaining glass eye, made it seem as though the stuffed animal winked at Steve. He paused and stared at the bear. Something seemed to hover on the edge of his consciousness, just out of touch of recollection. What was there about the bear?

Shaking his head, he gave up and dashed toward the front door. This time he kept his gaze riveted to the wooden portal. He had to get out of here.

As he swung the door open, the creak of the wrought iron hinges filled the silence. He grimaced and paused— listening. No sound. Nothing but the methodic ticking of the clock, the crackle of the cooling coals in the fireplace, and the heady smell of cinnamon and orange coming from the potpourri pot simmering on the mantel.

Opening the door wider, he slipped quietly into the moonlit night. Now, all he had to do was find his way back to the cabin. When morning came, he'd call the garage and check on the car. The sooner he got back to the familiarity of the city, the happier he'd be. Can't leave? He'd show her. As he strode across the footbridge into the night, he hummed softly.

Steve stepped off the footbridge and held his breath, waiting for the mist to reappear. When it didn't, he breathed a deep sigh of relief and then trudged on through the night. The snow crunching beneath his feet echoed through the stillness. The moon illuminated the footprints he'd made on his way here and would make a perfect guide to get him back to the cabin. It would simply be a case of following them. In the morning, he'd head back to the city, away from this place and these wacky people.

But as he walked, the image of Meghan clung to his mind like a persistent cobweb. Never had he seen a woman as beautiful as she was. Her hair reminded him of the spun glass his mother used to drape over their Christmas tree, and her eyes were the color of the sky on a really clear summer day.

Suddenly aware of what he was doing and that he'd wandered off the path, he shook free of Meghan and retraced his steps until he found where he'd gone wrong. Concentrating on the footprints, he hurried back to the cabin.

* * *

From her window, Meghan followed the form of the running man illuminated by the full moon. When he disappeared from sight, she picked up the lantern and in its milky depths watched as he raced through the moonlight-dappled trees. She continued to observe him until he disappeared behind the door of the cabin in the woods, the gateway to Renaissance.

What exactly drove Steve Cameron—the need to escape Renaissance or himself? Shaking her head, she replaced the lantern and padded off to bed. Settled beneath the patchwork quilt, she continued to ponder her newest Assignment, but not in relation to his fleeing.

What was it about him that affected her so differently? Why wasn't he like the rest? What prompted this strange weakness in her, this light-headedness, as if her feet no longer touched the ground and her head hovered somewhere in the clouds, every time he looked at her? And yet, at the same time, what prompted that ominous dread that tugged at her?

She never before had trouble assimilating her emotional response to an Assignment. However, with Steve, she read too much, yet read too little, sensed too much, yet couldn't sense enough, and, what she did sense, she couldn't fully analyze. Nothing of what she felt went beyond the emotions connected to his reason for being in the village.

No matter how hard she tried, she could not identify the unease he'd brought into her life, that nebulous something in him that called out to her, the invisible thread that drew them together, binding them as one. She snuggled down under the quilt. Fear slept beside her. Meghan had never known fear before today. Why then did its presence feel so familiar? Like an old enemy—waiting to attack.

CHAPTER 5

Clara Webb pushed the shuttle through the network of dark blue yarns stretched across her loom. She threw an I-told-you-so glance over her shoulder at Emanuel sitting in the rocker by the front window, the rising sun dappling his robes in soft pink hues.

"Didn't I warn you that your decision would come back to haunt you?" Behind the large wooden structure, a pile of navy-blue cloth grew steadily higher. Clara caught the shuttle. The soft click of the loom pushing the new thread into place echoed through the pensive silence. She pushed the shuttle back from where it came. The loom clicked again.

"I wish it were me being haunted." Emanuel frowned. "In this instance I'm afraid I deserve your scolding, my dear, but please, another time."

Clara smiled gently at him and went back to her work, knowing that the soft rhythmic clatter of the loom weaving yet another bolt of cloth for the villagers would soothe him. She understood well the effect of the sound on a troubled heart. When all else seemed to have lost its order, the assurance of one *clack* following another became heartening to the spirit. Many a time, when her mind grew heavy with the burden of healing an Assignment, Clara rose in the middle of the night and worked at the loom. Usually, by the time daylight emerged over the horizon, she'd sorted out her problem and could face the day with new direction and a smile.

A few minutes passed, then Clara's loom went silent, and she swung on the stool to face him. "So, have you decided what to do?"

He drew himself up from the old, wooden rocker, straightened the folds in his robe, and smoothed the length of his snowy beard with his hand and then favored her with a smile. "I will send Alvin Tripp at once. I cannot delay. The memories will begin returning soon, as in my heart, I knew one day they would. It is time."

She nodded. "Alvin's gone hunting, but he should be back any time." Clara glanced at the kettle boiling over the fire and reminded herself to freshen the water before making her tea. When she looked back, Emanuel had disappeared. She chuckled softly to herself.

Poor Alvin. He'd barely have time to eat before setting out on Emanuel's errand. But Alvin, being Renaissance's only link with the outside world, made unscheduled trips out there with ease. He hated being stuck in one place. She'd always believed that if he could no longer be the

Traveler he might leave Renaissance and become a Guide. What a loss that would be to their little community.

Once they'd decided to stay, none of the permanent residents had ever left the village. What would Renaissance do without the beauty of Josiah's flowers, the wisdom of Sara's teachings, and the guiding love of Emanuel?

"Gracious, Clara Webb," she scolded herself, patting the coil of gray hair at the back of her head and straightening her white mob cap, "you do get morose sometimes."

But even the stern scolding couldn't push to the back of her mind Emanuel's visit and what it would mean to the tiny, mystical village. How she wished he'd listened to her all those years ago and not kept this terrible secret. Sighing, she smoothed the wrinkles from her long, brown skirt and tightened the laces in the wide, cloth belt encircling her waist.

She shook her head. Emanuel, as wise as he was, had no idea of the strength of the emotions involved in this problem. She refreshed the tea water and hung the kettle back on the wrought iron crane, then swung it over the fire. Emanuel knew everything of the love of the spirit, but when it came to the love of the heart . . .

Going to the window, she watched Emanuel's robed figure move across the flower bedecked village square toward Alvin Tripp's house. Had Emanuel known of the love of the heart, he would have seen it shining from her eyes long ago. But she knew also that Emanuel's mission in life lay far beyond the yearnings of her heart—or his.

❄ ❄ ❄

Steve rolled his head slowly from side to side to remove the crick pinching the nerve at the back of his neck. The bed in this cabin left a lot to be desired. He kept his eyes closed, enjoying the feeling of the cramp easing away. As the pain gradually dissipated, he let his eyelids drift upward. His gaze came to rest on the handless face of a large, pine, grandfather clock.

He bolted upright. "What the hell . . ."

Meghan stood beside the chair, a knowing smile curling her lips.

"Dr. Cameron, you have an annoying habit of cursing." She glanced over her shoulder, then looked back at him, her eyebrows arched reprovingly. "Timothy is in the kitchen eating breakfast, so, if you please . . ."

He'd heard her words, but his attention centered on the shock of waking and finding himself not in the cabin where he'd gone to sleep, but back in Meghan's cottage, fully clothed as if he'd never left. But he had. He distinctly remembered following the moonlit trail of footprints he'd left in the snow as he traced his way back to the cabin. Had he just dreamt he went back?

"I told you you couldn't go back." Her soft words held neither anger nor reprimand.

"Was it a dream?"

"No. You went back. I saw you leave."

"Then—"

"Why didn't I stop you? Would you have paid attention?"

He frowned. "Then how is it I'm—"

"Here?"

Steve glared at her, then ran his hand through his tousled brown hair. "That little trick is entertaining at first, but becomes very annoying after while, not to mention intrusive."

"Trick?"

"Reading my mind."

She laughed. Despite his efforts to ignore it, the sound washed over him like a shower of sunlight. Pushed by his accelerated heartbeat, his blood drummed through his veins. He found himself wondering what her full, unadorned, red lips would taste like.

"I assure you, Doctor, I cannot read your mind."

"Then how did you know—"

"What you were going to say?"

"There. You're doing it again." Steve rose from the chair in which he'd found himself and faced her. Distractedly, he noted for the first time how his six-feet-four height dwarfed her. The top of her head barely reached his chin. To kiss her, he would have to bend . . .

"Do you think you're the first Assignment who's tried

to . . ." She paused, as if searching for the right word.

For a moment Steve was thrown, thinking her final words that would have finished that sentence were going to be *kiss me*. Then he recalled what they'd been talking about before his mind had taken a left turn into sensuality. "Escape?" He smiled, pleased at being able to play her mind game.

Meghan ignored him and moved to the other chair, then sank gracefully into it. What a remarkably composed woman. She looked up at him, her golden lashes framing her ice-blue eyes. Strange eyes, but warm and welcoming. And her lips . . . Quickly moving his thoughts to safer territory, he opened his mouth to speak, but she cut him off.

"*Escape* is a little strong. I was thinking more in terms of *withdraw*."

"I think *escape* pretty well sums it up." He waved his arm to encompass the village. "You've lured me here under some pretext—you, Irma, Hobbs, and God only knows who else. Now, you're holding me prisoner. *Withdrawal* just doesn't seem to cut it."

"You're *not* a prisoner. At least not by your definition of a prisoner." She looked at him steadily, until the heavy beat of his heart made him shift his gaze away from hers. "Prisons aren't always constructed of mortar and brick."

"Damn it!" As he swung again to confront her, Steve's voice exploded. Meghan jumped. "Why can't you just answer my questions like a normal human being? Why all the parables?" His stopped and his brows dipped into a frown. "Or is it because you aren't human?" Even as the question passed his lips, his eyes told him the answer. Meghan was all too human, all too beautiful, all too sexy.

Again her laughter filled the room—and Steve. The woman was a witch. Mentally, he once more shook free of her magnetism and this euphoria that overcame him whenever he looked at her.

"I can assure you, Dr. Cameron, I'm as human as you are."

While unreasonable frustration built in him, he stared at her for a long moment, his gaze coming to rest once again on her full, cherry red lips. "Let's just test that theory, shall we?"

He strode purposefully toward her. Before Meghan could stop him, he imprisoned her shoulders, pulled her into his arms, then lowered his mouth toward hers.

Something flashed through Meghan's mind. Something dark, ominous, and ugly. Something that left her cold and shaking. She gazed up at Steve. Her vision filled with his eyes. Eyes darkened with anger and determination. Once more, he started to lower his mouth to hers. Fear—stark, threatening, and ugly, coiled inside her like a snake ready to strike.

"No!"

The sound of her shrill voice echoed around the tiny room. She wrenched herself from his embrace. Staggering, she put the fireside chair between them, then clutched the chair back to support her weak knees.

"Meghan, I—"

Before Steve could finish, Timothy came running in from the kitchen. She searched the child's face. How much had the boy heard, seen? They'd been far enough around the corner to be out of his range of vision, but he must have heard her call out.

Timothy glanced at Steve, then to Meghan. The concern and fear in the child's eyes pushed her own to the back of her mind. Quickly, she hurried to him, squatted down, then embraced him.

"It's okay," she whispered. "It's okay."

Timothy pulled back. Then, as if checking to see that she'd told him the truth, he ran his small hand over her face. Seemingly satisfied that she hadn't been hurt, he moved his assessing gaze to Steve. When Timothy seemed content that Steve posed no threat, he stepped back and returned his attention to Meghan. He pointed at his mouth, shook his head, then indicated the door and nodded.

"Are you sure you don't want any more to eat?" Timothy's poor appetite worried her.

He shook his head vigorously, his straight, blond hair moving across his pale forehead as if alive, and pointed at the door again.

"Okay. Go play, but make sure you're back for lunch."

Once the door shut solidly behind the little boy, the room grew oppressively quiet. To Meghan's ears, the telltale sound of her shallow breathing filled every corner of the house. Carefully keeping her gaze aimed at the floor, she made her way back to the kitchen.

As she removed Timothy's nearly untouched cereal bowl from the table, Steve entered the room and took a seat. "Does he always have such a poor appetite?"

Meghan turned away. Fighting to display the same nonchalance as Steve was about the incident in the living room, she put the dish in the sink. "He rarely eats anything. He's been that way since he got here. I wish he would eat as well as he sleeps."

"Oh?"

Feeling more in control, but not enough to make eye contact with him, she poured coffee into Steve's cup, and then returned the pot to the stove. "He goes to bed extremely well and is off to sleep in a matter of minutes." No need to fill Steve in on Timothy's nightly ritual of crying himself to sleep. Sharing the same room, he'd find out soon enough. She laughed lightly. "Considering he takes a long nap every afternoon, I would expect him to stay up later."

Steve said nothing. She turned toward him to find him studying the table with fixed concentration. "Is there something wrong?"

Raising his gaze to meet hers, he shrugged. "You mean, of course, beyond the fact that I seem to have fallen through a rabbit hole into Wonderland?" The corners of his mouth lifted in the first genuine smile she'd seen him exhibit since coming to the village. She sucked in her breath.

"No. That's not what I meant. You seemed deep in thought. I wondered if something I'd said about Timothy . . ."

He stiffened against the chair's back. "He's a little boy with a lot of energy. Burning that energy will tire him out. As for his appetite . . . any child would rather run around in the woods than stay inside and eat meals." His voice emerged curt, his tone sharp. He looked away. "When he's hungry, he'll eat. Don't force him," he added in a softer tone.

"I understand all that, but—"

"I'm going to take a walk." He stood and started toward the door, stopped, then swung back to face her. "I'm not going to be transported back here if I step outside, am I?"

"What?" She'd been thinking about Timothy, deciding that Steve was probably right, and she worried for nothing. She turned the faucet to fill the sink with hot water for dishes. "Oh, no. That only happens when you leave with no intention of returning. You can even go outside the village, but if you plan on staying, you will be brought back." She glanced over her shoulder. He turned back toward the door and again stopped.

"Meghan, about what happened before . . ."

She couldn't risk looking at him. She directed her gaze to the mounds of white suds forming in the sink. Her fingers curled into tight balls that forced the suds up into soft peaks. She was still uncertain as to whether Steve had been the cause of the fear she'd experienced. Until she knew for certain, she would deal with it alone. Besides, he had enough problems already without her burdening him with what could well be false accusations.

Meghan forced herself to begin washing the dishes. "It's forgotten."

For a long time she could feel his presence, then very quietly, she heard him say, "Is it?" Moments later, the door closed softly behind him.

She sank into the closest chair. What was happening to her? Her entire world had suddenly turned upside down. Nothing made sense. Least of all what had taken place in the living room earlier.

Emanuel often said that if a person were to conquer his fears, he must face them head-on. She rested her forehead against her hand, closed her eyes, and intentionally tried to bring back the vision of whatever had frightened her enough to call out.

For a long moment, nothing came. Then suddenly, half-formed images raced across her closed eyelids, blurred, indistinct. Even though she was unable to make them out, she felt that cold, icy fear again. She shivered. Wrapping her arms around her middle, she hunched over the table, trying to make herself as small as possible. A voice called out, but she couldn't tell who it was or what it said. Then the figure turned toward her. A man. Tall. Muscular. He took a step in her direction.

She screamed and bolted from the chair, her eyes wide, perspiration dotting her brow. Taking a deep breath, she hurried to the sink. She splashed cold water over her face. Her temples throbbed and a piercing pain began forming at the nape of her neck. She massaged it with her fingers, turning her head this way and that to ease the sudden stiffness. Though she wanted to close them against the bright sunlight pouring through the windows, she kept her eyes wide open, afraid the images would return if she dropped her eyelids for a second.

When the pain subsided, she tried to understand what had just happened to her, but no explanation she could devise explained it. Since fear was a stranger to her, she had no idea what could have fostered the images or what they meant.

Emanuel. Perhaps he could tell her what demons had suddenly chosen to stalk her and why.

❊ ❊ ❊

Steve brushed the dusting of snow from an outcropping of flat-topped rocks overlooking the glen, then sat, facing the village. In the distance lay the Hudson River, frozen solid, except for a dark, jagged wound of free water up the middle, ripped open by the river barges on their trek to Albany. As he gazed over the serene scene, a ripple of awareness coursed up his spine. He looked around him. Nothing. Still, he had the distinct sensation that he wasn't the only one gazing out at the river.

Shaking his head, he chuckled. "Get a grip," he told himself.

The strangeness of the last few days' events had thrown him into a spin. But why shouldn't it? A person didn't stumble on something like Renaissance and Meghan everyday. And even if a reasonable explanation existed for the whole thing, she certainly believed what she'd told him to be true, even if he still harbored serious doubts.

His thoughts centered on the beautiful Meghan. Nothing about her indicated she made a habit of flights of fancy. Thoughts of Meghan brought to mind how close he'd come to tasting her lips. He could still feel the soft brush of her breath on his face, her body molded to his, fitting in all the right places, as if they'd been made precisely for that purpose.

This admission had him fidgeting on the cold rock. To begin taking all this seriously would be a big mistake. Still . . . The lack of a logical explanation for his reappearance in Meghan's cottage, the incident with the envelope and his car breaking down at exactly the right spot at the exactly the right time proved a bit difficult to digest otherwise. He had always prided himself on being a sensible man, not given to flights of fancy or believing in things he couldn't see with his own eyes or could not prove through science and medicine. Nor did he believe in villages that supposedly appeared out of the mist, even if Meghan did.

Out of nowhere, sudden memory of her reaction to his attempt to kiss her flooded his mind. The woman had been frightened beyond the fear brought on by a man she barely knew trying to kiss to her. She obviously hadn't wanted to discuss it, but Steve knew the incident hadn't been the kind a person dismissed out of hand. Nor was it one that popped up on the spur of the moment. These problems Meghan faced were ones of long standing. Meghan, it seemed, wasn't so different from him after all. She too had ghosts with which to contend.

For the first time in two days, Steve slid his hand into his trouser pocket and pulled out the keychain. He slid his thumb over the solid surface, taking comfort in its familiarity.

This time, however, instead of bringing the vision of Ellie and her sweet smile to mind, it conjured a small boy's face, framed by a shock of golden curls and with skin as translucent and white as the snow at Steve's feet. Deliberately, he shoved the keychain back in his pocket and with it, the visions of a child's face, a vision far too familiar to Steve. Had Meghan noticed the bruise under Timothy's right ear or the one Steve had seen the night before on the boy's bare foot as it lay outside his blanket?

Steve dropped his face to his hands, forcing away the mind-pictures and the inevitable conclusions of his medical training. Why couldn't he just wipe that from his mind?

He'd tried for six long years to no avail. Would he ever find the secrets to the peace of mind he sought?

Feeling a presence at his side, he raised his head. On the rock next to him sat Emanuel.

The old man smiled and patted Steve's hand. "Sometimes the simplest answers are the hardest to see." He patted the rock on which they sat. "It was right here that I found my answer long ago."

Steve said nothing, knowing in his gut Emanuel would tell him what that answer had been. And he didn't have long to wait. Emanuel launched into the story of his mother and father, their cabin, and how his father had discovered the mist and told his small son of it.

"After they died, I was brokenhearted, lost, lonelier than I'd ever been in my whole life. I wandered these woods for days looking for something that I wasn't sure existed except in my own mind—peace. Finally, I realized that the answer lay here, so I came here every day, sat on this rock . . ." He patted it again. ". . . and waited. In my heart of hearts I knew the mist my father had spoken of would come back and when it did, I was going to find the peace he'd found inside it for myself."

"And?" Steve prompted

"And I did. Once inside the mist, I decided not to leave again. There was nothing out here for me, and I knew that in there was all I'd ever dreamed of having: peace, contentment and love."

Steve thought about Emanuel's story, then stopped dead. "Wait a minute. You said your mother and father settled this area. This area was settled back in the early 1700s. That would make you. . . ."

Emanuel looked at him from beneath his bushy white eyebrows. "Yes, it would, wouldn't it?" He smiled wisely, rose, and trudged off through the snow toward the village.

CHAPTER 6

Meghan gazed thoughtfully into the lantern's globe. Steve sat on the hill above the village, his brow furrowed in thought. His obvious pain and confusion called out to something in her, tugging at it, and pulling her toward him. She fought it off, still confused by these foreign emotions. Shaking her head, she set the lantern aside and watched as the mist thickened and blotted out the man who occupied her thoughts.

She'd already concluded that even though Steve had been assigned to her, this strange and unexpected reaction to him would preclude a clear perspective. She would need help in healing him. It wasn't as though the villagers hadn't shared their Assignments before. But whom could she ask? It must be someone who can teach Steve that the deaths of his children were not an end, but a beginning.

Mentally, she began going down the list of the villagers. There was Clara Webb, the weaver, who skillfully repaired the fabric of broken dreams and torn souls with her threads of wisdom and mended the lacerations in the soul.

Clara often wove flaws into her designs, because, as she says, "Nothing's ever perfect, is it?"

Clara was a strong possibility until Meghan recalled that Emanuel had told her Clara would soon be getting an Assignment that would "keep her busy for a while." Meghan couldn't burden her with more work.

What about Sara Spencer, the storekeeper and laundress for their small settlement? Sara's stores fed the body, but she had special provisions for the heart and soul that would nourish those starved for compassion and love. Somehow, Meghan didn't feel that Sara, though loving and wise, was just right for what ailed Steve. Steve needed to see that the cycle of life and death was not just a beginning and ending, but a journey to renewal.

Then the answer came to her. Josiah Reeve, the grower of produce for the village. No better example of the circle of life could be found than in the living things that Josiah, unable to see with his eyes, sees with his heart. Josiah, who nurtured the soul with the same care he did his beloved plants, had his own version of the three R's—Redemption, Restoration and Rebirth. Yes, Josiah would be perfect for Steve.

She laid her embroidery aside and slipped from the house to search for Josiah. She found him on his knees tending a rose bush that boasted large, yellow blooms that perfumed the air.

"You need to talk to them, my dear," he said, sensing

Meghan's presence. "I truly believe they can hear us and take nourishment from our voices. Don't you, my lovely one?" he asked, caressing the rose's petals with his gnarled, callused fingers. "People in the village where I came from laughed at me when I told them the flowers had souls." He looked at Meghan with sightless eyes. "They do, you know." He struggled to his feet with Meghan's help and brushed the dirt from his hands. "I think that when we die and are buried in the soil, the plants absorb our souls, and they become theirs. Our entrance into heaven is to bloom as a lovely flower. Only after we have graced the earth with beauty can we pass on into the Hereafter."

Meghan had heard Josiah's beliefs many times before. Whether she believed as he did or not, she could not deny that because the old man saw it with his heart, it was a beautiful thought.

"Josiah, I need a favor."

He took her arm and led her to a crude wooden bench beside the rose garden. "What can I do for you?"

She sat beside him, the sun warming her face and arms. "It's my new Assignment."

"Ah, yes, Dr. Cameron."

"I need someone who can teach him of life, rebirth, beginning, and renewal. I think you'd be admirable at it."

The old man's chest swelled with pride. A grin broke across his face. "I'd be delighted to help you, my dear, delighted."

❋ ❋ ❋

Having set up a meeting between Josiah and Steve, Meghan left word with Clara Webb that she needed to see Emanuel, then went home to hem handkerchiefs to embroider for upcoming Assignments, while she waited for the one person who could possibly tell her more about the vision she'd had that morning—Emanuel.

Settled into her chair once more and feeling a bit more secure about her new Assignment, Meghan picked up her sewing. Always in the past her handwork had soothed her and brought peace to her days. Today neither happened. The unease she'd experienced that morning hovered over her like a persistent, black storm cloud.

She re-threaded her needle, but before she put needle to fabric, she craned her neck to see out the window and down the road, searching for any sign of Emanuel. All the movement she saw was Josiah tending his flowers and Clara Webb delivering a bolt of navy blue material to Sara's store.

Sighing, she tried to clear her mind of her troubling thoughts by going into the kitchen and preparing a tray of coffee and cookies. Once done, she settled back in her chair and went back to her handwork. But the busy work couldn't chase away the horrifying visions that dogged her every moment or the memory of Steve and what would have been her first kiss.

She dropped her needle and touched her fingers to her lips, trying to imagine what it would be like to kiss a man, in a romantic way. She'd kissed Emanuel's wrinkled cheek and even Josiah's this afternoon when he'd agreed to take Steve's lessons on, but she had never kissed a man with anything more than gratitude prompting it.

What would it be like? Would it be pleasurable? Would she want more? Would he? Her embroidery forgotten, she mused about kisses for a long time.

The sun had started to drop toward the horizon when she sensed another's presence in the room.

Meghan folded the handkerchief, tucked it in her basket, and turned toward the door. Afternoon sunlight shafted through the opening and spilled across the pine floor. The sweet scent of Josiah's flowers wafted into the room. A breeze ruffled the curtains at the windows. Despite all that, Meghan felt tense, anxious.

Emanuel filled the doorframe, the light behind him washing his shoulders and head in a golden hue. "You needed to speak to me?"

Not trusting her voice now that she faced him, Meghan nodded. Out of habit, she filled his cup from the silver coffee pot and waited while he took a seat in his favorite wing chair. He lifted one of the delicate cups from the waiting tray on the table between them, and then selected one of the sugar cookies from the plate. Settling back, he waited for her to speak.

"I . . . I . . . uh . . ." Where were the words to explain the strange feelings she'd had when Steve tried to kiss her, then the blurred visions she'd experienced later?

"You had a vision," Emanuel said quietly, studying her over the rim of his coffee cup.

"Yes."

"And?" He sipped the fragrant brew and returned the cup to the saucer, the porcelain making a soft *click* as the cup fitted itself into the indentation in the saucer.

"What does all of it mean?"

He sighed and replaced the cup and saucer on the tray. The indecision Meghan saw in his features alarmed her. Without consciously thinking about it, she slid forward to the edge of her chair.

"Can you tell me?"

"For now, child, it will have to be enough explanation that you will soon understand."

"But—"

He raised a silencing hand. "I promise it will be very soon. Until then, you must trust that the visions can only hold power over you if you allow them to." When she would have protested, he smiled and shook his head. His long white hair swished over his shoulder like an ancient wave and his long beard dusted the front of his robe. "Patience, child. This is not my tale to tell."

Meghan leaned back. She knew that to press Emanuel

would be nothing more than an exercise in futility. Still, the idea that these demons would come back to terrorize her again, made her push for more.

"Why? If it's nothing more than a story, why can't you tell me?"

"It's more than that. I promised, when the time came, I would allow another to tell the tale. If I did not, I would be breaking my word." He sighed and stood, his robes coming to rest in soft folds about his robust body. "Even now, Alvin is summoning that person to us."

He patted her shoulder as he passed her on the way to the door. A modicum of peace washed over her, but not nearly enough to ease the apprehension. A gust of cool air scudded past her bare legs, then she heard the *click* of the door latch.

Finding herself alone, she still had no idea what these visions meant or why she was having them. But of one thing she was almost sure. The visions had some connection to Steve, otherwise why would they have made their first appearance when he tried to kiss her?

❊ ❊ ❊

The following morning, Steve sat down at Meghan's kitchen table for breakfast and glanced at Timothy. The boy stared back. What Steve saw in the child's eyes unnerved him. Trust.

Steve had forgotten what it was like to see that reflected in a child's eyes, but he couldn't understand why this child who didn't know him trusted him, especially when he didn't even trust himself. He tried to look away, but his gaze kept being drawn back to the boy.

Other times he'd had to earn that trust with long hours of interaction and cajoling. Timothy seemed to give it without question. This really surprised him, especially in light of what Timothy had overheard between him and Meghan the day before. Only one other child had endowed Steve with unquestioning trust . . . Ellie, and he'd let her down.

Steve watched the boy, waiting for the trust to go away, but it didn't. Timothy scrubbed his waffle around his plate, never eating one morsel, but each time he looked at Steve, the same light filled his eyes.

Despite his vow to stay away from children, Timothy's reaction created an aching emptiness inside. He hadn't realized how much he'd missed the children until now. Steve glanced up to find Meghan watching them.

She slid a golden brown waffle onto Steve's plate, then turned to Timothy. "After you eat, you can go outside and play," she said.

Steve added butter and syrup to his waffle, and slid the bottle and butter dish toward Timothy. He mimicked Steve and added butter and syrup to his own waffle. Even then, Timothy continued to just slide the waffle around the plate, never offering to eat one bite.

Glancing up, Steve saw Meghan staring at him again. This time, her eyes begged for his help. He couldn't give it. He knew that, when added to the other symptoms he'd observed in the boy, Timothy's lack of appetite was a sign of something far more complicated than just a small boy's eagerness to get outside to play, something Steve had no desire to explore or become involved in.

In the days when he'd worked with children, he would have tasted something on the child's plate, plied them with a tale his mother had told him and, eventually, get them to eat. But the days of coercing a child to eat with silly tales were behind him.

"I think I'll skip breakfast," he said, pushing his untouched plate away, rising from the chair, and avoiding Meghan's quizzical gaze.

Meghan stepped around the table and blocked his path. "Josiah is expecting you to help him this morning."

"Josiah?"

"Josiah plants all the flowers in the village and produces all the fruit and vegetables we consume. He can make anything grow. He's about to plant the spring vegetables, and he needs help. I told him you'd be happy to lend a hand." She punctuated her instructions with a smile.

Her smile had his heart turning somersaults, but, when her words sank in, Steve frowned. "You've got the wrong person. I haven't a clue how to plant anything."

"You'll learn," she said, smiled, and went back to cleaning up the remains of breakfast from the sunny kitchen. "His house is right across the square. You can't miss it."

❋ ❋ ❋

Even without Meghan's directions and her description of Josiah's role in the village, Steve would have recognized the home of the man purported to possess a green thumb.

A smooth carpet of flawless, emerald green grass surrounded the house on all sides. Pink, red, white and bright yellow roses, their stems and blossoms entwined like the tangle of threads in Meghan's sewing basket, clung to several trellises that almost obscured the front of the house. Flowerbeds, that looked as if an artist had haphazardly emptied his paint tubes on either side, boarded a walk leading to the front door. Aside from Meghan's smile, Steve had never witnessed anything so beautiful in his life.

Steve raised his hand to knock on the solid wood door.

"In the backyard," a man's voice declared, the strange accent very much like Emanuel's.

Hoping Josiah had gotten someone else to help him, and that he'd be off the hook, Steve proceeded toward the back of the house. It wasn't that he didn't want to help Josiah. The lack of activity in the past day had begun to get to him. Not knowing what to do, he feared really messing something up.

As Steve rounded the corner of the house, he caught sight of a rather small man removing a plant from a clay pot, then placing it gently in a larger pot. From the Memorial Day visits to his mother's grave with his father, Steve recognized the blood red flowers as geraniums. But never had he seen anything to equal the size of this plant or the abundance of flowers covering it.

With the same loving care a mother would use to tuck in a child, the man folded soil around the base of the plant. Grabbing a metal watering can, he doused the geranium, then stood back and appraised his work.

"Beautiful, isn't it?" he said, then turned to Steve.

His gaze transfixed by the beauty of the plant, Steve had to agree. "It certainly is." He glanced up at the man facing him and went stone still.

Of small stature, the man seemed to have stepped out of a Revolutionary War painting or missed a few centuries of changing dress codes. His colonial style knickers, black buckled shoes, and blousy, white shirt belonged in the seventeenth century, along with the black tri-cornered hat perched atop his silver hair.

But something really set him apart in a way that Steve hadn't expected. The man before him had eyes that, though brown, were covered by a cloudy gray film that told Steve he was blind. Blind? A blind man had created all this beauty?

"Ah, Meghan didn't tell you I can't see."

Steve didn't answer. Struck speechless, he could only stare in absolute wonder at the man and the flower in the pot. Dragging his attention from the single plant, he gazed around him. The front of the house paled in comparison to the backyard. A space the size of a basketball court resembled a jungle, abounding in plants and flowers in all colors, sizes and species. The air, redolent with their perfume, each vying for supremacy and blending into an exotic scent, brought one thing to Steve's mind—the woman in the house across the square.

"Where are my manners? Should have introduced myself right off." Josiah wiped his soil-encrusted hand on his brown knickers. He held his hand out to Steve. "Josiah Reeve."

Shaking himself from his state of shock, Steve grasped Josiah's hand and shook it briefly. "Steve Cameron."

"Well, we best get started. You grab that flat of tomatoes over there," he said, pointing to a wooden box filled with seedlings, "and we'll get to work." Unaided by a cane, Josiah began walking straight toward a large plot of freshly turned earth toward the back of the yard.

Steve picked up the flat of tomatoes and had all he could do to catch up with Josiah as he hastened down a stone path nestled between rows of deep purple flowers. Their shape reminded Steve of the bells he'd heard ringing in the steeple of a small church he'd passed on his way to Tarrytown.

Feeling the need to be up-front with this man who was relying on him for help, Steve called out to Josiah as they hurried along. "I should tell you that I have never planted anything in my life."

Never missing a step, Josiah waved a hand. "You'll learn," he said, echoing Meghan's words. "Didn't know how to plant a thing before I came here either. I soon found out how." To Steve's amazement and as if he could see it, Josiah plucked a brown bud from a small flowering plant. "Have to pick off the dead ones to make way for the new growth." He tossed the dead blossom at the foot of the plant. "Best fertilizer in the world," he said, hurrying on down the path. "Losing a blossom always saddens me, but when the new flowers come out, I know the old one helped make that happen."

Steve assumed Josiah was imparting something important about horticulture that he should have gotten from that statement, but for the life of him, he could not zero in on what it was. He shrugged and hurried after the old man.

Three hours later, Steve had proven Josiah right. He'd learned. He knew how to separate a seedling from its companions, slip it into a shallow hole, then tuck the dirt around its roots and give it just enough of the water Josiah had mixed with his special fertilizer to start the growth process.

At then end of the day, Steve ached in every unused muscle and felt more exhausted than if he'd put in a full day in surgery, but he felt a sense of accomplishment that had been missing from his life for far too long.

As he left the backyard, Josiah had called out "See you tomorrow."

"I'll be here." Steve called over his shoulder and walked away trying to tamp down the exciting anticipation of another day working at Josiah's side.

❋ ❋ ❋

Too keyed up to go straight home and his mind occupied with the day's events, Steve crunched through the ice-coated snow outside the perimeter of the village. Laboriously, he made his way toward the outcropping of rocks above the glen. He needed time alone to digest what he'd just done.

As he ascended the hill, the sounds of footsteps behind him interrupted his reverie, but each time he swung around, no one was there. After doing this several times, he decided that it had to be Emanuel, and that he'd make himself known when he saw fit.

He laughed to himself. In the short time he'd been in Renaissance, he was coming to accept the strange happenings there as easily as everyone else did. Well, almost as easily. Basically, he'd decided that rather than make himself crazy trying to give rhyme and reason to everything that happened, he'd chalk it up to coincidence. Although, watching a blind man complete tasks that would have given a sighted man pause, could not be considered coincidental in any way and still unnerved Steve.

His mind occupied by the remarkable Josiah, Steve continued up the hill until he reached the flat rocks, then he sat down and waited for whoever had followed him to show themselves. To his shock, it was not Emanuel who appeared at his side, but Meghan.

"I saw you headed this way and thought you might need this," she said, handing him his wool jacket.

He took it from her and slipped it on, not bothering to button it up. "Thanks."

"How did things go today?" she asked, sitting beside him. She could feel the heat emanating from his body to hers. She shifted slightly, trying to dispel the sensation.

"Quite honestly, I can say I have not enjoyed myself that much in a long time. Josiah is truly a remarkable man. It's just too bad he can't see the beauty he creates."

She glanced at his profile and caught her breath at the animation in his features. He had shed a bit of the depressed, uninterested man he'd been when he first came across the footbridge, but they still had a long way to go in restoring Steve's faith in himself as a doctor.

"Oh, Josiah sees all the flowers," she said, dragging her gaze from Steve's face and concentrating on a barge splitting the thick ice as it crawled up the Hudson River.

"That's not possible."

"It is when you see with your heart," she said quietly.

She could feel his gaze on her. Not daring to look at

him, knowing how easy it would be to be drawn into the vortex of his charm, she continued to stare at the river.

She'd followed him up here to see if the visions would return, but nothing but the silence of the waning day and sound of their breathing kept them company. Soft puffs of gray smoke emerged in intermittent clouds from their mouths as they took each breath. However, though the visions didn't return, the magnetic draw of this man did.

She was aware of every move he made, every breath he took. Not the feeling she usually had for an Assignment. It was more, stronger, more intense. A sense of helplessness invaded her, a need so strong that she was sure if she sat here any longer, she would ask him for another kiss. Meghan pulled the thick, gray, knitted shawl closer around her shoulders. As she had that afternoon, she thought about what it would feel like to have his lips touch hers.

When she realized the direction of her thoughts, she vaulted to her feet and stared down at him. "I have to go start supper." Before he could say anything, she hurried down the hill.

Meghan had only been gone a few minutes when Steve felt the presence of someone else behind him. He turned to find Timothy standing there, a look of hesitation on his face. Shifting his seat, he beckoned the boy over to join him. Timothy sat, folded his hands as Steve had, and together, they watched Meghan as she made her way toward her house.

"Did you ever finish your breakfast?" Steve asked.

Timothy shook his head.

Steve smiled. Without thinking, he lapsed into the tale his mother had always used to get him to eat. "When I was about your size, my mother told me if I didn't eat, Santa's elves would come in the night and tickle me." He leaned closer to the boy. "I hated to be tickled, so I would eat every bit of food on my plate."

Timothy chuckled.

Steve picked up a handful of snow and molded it between his hands until he had a snowball. He threw it haphazardly at a tree and watched it explode into millions of white fragments. Timothy followed suit. Then he tapped Steve's shoulder.

Steve turned to him. Timothy flattened the snow then drew three stick figures, one tall with just a few wisps of hair on his misshapen head, one shorter with a dress and long hair that curled on the ends, then a little one with long pants. Timothy pointed at the big one, then at Steve.

"Me? No, I don't have any kids."

The boy shook his head and pointed first at the little figure, then Steve, then at the big figure, then Steve.

Steve studied the drawing. He thought he knew what Timothy was asking. "The father?"

Timothy nodded and pointed first at Steve then the largest stick figure.

"My father?"

Timothy nodded vigorously.

Steve tried not to think about his father, much less talk about him. "I haven't seen him in a long time. We never . . . well, we never really got along."

Timothy frowned, and drew a question mark in the snow.

"Well, when I decided to be a doctor, he said I couldn't do it and that I wouldn't be a very good doctor."

Timothy shook his head vigorously.

"You don't agree with that?"

He shook his head again.

"How do you know I'm a good doctor?"

Timothy covered his heart with his hand.

Steve looked quickly away.

A chill breeze blew off the river. Steve shivered and found himself longing for the spring temperatures inside the village and, in particular, the warm crackle of the big fireplace in Meghan's house. Or was it just Meghan he longed for?

"We better be getting back." He stood and reached for Timothy's hand. When he felt the small fingers curl trustingly around his, a jolt went through him that jarred him to his toes.

Quickly, he untangled the boy's grasp, then, making certain Timothy followed, started down the hill. He didn't want trust from any child, and for some inexplicable reason, especially not this one.

CHAPTER 7

The next day, the morning sun hung low in a cloudless, bright blue sky when Steve arrived at Josiah's, anticipating another day of digging in the warm earth and setting seedlings on their way to maturity. He rounded the corner of the cottage and found the old man waiting at the edge of the plowed field with Timothy and Meghan.

None of them noticed his approach, and he took advantage of it to drink his fill of the beautiful woman beside Timothy. The morning sun transformed Meghan's long, wavy hair into spun gold. A breeze played with the hem of her long, blue skirt, giving him fleeting glimpses of the shapely legs hidden beneath. The same breeze plastered the flimsy material of her snowy blouse to her upper torso. Not voluptuous by any measure, her small, well-shaped breasts pushed against the material with a prominence that made Steve stumble.

Large-chested women had never attracted him, and he judged that Meghan's would nestle quite comfortably in the palm of his hand. His groin tightened.

Thankfully, Josiah's head raised and turned in Steve's direction, saving him from any further self-torture.

"Mornin', Steve," Josiah called.

Yesterday, Steve had attributed Josiah's ability to sense him, before Steve could say anything, to coincidence. This morning's repeat proved that Josiah's unimpaired, working senses had developed far beyond that of most of the visually handicapped people Steve had come into contact with in his career as a doctor.

This fascinated Steve. He hoped that one day he would find the opportunity to sit with Josiah and talk to the old man to find out how he had managed to fine tune his remaining senses to such a high degree. Some of his fellow physicians at St Joseph's would be greatly interested in information like that. That is if he ever got out of this crazy place and back to the normal world. Until then. . .

"Good morning, Josiah." Steve nodded at Timothy and Meghan. "Morning."

"Meghan has brought this young man here to help us," Josiah announced, putting a hand on Timothy's shoulder.

Timothy looked up at Steve with those wide, trusting blue eyes and smiled. Steve looked away and caught Meghan staring at him. Her expression held a plea to go along with this new arrangement. He avoided her gaze. He may still be dazed by the inexplicable things that had happened to him in the last days, but he had enough of his common sense left to determine Timothy wasn't here just to help him plant tomatoes.

What in hell was she up to? Was she deliberate trying to prolong his pain? Was this part of that healing crap she'd told him about when he first arrived here? If it was, Steve had a big surprise for her. Nothing she could say or do was going to tie him to this kid. Nothing.

"Is that all right with you?" she asked Steve.

"Whatever Josiah wants. His field. His vegetables." Steve picked up a flat of pepper seedlings and stalked toward the unfinished row of plants he'd left the previous day.

Meghan followed him, nearly running to keep up with his long strides. "Why don't you want Timothy here?"

Stopping short, Steve turned and only by putting the flat of seedlings between them did he prevent a head-on collision.

"Do I have to spell it out for you? I swore off kids six years ago." He turned and trudged on.

"You can't just swear off kids," Meghan said, once more following in his footsteps. "Children are a part of the endless circle of life. Besides, Timothy needs a man to relate to."

"He has a father for that," he growled back over his shoulder.

When he reached the end of the partially planted row, he dropped the wooden flat to the ground, then knelt next it. Her shadow fell over him, reminding him of her presence, as if he needed reminding. He was much too aware of every move she made, every breath she took, and, to his dismay, his attraction seemed to be intensifying with each day. The woman was creeping under his skin, and he didn't seem to be able to stop it, and, truth be known, he wasn't sure he wanted to.

But despite his growing attraction for Meghan, he was not about to allow this child to creep under his skin and worse, into his heart. There were too many children residing there already. Any more and Steve wouldn't be able to endure it.

"His father isn't here. You are." She squatted down so they were on the same level. "He likes and trusts you."

There it was. *Trust.* The one thing he neither sought nor wanted from a any child.

His chest constricted. He caught his breath. It was one thing to see it in the kid's eyes and quite another to have it confirmed for him in words. The ice that had encased Steve's heart for six years began to crack, and the minute return of emotion almost bent him double with the pain.

"Meghan, I . . ." A small, warm hand closed over Steve's and gently removed the pepper seedling he'd been holding.

Steve watched silently as Timothy dropped the plant into the hole he'd dug. Cupping his hand, the child gently scooped the soil around the plant, then patted it into place. He looked expectantly at Steve.

Rousing from his study of the boy's movements, Steve grabbed the watering can and doused the plant liberally.

He looked back at Timothy, who smiled up at him with a radiance that caused that crack in his emotional prison to widen another fraction.

Unable to help himself, he grinned back at the little boy. "I can tell you've done this before."

Timothy nodded vigorously. The wave of blond hair on his forehead danced merrily in response.

Steve pointed to the flat of seedlings. "Well, don't just sit there then; we've got a lot of work to get done today. Grab another one of those plants and get it in the ground." He softened his command by patting Timothy on the head and smiling broadly at him.

Steve knew the exact moment when Meghan left. The familiar emptiness he'd come to associate with her absence took hold. He glanced toward the cottage in time to see the hem of her blue skirt vanish around the corner.

Timothy plucked the next seedling from the flat and waited for Steve to dig the hole. Without a word, Steve complied. Hole after hole went that way until the entire flat of seedlings was nestled in the rich, dark earth.

He and Timothy worked for another hour or so cultivating the soil around the newly planted seedlings, then stopped. Their hands were coated with thick mud, and the knees of their pants bore witness to the wet soil they'd been crawling through, but they both smiled broadly. Fatigue showed in every movement of the boy's body and in every line in his face. They'd worked hard, but not nearly hard enough to produce that degree of exhaustion. Steve pushed aside his concern, unwilling to address the prodding of his conscience. He wouldn't do Timothy any more good than he'd done the rest of the kids.

"Well, what do you think, buddy?"

Timothy surveyed the plants and curled his thumb and forefinger together to form an *O*.

A deep laugh rumbled from Steve. "My feelings exactly. We are good."

The boy raised his forefinger.

"Yup. Number one is right."

They slapped their palms together in agreement and laughed.

Standing, he drew Timothy to his feet. They surveyed their work one last time. Timothy slipped his hand into Steve's. Steve almost pulled away, but then he gazed around them at the new growth reaching toward the sun and the pride on Timothy's face, and he couldn't bring himself to let go of the boy. Suddenly, he knew contentment he hadn't experienced in a very long time, and he had an immediate need to share it with Meghan.

❋ ❋ ❋

Timothy decided to help Josiah put the tools away. After Josiah assured him his help was not needed, Steve rinsed off the mud and dirt and hurried toward Meghan's cottage.

Despite being eager to see Meghan, Steve found the idea of being alone with her discomforting to his libido. Each time he was with her his awareness of her became more intense. Instead of only a few days, he felt as if he'd known her for an eternity. Feeling that comfortable around her meant it was just a matter of time before he did something stupid like kissing her.

Since he didn't plan on staying in this place and she couldn't leave, getting attached to her would be the equivalent of emotional suicide.

Hoping he was tired enough that his emotions wouldn't erupt on him, he opened the door. When he stepped inside, he found Meghan balancing on a ladder, draping strings of cranberries across the mantel.

Puzzled, for a moment he watched her. Then it occurred to him what she was decorating for. Because the village seemed to reside in a perpetual spring, Steve had forgotten that it was December, and Christmas was approaching.

He took in the decorations she had already put in place. Garlands of princess pine covered the mantel and outlined each doorway. A large, long-needle pine wreath tied with red bows, each holding clusters of pinecones, covered the wall over the mantel. The heat from the fireplace magnified the rich, woodsy fragrance emanating from the wreath.

However, what caught his attention and held it prisoner was the woman decorating. Her long green skirt had ridden up her shapely calf. The pale green peasant blouse had escaped from the waistband and bared a section of her midriff. Her long blond hair had been caught up on the top of her head with a comb, leaving the nape of her slim, white neck exposed to Steve's hungry gaze. He took a step toward her.

Just then Meghan stretched to drape the cranberry string over a nail above her head. The ladder swayed precariously and then pitched to the side. Steve sprang forward and caught Meghan in his arms just before her head struck the stone hearth.

Stunned by her fall, Meghan could only lay in his arms blinking up at him, trying not to think about how safe and secure his arms felt. "Thank you."

He continued to hold her, his large hands cradling her back, his warm breath brushing her cheeks. "My pleasure," he said, his voice almost a sigh.

The smell of fresh air, sunshine, and the rich earth of Josiah's garden surrounded him—an aphrodisiac to her already over-burdened senses.

Blood pounded through her temples. She tried to free herself, but he held firm, his arms neither demanding nor imprisoning, just too comforting to abandon. Little by little, an awareness of his large body and the heat of his hands on the bare flesh where her blouse had ridden up flooded through her, drowning out the voice of caution whispering in her ear to stop now, before it was too late.

"You can let me go now," she said, her voice low and

lacking conviction.

"Not yet," he whispered. His dark gaze locked with hers, and he dipped his face toward her parted lips. "I haven't held you nearly long enough." He shifted his body so he was sitting on the floor with her cradled across his lap.

This can't be happening, she told herself. *I can't let this happen. I'll jeopardize everything.*

But while her head denied it, her body arched toward him, her arms slid around his wide shoulders. A foreign longing grew inside her, one she'd never experienced before, but one she could not deny.

"Steve."

"Shh," he said, laying a warm finger across her lips.

Inside, he knew that if they spoke, this moment might disappear, and the thought of never holding her again was more than he could bear. He gazed into her face, and it struck him full in the heart. Illogical as it seemed, he had fallen in love with this woman. He wanted to be with her forever—hold her just like this, make love to her, have kids with her, grow old with her.

Slowly, he lowered his mouth to hers. The first touch of her lips was like being brushed briefly by a cloud, leaving him unfulfilled, unsure if it had really happened. Needing the assurance that it *had* happened, he gathered her closer and captured her mouth with his, kissing her with an intensity that bespoke all the need bottled up inside him. Heat rushed through him, flowing like an ocean current as it skimmed across the sea and gathered strength to break and crash against the shore.

He tasted the tartness of the cranberries she must have been eating and the warm, velvety softness of her lips as they nestled against his. But there was more. He could detect the innocence in the untried woman and knew he was the first to experience her passion. And experience it he did.

Sitting back on the floor, he pulled her even closer. He delighted in the way she clung to him as if afraid he'd go away and all this would end. He slid his hand down her side, barely skimming the side of her breast. She gasped and held her breath. A shudder coursed through her.

His fingers touched bare skin, and he drew in a deep, shuddering breath. God, was it possible that anything could be so soft, so warm, so inviting? Carefully, he lifted the hem of her blouse and slipped his hand beneath the thin fabric.

Just as he'd known it would, her breast nestled in the palm of his hand, filling it comfortably. He massaged it gently and rubbed the hardening tip against his palm. She moaned deep in her throat and strained against him, silently begging for more. His groin tightened and throbbed with need.

Looking down into the blue pools of her eyes, Steve could see her desire rising to the surface, making itself known to both him and her. At the same time, he could read her hesitation and her wonder at these new sensations wracking her body.

"It's okay. We'll take this slow."

He pulled back and glanced around them. The living room floor was hardly the place he would have picked to make love to Meghan. He would much rather they were stretched out across the colorful patchwork quilt on her bed, but . . .

The door opened, and Timothy walked in. Meghan and Steve sprang apart and scrambled to their feet.

"Hi, Timothy," Meghan said, straightening her clothes and obviously fighting to control both her breathing and her tone of voice. Her porcelain-like, creamy complexion had turned a deep pink.

"Hey, buddy," Steve chimed in. "How's it going?"

Steve held his breath while the boy looked from one adult to the other. Then suddenly he grinned and, with a whoop, tackled Steve, throwing him off balance and tumbling to the floor on top of him. Once down, the boy straddled Steve's middle and laughed aloud.

It took Steve a moment to realize that he thought Meghan and Steve had been wrestling when he came in and was joining in the fun. Over the boy's shoulder, Steve could see Meghan still struggling for composure.

"I'm going to start supper." She scurried from the room, leaving Steve and Timothy in a heap in the middle of the floor.

Steve watched her go with a growing need to follow and . . . And what? Apologize? No, he wasn't sorry it had happened. Assure her? Of what? That it would never happen again? He'd be lying to both of them if he tried to make her believe that.

He knew the first chance he got, it *would* happen again. If he had learned nothing else by kissing Meghan, he had learned that he would never get enough of her.

* * *

Dinner turned out to be a very quiet meal. Timothy once again played with his food, but this time neither Steve nor Meghan seemed to notice. What Steve did note, however, was a new bruise on Timothy's forearm. Normally, the brief wrestling he and Timothy had engaged in earlier in the living room would not have caused a bruise on any of the participants, but Timothy wasn't normal. Steve looked away.

His gaze fell on Meghan, and instantly the memory of holding her, kissing her, came rushing back. Shifting in his chair in an effort to find comfort, he dropped his gaze and tried to wipe away the memories. But they were too stubborn to be dismissed. The softness of her hair, her warm lips, her body against his—all of them played through his mind.

"How's the garden coming?" Meghan asked, obviously using small talk to dispel the air of discomfort that hung over the table.

For a moment, Steve groped for an answer, any answer. He grabbed at the first word that entered his mind. "Good," he said, finally managing a modicum of control. "We're almost done with the planting. Tomorrow, we'll put in the last of the peppers."

"Are you enjoying it?"

He paused in the act of stabbing a piece of juicy roast beef. "I didn't think I would, but, yes, I am enjoying it." He laid the fork down on his plate. "It's kind of hard to imagine that I had a part in those plants growing and producing vegetables." He smiled at her. "My family had . . . well, let's just say we wanted for very little. I never was allowed to . . . get dirty. It probably sounds silly, but I've never had an experience like this before."

"Yes, you have." Meghan looked at him, her gaze intent.

"Excuse me?"

"The children you care for. It's the same thing. Taking care of them, giving them what's needed to nurture them back to health."

Steve went stone still. The pain he'd buried deep down where he could ignore it, live with it, began rising to the surface. His hands tightened into fists. "No. It's not the same thing at all. The plants are thriving, growing, maturing, as they should. The children died."

"But—"

"Let it go, Meghan," he growled, glaring at her.

She glanced toward Timothy, whose head pivoted from one adult to the other, his eyes full of questions, his bottom lip quivering.

She patted his hand reassuringly. The boy seemed to relax. Her ability to calm the child amazed Steve. A word, a gesture, and the boy forgot whatever had alarmed him. Never in his life had he met a woman who was so gentle, so loving.

Oddly, his anger had dissipated without his knowing it. He had no idea why or how, he just knew that suddenly it was gone. But the pain was still there, always reminding him of the failures, the losses.

"Dessert, anyone?" Meghan said, rising and beginning to collect dishes.

Just then a knock sounded on the door. Steve went to answer it. He threw open the door, and standing there was a woman wrapped in a fashionable dark brown coat. The combination of chestnut hair and clear blue eyes produced a deceptively youthful face that made it difficult to assess her age. Her wide smile revealed a straight row of perfectly white teeth. She reminded Steve of someone.

Then he noticed the star-shaped scar between her eyebrows.

"It can't be," he whispered.

CHAPTER 8

"H ey there, Mr. C," the woman standing on Meghan's doorstep said, then she smiled as if they were back in Central Park feeding the pigeons.

Steve blinked several times, then questioning his own conclusions whispered, "Irma?"

"One and the same," she announced, throwing her arms wide and executing a curtsey.

"But, how . . ." He swept her from head to toe with his gaze, trying to equate the homeless bag lady of Central Park with the lovely, well-dressed, middle-aged woman before him.

"Who is it, Steve?" Meghan emerged from the kitchen wiping her hands on a dishtowel. She stepped around Steve and stopped short. "Irma!" Immediately, she engulfed the woman in a hug and pulled her into the house and into the living room, leaving Steve standing by the open door, gape-mouthed. "When did you get here? Emanuel said nothing about you coming so soon."

"It was a spur of the moment thing," Irma said,

returning Meghan's embrace and placing a brief kiss on her cheek. "Emanuel had something for me to take care of here so I am a little early, but enough about me. Tell me how you've been. How is Mr. C doing?"

Meghan cast him a worried glance and quickly looked away.

While Steve stood transfixed in utter amazement, Meghan helped Irma off with her coat. Beneath it she wore a tailored dress of baby blue silk that perfectly matched her eyes and hugged her trim figure. Even to his untrained eye, the garment looked far too expensive for the woman he last saw pushing a shopping cart around the park.

"Steve, would you please put Timothy to bed and, on your way back, bring Irma a cup of coffee?" Without waiting for his answer, Meghan turned back to her guest. "Let's sit." Meghan ushered her visitor toward the winged chairs flanking the roaring fireplace.

Still baffled by this new turn of events, Steve could not take his eyes off Irma as he moved slowly toward the kitchen. Many strange things had happened since he got to Renaissance, things that he'd tried to explain with reason and logic and failed, but this had to be the strangest. How had Irma shed close to twenty years and become this charming, lovely lady? And why had she suddenly shown up here?

What had she said? Emanuel had something for her to take care of? He sure hoped it wasn't him. He had all he could do to withstand Meghan's campaign to "heal" him. He wasn't sure he could handle both of them. He roused himself and headed toward the kitchen, still trying to apply logic to a situation that obviously defied it.

✳ ✳ ✳

Meghan settled into the chair opposite Irma. "So, tell me why you've been called back to the village."

"I wanted to check on Mr. C." Irma gazed into the blazing fire rather than meeting Meghan's gaze.

Her natural instincts told Meghan that Irma was not being totally forthcoming with her. "But that's not the only reason, is it?"

Irma's gaze flew to Meghan, then immediately went back to the fire. Her hands twisted in her lap. "No."

"Then what is it?" Meghan had never seen Irma nervous and unsure of herself. The Irma she knew was always in control of any situation, always confident and strong.

Once more, Irma turned to Meghan, the shook her head. "I can't say right now, but I promise, you'll know soon."

Almost Emanuel's exact words when Meghan had asked him about her visions.

Did Irma have something to do with it? Was it her tale that Emanuel couldn't tell? Is that why she was here?

That was silly. She only saw Irma a few times a year. What could the woman possibly have to do with anything

135

that affected Meghan so personally?

Irma suddenly brightened, but the hints that her apparent good humor was forced did not escape Meghan's sharp eye. "Enough about me. Tell me about Mr. C."

Meghan leaned back in the chair. "It's not going as easily as it should be. He's fighting it."

Irma nodded sagely. "That's because he's afraid of the pain." She frowned in thought. "Maybe we need to bring Ellie back here so he can see she's alive."

Meghan shook her head. "No. He needs to understand this in his heart without material proof. Once he's accepted that he's a good doctor, and that none of those children's lives were wasted, and none of their deaths were his fault—then we can show him the proof."

For a long moment, Irma was silent. Then she looked at Meghan and smiled. "You're right, of course, which is why you are a Healer, and I am a Guide." She shifted in the chair and re-crossed her legs so that she faced Meghan more squarely. "That child holds the answer."

Meghan agreed, but she had reservations. "I think Steve sees that I'm throwing them together. I'm afraid he'll balk."

Leaning forward, Irma patted her hand. "No one can resist a child for long."

"He is very good with him. He's gentle, patient, and, when he's not fighting it, I can see he cares for the boy." She could add that his kisses rocked her world and his hands were those of a skilled lover, but she kept that to herself.

Irma studied Meghan silently for a while, and then smiled gently. "You speak very highly of him. A body might think that you—" She stopped short and gave her head a brief shake. "None of my business."

Meghan leaned forward eagerly. She loved Irma and had often confided her deepest thoughts to her. Irma's opinions mattered greatly to Meghan. "What? What would they think?"

Standing, Irma walked to the blazing fire. She leaned forward to warm her hands in the radiant heat. "I live in Central Park, and I see many things: children playing, animals being walked, seasons passing. But the one thing that warms my heart as nothing else can is seeing the couples walking hand in hand. I've seen the look in their eyes, the same look that's shining in yours."

Meghan blinked, not understanding any of this. "I seem to be missing your point."

Irma smiled gently and touched Meghan's hand lightly. "It's love, Meghan. You're in love with Steve."

Opening her mouth to deny Irma's words, Meghan stopped cold at the sound of footsteps approaching from the kitchen. Steve walked into the room with Timothy straddling his shoulders.

"This cowboy came to say goodnight." He strode toward them, grinning and bouncing Timothy as he walked. The child giggled and clung to Steve.

Though Meghan should have been pleased at this turn of events, Irma's words had driven everything from her mind except a barrage of burning questions. Could Irma be right? Had she fallen in love with Steve? How, when she'd had her guard up, had it happened?

Meghan looked up at Steve and felt her heart pound faster, her breath catch in her throat, and her head become light when she dropped her gaze to his lips. Slowly, the truth advanced on her.

A chill chased down her body. Dread settled over her. In her mind, she could see her home, her lifestyle, and her very happiness slipping away, and she was helpless to stop it. All because she'd done the unthinkable.

She'd fallen in love with Steve Cameron.

"Meghan?" Steve stared down at her. "Are you all right?"

She shook herself, her thoughts slowly righting themselves. "Yes. Yes, I'm fine. Please take Timothy to bed for me." She rose unsteadily and kissed the boy's offered cheek. "Good night, little one."

Steve waited a moment before turning to Irma. "How about a good night kiss for this cowboy?"

Irma rose from the hearth where she'd taken a seat earlier. She glanced at Meghan, concern evident in her face, before forcing a smile and kissing the boy's cheek. "Night, Timothy. Sleep tight."

Timothy slapped Steve's side as if urging a horse to a gallop. He obliged and trotted off toward the kitchen.

In the doorway, he paused and scanned Meghan's face. "I'll be right back with the coffee," he said, more to Irma than Meghan.

When Steve had gone, Meghan collapsed back in the chair. Irma came to squat in front of her and grasp her hand.

"The last thing I ever wanted to do is upset you. I thought you knew."

Shaking her head, Meghan raised her gaze to the woman. "I suspected, but I had hoped it wasn't true."

"Why? Steve's a wonderful man."

"Yes, he is, but he'll be leaving Renaissance. You know I can't go with him unless I'm willing to give up everything here." She glanced around the room, her gaze taking in all the things she held dear.

But deep down, she knew. It wasn't the material things that she would not want to leave. It was the security, the peace of this place. She'd heard tales and seen the result on her Assignments of the world beyond the mist, and she had no desire to become part of it. But she could not ask Steve to give it up either. He had a destiny to fulfill.

Besides, if she went beyond the mist with no intention of returning, her memory would be wiped clean, and she would not remember the love or the man. It was an unreasonably hellish choice. Either she spent a lifetime with only memories as a companion or a lifetime with no memory of the things she never wanted to forget.

❋ ❋ ❋

Alvin Tripp faced his longtime friend across the rough-hewn trestle table in his dining room. "She's here."

His athletic build and tanned face testified to the many hours he'd spent in the outdoors looking for game to feed the village. He still wore the outside world's clothes, jeans and a dark green sportshirt, but Emanuel knew Alvin couldn't wait to get back into his beloved buckskins.

Emanuel nodded. "Thank you."

"She wasn't at all happy about coming back."

"I didn't expect she would be," Emanuel said, his high forehead creasing in thought. "But it's time. Meghan has started to have visions, and Irma has to explain them to the girl. The village is a haven in which to heal and find peace, not a place in which to hide from things we don't wish to face. Irma has known that since she first came here. She's always been aware that one day she would have to face her past and tell her story."

Alvin nodded. He helped himself to another thick slice of Sara's bread. He frowned as he slathered butter over the white surface. "It's gonna be hard for the girl to hear."

"Yes, yes, it is."

"I wish I could do it for her. Irma is a good woman. Is there no way she can get out of it?"

"I'm afraid not." Emanuel sighed. "Much in life is hard, Alvin. That doesn't mean it's to be avoided.

Sometimes, facing the thing we fear most can strengthen us for other tasks."

Forking the last of his hasty meal of rabbit stew into his mouth, Alvin swallowed. "And sometimes, it tears the heart into so many pieces it can never be put back together again."

Emanuel rose and placed a comforting hand on his friend's shoulder. "Faith and trust, Alvin. Faith and trust."

❊ ❊ ❊

Meghan had said a brief goodnight to Irma and gone to bed shortly after Steve had left the room with Timothy. After what she'd had to admit to herself and Irma, she had no desire to see Steve again until she'd had time to think about it and try to come to terms with what it would mean to her very existence.

Donning her nightgown and slipping into bed, she laid back and thought about when she'd first seen Steve come over the footbridge. She'd known then that something was different. She felt too much, but not enough. Never before had her Assignment's thoughts and deep feelings been shut off from her. However, she'd known from the start that Steve was not going to be like her other Assignments.

She had assumed it was because his injuries went far deeper than any she'd encountered before. So, what made her change her mind? The observations of a woman who barely knew her? Her own frantic search to put a reason to her visions? All of the above?

What she felt for Steve was concern for a fellow human being, a desire to help him find his way back to who he was and what he did, a need to show him his worth. None of that added up to love.

As far as what had happened on the floor of the living room, that was nothing more than two people coming together and experiencing primal instincts that had been held at bay for too long. The same would have happened with any man.

Bypassing any arguments to the contrary, she snuggled down under the quilt, satisfied that she had sorted through the tangled web of her emotions and at last had them in perspective. Maybe she did love Steve, but love came in many forms. The love she felt for Steve was nothing more than the kind she felt for Emanuel.

Why then did her blood heat only when it was Steve touching her?

Before she had time to answer this troubling question, her eyelids closed and the dream came.

* * *

The alley was dark and rank with the odor of rotting garbage. Shadowed figures prowled in dark corners, their eyes glowing with an eerie yellow light. Meghan shivered and hurried on. Trash scattered before her as she increased her speed to reach the end. But the alley just grew longer, stretching on forever.

Frantically, she ran faster toward the pinpoint of light she could see at the far end, but it kept moving farther away from her. She ran faster. Suddenly, she was out of the alley, but into another one—smaller, dirtier, and smellier. Hunger gnawed at her stomach, and she looked around for . . . For whom?

She wanted to go home, but she knew she had no home. She leaned against a slimy, damp wall and slid to the ground, tears streaking her dirty cheeks. A strange cold seeped into her. Her teeth clattered against each other. Not understanding why, only knowing she had to, Meghan slid behind a large dumpster standing near the wall. She huddled down and made herself as small as possible. Then she waited. Shivers wracked her little body.

Little? She looked down at herself and realized she couldn't have been more than four years old. This was bizarre. She was a grown woman, not a child. Nevertheless, when she looked at her body again, she saw a child.

Suddenly a scream rent the air. Meghan looked toward the sound but could only see rapidly moving shadows. Carefully and slowly, she crawled from her hiding place.

Then she saw it. Something black and foreboding and without form. Terror gripped her. She opened her mouth to cry out, but no sound emerged. The silhouette came closer. Its shadow blotted out the light. It grabbed her, but she tore free of its hold and started running again. Her feet tangled in the trash on the ground, and she couldn't get loose. She couldn't get . . .

* * *

Meghan sprang up in bed, blinked several times and looked around. The familiar silhouettes of her bedroom came into view. Her blankets were tangled around her legs. Sweat plastered her thin nightgown to her body. Her breath came in rapid spurts.

Never, in all her life, had she experienced anything to equal that nightmare. She lay there panting for breath and shivering as the night air hit her wet gown. After a few minutes, she managed to get out of bed and change.

Flipping on her bedside light, she climbed back into bed. She lay beneath the warm quilt—afraid to go back to sleep, afraid whatever it was in the shadows of her dreams would return, and, this time, she would not be able to outrun it.

* * *

After taking Timothy to bed, Steve returned to the living room with the promised coffee and found Irma still sitting on the hearth, alone.

Not wanting to disturb what appeared to be deep thought, he set the tray on the side table, poured himself a cup and leaned back in the chair. He sipped his coffee quietly and waited for Irma to speak. Long moments passed, and still she said nothing. Instead, she continued to stare at the mesmerizing flames dancing over the charred wood.

Steve silently studied her. He was still having trouble equating this lovely woman with the bag lady he'd shared coffee with for over a year. Gone were the holey clothes, the grime and dirt, the gap-toothed smile, and the gray hair. All the time he'd spent with her and not once had he ever glimpsed the woman before him.

How had she managed it? Had she really been penniless and lived in the streets? Were the contents of the shopping cart really her worldly possessions?

Questions bombarded him. He could stay silent no longer. "Irma?" he said quietly, hoping not to startle her.

She jumped anyway and turned to him. "Oh!" She laid her hand on her chest. "I didn't hear you come back in."

"I'm sorry. I didn't mean to scare you." He laughed and held his hands wide. "I was just looking at you. I can't believe you're the same woman from Central Park. You don't even sound like her."

Smiling, she swung away from the flames. "That was Irma the Guide. This," she waved her hand across her a trim body, "is Irma the . . . woman."

He frowned. "Then you're not here as a Guide?"

A shadow passed over her expression. She picked at imaginary lint on her skirt and shook her head. "I wish I were."

"Would I be prying if I asked why you're here?"

For a long time, she stared at him, until he thought she'd confide her reasons for showing up in Renaissance without warning. In the end, she chose to guard her silence.

"Simple curiosity is not prying, but I'm afraid I can't tell you."

He'd learned not to question things that happened in Renaissance. On those few instances when he did, rarely did he ever receive a satisfying answer anyway. If the people in this village could do nothing else, they had evasion down to a fine art. Silent ignorance was far less frustrating.

Still, since she'd been initially responsible for him being here, he needed to ask one thing. "Are you here because of me?"

She smiled the smile he had seen innumerable times in the park and, despite the absence of the missing teeth, one he would have recognized anywhere. "No. My job with you finished with that envelope you found in your pocket."

Steve opened his mouth to ask how she'd done that, but the twinkle in her eye told him he would get nothing more than another evasion.

"You love Meghan, don't you?" Irma said without preamble.

Irma's statement almost knocked Steve out of the chair.

How, when he'd just discovered it himself, had she guessed after just a few minutes? "How . . ."

"I've grown adept at reading people, and you have very expressive eyes."

"I . . . uh . . ."

Steve could find no words or a voice to express them with. He'd known for a long time that Meghan was coming to mean a great deal to him, but he'd only recently applied the word *love* to his feelings. So how had this woman, who only just arrived here, guessed? Did it show on his face? That was perfectly understandable, given the changes Meghan had wrought in him in the short time he'd been here.

With the mention of Meghan, his mind inevitably wandered to thoughts of her.

He pondered how Meghan warmed all the cold corners of his soul when she smiled, how just her presence beside him brought a peace he'd never known before, how she'd almost made him believe that he had not failed the children. That last thought brought him up straight in the chair.

When had that happened? He thought back to the feel of a small boy's hand in his, the joy of working side by side with him to plant the garden, sitting on a rock throwing snowballs at a tree.

He had no idea when it had happened or how, but it had. Not only had he fallen in love with the woman who had pushed them together and made it happen, but he'd also fallen in love with a little boy who trusted him without question. Knowing what Timothy's health problems meant, the idea of loving the child tore shreds from his already lacerated heart.

"I'm right. You do love her." Irma smiled, contentment coloring her expression.

Steve looked at Irma. "Yes, I love her."

"Good," she said, rising from the hearth, "that will help make the next few days easier for her to bear."

❄ ❄ ❄

Steve shifted the weight of the big ax from one hand to another. He pulled the collar of his jacket up and turned to Meghan. She and Timothy were assessing the pine trees around them.

"Good grief, it's just a Christmas tree. Decide on one before we all turn to solid ice." He shivered and made a funny face. "I'm beginning to feel like a snowman."

Timothy laughed.

Meghan smiled.

Steve inhaled sharply.

It had started to snow and some flakes had gotten caught in her hair, twinkling like diamonds against the blond tresses. He recalled her description of the snowflakes the day he'd arrived in the village—*tiny lace doilies, each perfect, each different.* That was Meghan—perfect, and different from any woman he'd ever known.

He could not believe how lovely she was. Her cheeks were red, and her blue eyes sparkled with a child-like anticipation as her gaze danced from tree to tree, searching for the exact one to take home. He ached with the need to hold her, to press his warm mouth to her cold lips. To throw her down in the snow and kiss her until neither of them could breathe.

"I can't make up my mind. They're all perfect." She turned to Timothy. "You decide."

They watched the boy take off into the trees, checking each one as he made his way. When he came to a tree he wanted to consider, he stepped back and looked it up and down, like a man assessing a woman. Then he'd shake his head and move on to the next to repeat the process. More than a dozen trees fell under his critical eye. Steve was beginning to think it would have been faster to have left the choice to Meghan after all, when Timothy paused overly long before a short, plump spruce. Hope blossomed in Steve's cold limbs. Then Timothy once more shook his head and hurried to another tree.

After inspecting at least a half dozen more, he stopped and pointed. Steve and Meghan followed the direction of his finger. Standing on a slight rise was a perfect blue spruce. It was tall enough to just fit into the living room and leave room for the treetop. Its graceful limbs swept the snow at its feet. The needles, while neither blur nor green, cast off a fragrance that simply said *Christmas*.

"That's it," Meghan cried and ran toward the tree. She circled the trunk and checked it from all sides. "Timothy, from now on, you are the official tree picker-outer."

Timothy beamed.

Meghan continued to admire Timothy's choice. "I proclaim that every year, from this day forward, you will—" She stopped short, lowered her head, then stepped back. "Steve, we'd better cut the tree and get home. It's getting late, and Timothy needs to eat supper."

He noted the abrupt change in her. The sparkle had gone. The fun she had been having a moment earlier had vanished. He knew that she had realized this would be the one and only Christmas they would ever spend with Timothy.

Despite his vow to keep himself removed emotionally from the young boy, Steve's heart felt as if someone were squeezing it.

❄ ❄ ❄

The next afternoon, in an effort to put the replay of the nightmares and the inevitable loss of Timothy and Steve out of her mind, Meghan threw herself into decorating her tree for the upcoming holiday. Deep into her task, she stretched to put a shiny gold ball on the branch of the blue spruce just below the treetop ornament, an angel in a flowing white satin gown with gold accents. When she found she couldn't reach the branch, she moved a chair in front of the tree and started to climb onto it.

A warm hand grasped her upper arm and stopped her. The odor of wet earth and fresh air surrounded her, but even without it, she knew, from her reaction to the touch of the warm fingers, who stood close behind her.

"Let me." Steve took the ball from her and, with little effort, hooked it on the branch that had been so tantalizingly out of Meghan's reach.

Meghan held her breath. Imprisoned between Steve and the tree, she could feel every line of his firm, muscular body against hers. As if an unseen force had stolen all her breath, she gasped for air. Quickly, she stepped aside and put space between them.

"Thanks." Looking first at him, then the tree, she smiled. "What do you think?" she asked, playing for time to control her runaway senses.

Steve stood back and studied the fully decorated tree for a time. "Gorgeous, but why didn't you wait for Timothy and me to help? Decorating a tree is supposed to be a family project."

Taking a deep calming breath, Meghan began to pack away the empty ornament boxes. "I'm used to doing it alone," she said. Then, taking another deep breath, she prepared to say the words she knew she had to say to prevent Steve from forming such strong ties with the village that he'd never leave. "Besides, we aren't a family."

Steve looked as if she'd slapped him. She hadn't meant

for it to sound so curt, but it was the truth after all. Now that she'd had plenty of time to think about how she felt about Steve, she'd concluded that it was not love she felt for Steve, but the deep bonding she always experienced with an Assignment. She'd also decided that they had grown too close, and that closeness might encourage Steve to look for a life inside the mist. That couldn't happen. Too many people needed him. His destiny could not be with her.

"What do you mean?" Steve asked. "Maybe we're not family in the traditional sense of the word. But living as close as we do, sharing our everyday lives, and caring for each other, for all intents and purposes, I'd say we are a family."

"No, we aren't, and it's not going to do anyone any good to think in such terms." Drawing herself up, she faced him. "We're simply three people who have been thrown together for a short period of time. Nothing more."

"Once you're healed, you'll leave. Once Timothy speaks and they locate his parents, he'll leave." *And I'll be alone again.* The thought sent a piercing pain knifing through her.

No denying it, she'd miss them both terribly. But then, she rationalized, she always missed her Assignments after they left. She always got over it, and she would this time, too. Wouldn't she?

"I don't think you believe that," he said, studying her face. "Besides, I don't have to leave. You even said I had that choice. I can stay or go." Steve's voice held a note of desperation.

"But the children—"

"Will manage quite well without a doctor who can't do anything to save them."

Meghan grabbed his upper arms, surprising herself with the strength of her grip. "Do you, in your heart, really believe that anymore?"

Steve opened his mouth to answer, but closed it. "I don't know what I believe anymore." He did know two things for certain.

Against his better judgment and every survival instinct he possessed, he'd come to love the little boy who dogged his every step. He wished the child nothing but good things in life. But Steve could not be a part of any of it. The boy was going to need a miracle to get past his imminent health issues, and Steve had yet to find his own miracle.

More importantly, he loved Meghan, and he would do whatever it took to be with her, even if it meant giving up any life beyond the mist.

CHAPTER 9

Steve skirted the empty Christmas ornament boxes piled in Meghan's living room and took her by the shoulders. "I've thought about this for a while. I don't want to leave. I can stay here, be part of the village. There's nothing back in the city for me."

Meghan stared into his eyes, and what she saw there made her heart beat faster, her knees go weak, and her emotions soar. She wasn't at all sure what this romantic love was supposed to feel like, but one thing she did know for sure, her calmly thought out reasoning as to why she didn't love Steve had been nothing more than a series of excuses. What she felt for Steve Cameron had nothing to do with the Assignment and everything to do with the man.

She wanted to fight his magnetic pull, tell him he had to go, he had work to do, kids to save, a life to live. But God help her, she couldn't. She wanted him to stay more than she wanted her next breath.

When he drew her toward him, she went willingly and reveled in the joy of being in his arms. His chest made a cradle for her head. His arms provided the safety and security she so desperately needed right now—a place that would protect her from the demons of her nightmares, if only during the daylight hours.

She took refuge in the feel of his heart throbbing against her, the steady rhythm reverberating in her ear, the racing beat matching her own. His big hands splayed over her back, caressing her through the fabric of her blouse and sending unnamable sensations coursing through her.

Maybe, she thought, just for today, she'd pretend that they were an ordinary couple with a future to plan and a love to hold them close, protecting them from anything that could hurt them. Maybe, just for today, she'd give in to the intense need growing inside her. Maybe, just for today, just for this moment in time, she would love Steve as she yearned to, wholly, completely, and devoutly.

"I want to be with you in every way a man and woman were meant to be together," he whispered into her hair.

Somewhere deep inside, that persistent voice warned her that this was wrong, that she should be encouraging him to go back to the outside world, that he should leave her. But she pushed the warnings aside to allow these strange and wonderful sensations to flood her and wash away all her misgivings.

Perhaps she'd been wrong. Perhaps Steve's destiny was here, with her. Perhaps that was what Emanuel had meant by Steve being a very special Assignment.

Steve drew back a little and cradled her face in his large hands. "Meghan, I love you. Don't ask me to leave you."

He loves me, and he wants to stay!

Elation blossomed in her like a new spring flower experiencing the touch of the hot sun for the first time. And like the flower, she strained toward its warmth. Never in her whole life had she heard those words spoken just for her. Oh, she knew everyone in Renaissance loved her, but no one had ever said it, and no one had ever loved her with the intensity that shone from Steve's eyes. How could she turn away from that? How could she turn away from Steve? How could she send him into a world where she could not follow?

Steve knew the moment of Meghan's surrender. Her entire body sagged against him while her arms encircled him and tightened. Her fingers dug into his shoulders. He pulled her closer, so close that nothing or no one could ever come between them.

He heard her whisper something against his shirt-front. Pulling her back a fraction, he gazed down at her. "What did you say?"

She smiled up at him, her expression timid and unsure. "I . . . I think I love you, too. I've never loved anyone in a romantic way before, so I'm not really sure it's what I feel."

Her admission took him by surprise, but it shouldn't have. Being tucked away in this isolated, strange little village for God only knew how long, he should have realized that Meghan was a virgin, untried in the ways of love. Steve chuckled with delight at the idea of being the one who would teach her the intricacies of love and the joy in expressing it by joining together as one.

"Well, this romantic love stuff is new to me, too, so why don't we explore it together?" he said, then waited for her reaction. When she gave a hesitant nod, he gently lifted her from her feet and carried her toward her room.

Once there, he placed her carefully on the multi-colored patchwork quilt, sat beside her, then gathered her to him. She looked up at him with such trust that for a moment he was stunned. It reminded him of the trust he'd seen shining from Ellie's eyes when he'd put her in the cab with her grandparents. He'd failed Ellie. Would he fail Meghan, too?

Before he could question himself any farther, Meghan pulled him toward her.

"Please, kiss me again, like you did the other day," she whispered, her voice throbbing with aroused emotions.

"If you recall, we didn't really kiss. We were interrupted."

"Well, there's no one to interrupt this time. Timothy will be having dinner with Josiah, and Irma is busy helping Clara." She tugged on his neck. "Kiss me, please," she whispered against his mouth.

If he'd been able to think rationally, Steve might have pulled back, given her more time to absorb what was happening. But rational thought vanished the moment he felt her soft lips conforming to his. Her hesitant, tight-lipped kiss confirmed her lack of experience.

Slowly, he moved his mouth over hers, coaxing her to relax. With the tip of his tongue, he teased her lips. Then delivered a series of soft butterfly kisses, touching her, then moving away.

A frustrated sigh escaped her. Her hands tightened on his neck. She pressed her body closer to his, inflaming desires he fought to keep in check. When he could stand it no longer, he placed his mouth on hers and slowly but steadily increased the pressure until finally her mouth opened under his. When his tongue slipped inside, she stiffened for a second, then gradually, her body went limp, leaving him to have his way, to explore the sweetness only he had tasted.

Meghan moaned and clung to him, not understanding what was happening to her, but at the same time, not wanting it to stop until the gnawing need inside found satisfaction. Never had she experienced such emotions, this insatiable longing that grew stronger, more insistent each time Steve kissed her.

Then his hand slipped from her back. Slowly and tantalizingly, it made its way around her side and up to cup a breast, the thin material of her blouse the only thing separating her skin from his. Gradually, he began moving his fingers in a gentle massage of her pliant flesh. His thumb skidded across her taught nipple, sending fever chills down her entire body. Her skin came alive with pinpricks of pleasure. Moans filled the silence. It took a moment for her to realize that they were coming from her.

"Relax," he whispered into her ear, his hot breath further increasing the sensations washing over her body in wave after wave of delightful rapture. "Let me touch you, teach you, love you."

She tried to speak, but forming words seemed beyond her capabilities. She could only feel. Meghan looked up at the love shining from his dark eyes, gentle eyes, eyes heavy with desire.

Gently, she cupped his cheek and outlined his lips with the pad of her thumb. "Please," she whispered haltingly.

His answer was to kiss her with such force that she was swept up in a current of pleasure so overwhelming that she lost touch with everything but Steve. She strained against him, wanting to literally become this man she loved, so that they would never be parted.

He eased her back against the pillows and stretched out beside her. His body molded itself to hers, his hand resting on her flat stomach. Very slowly, he gathered the material of her skirt in his fingers, sliding it tantalizingly up her legs, then her thighs. His gaze never left hers, almost as if he were gauging her reaction and waiting for her to stop him. But she didn't. She couldn't.

Every part of her was screaming for . . . what? Meghan had no idea what she was striving for so passionately; she just knew she had to have it.

Coaxed by him, her skirt rode higher, until she felt his hand rest on the V of her thighs. Heat rose up in her. She pushed her body against his fingers, begging silently for him to touch her, to ease the ache pounding inside her.

When he pulled away, she cried out, clutching at him.

"I'm not going anywhere," he said softly. "I want to feel your skin next to mine, so we need to get rid of these clothes."

His words came to her through a haze of desire. Vaguely, she understood. Then she felt him removing her clothes, one piece at a time, and exploring the skin that was left bare to his touch. When he'd removed all her clothes, he shifted on the bed, then moments later his naked body pressed against hers. The ache inside her flared into a raging inferno.

His skin felt so smooth, so warm, his musky smell intoxicating. She explored his chest with eager hands, touching and playing briefly with the tiny nubs she found there. Eager to know all of him, she moved her hand down his chest to his flat stomach. His breathing stopped on a sharp intake of breath. The muscles beneath her fingers contracted. His fingers tightened on her thigh. She smiled. With the realization that she could make him react to her touch as strongly as she had to his, she became emboldened, and her hand slipped lower on his body.

When she touched the hard shaft of flesh protruding from the V of his thighs, he moaned as if in pain. Her exploration stopped abruptly. She stared up at him. Pained pleasure etched his face. His back arched, encouraging her to go on.

Meghan closed her hand over him. She paused, marveling at his size. She knew about the difference between the sexes—after all, she'd bathed Timothy and other little boys who had come to the village. But never in all her wildest imaginings had she guessed . . .

Cautiously, she moved her fingers. He moaned again. Instinctively, she knew that pain was not what he was feeling. Oddly, as his pleasure increased, so did hers, and she found herself squirming, the heat between her thighs almost unbearable.

His hand closed over hers, guiding her movements. Suddenly, he stopped her.

"No. No more." He took a deep breath. "This first time is about you, not me."

Steve waited for a second to get his own desire under control, then laid his hand on the V of her thighs. Slowly, he inched his fingers down until they nestled in the folds of her heat. When she seemed okay with his touch, he introduced a single finger into her, slowly moving it in and out.

She arched her hips against his palm. Her fingernails dug into his arms. She was wet and hot and more than ready for him, but he held back. Her first time had to be something very special, and he intended to see to it that it was, even if it killed him, and, if the throbbing in his groin meant anything, it just might.

Her body thrashed and squirmed against him until her breathing became erratic and her hips matched the rhythm of his finger.

Meghan moaned, her hips rose higher and higher, straining for more. Gently, as her movement increased, he coaxed her to her first climax. She could feel a strange pressure building inside her, arching out from the V of her thighs. The, when she though she'd go mad, the pressure exploded, sending her spiraling down an endless shaft of pleasure. She shivered and lay quiet.

Before she could catch her breath, he eased himself on top of her and gazed lovingly down into her desire-clouded eyes. With great care, he entered her slowly, giving her time to get use to the size and feel of him.

She felt the pressure against her. She gasped and pulled her hips back, but he cupped her buttocks and held her to him. For a long moment, he remained still. Slowly, the heat began to build again. The need she'd felt before seemed to grow and magnify. She had trouble keeping still any longer. Her hips began to move of their own volition. That now familiar pleasure flooded her being.

When she thought she could stand it no longer, he lowered his head to hers. "I wish this could be painless for you, but it can't. Hang onto me, and I'll be as gentle as possible."

Painful? How could anything that brought so much pleasure be painful? But she did as he had instructed and held onto his broad shoulders.

Little by little he pushed forward and then stopped. The need for him to continue filled her, but she let him take the lead. He gathered her closer, then pushed.

Pain razored through her. Her eyes flew open. Above her, Steve's face reflected the pain she had just felt, the pain that still burned insider her.

"I'm sorry," he said, his voice full of compassion. "Had there been a choice, I would never have caused you this pain."

Even as he said the words the pain started subsiding. As if a magic salve had been applied, it ebbed until it disappeared and a gnawing need replace it. She moved her hips experimentally. No pain, but the need increased until she could barely hold it in check.

She kissed him and then drew him to her. "I love you," she whispered against his ear. "Please, love me."

Steve reared back and gazed down at her. "My pleasure," he said, and then kissed her long and deep.

At first, his movements were slow and careful, but with her encouragement, he increased his speed. Soon they were riding a stormy sea of passion and being tossed from the top of one wave to the other, each higher than the last.

When Meghan was sure she would die with the pleasure of it all, the waves crested, tossing them into a vortex of pleasure that seemed bottomless. For what seemed like forever, they spun and whirled. Then eruptions of ecstasy wracked her body and Steve's. They came so fast, each more intense and powerful than the last, that she couldn't catch her breath.

Slowly they drifted down into a placid lagoon of spent emotions. Steve rolled to his side and held her close against him. His labored breathing filled the silence of the room. He nuzzled the top of her head, placed fleeting kisses in her hair. Against her ear, she could feel the frantic beating of his heart.

Unable to put words to the amazing experience they'd shared, Meghan could only clutch Steve close and try to catch her breath. Fatigue flooded her. But a euphoric happiness, such as she had never known existed, made her feel as though she would never come completely back to earth.

Cuddling as close to Steve as she could, she closed her eyes.

Steve's breathing slowly returned to normal. By her even breaths, he knew Meghan had fallen asleep. Though his body felt totally devoid of energy, sleep eluded him.

He had asked many things of life, some granted and some denied him. At this very moment, however, he could forgive fate for taking away everything that mattered to him, if he would never have to know a day without Meghan by his side.

As he settled closer to the woman he loved, a light coming from her night table caught his eye. The lantern sitting there had begun to glow from the inside. The milky mist swirled and moved, slowly revealing the face of a little girl he'd last seen through the back window of a taxicab as it pulled away from the hospital.

Her voice echoed in his head. *Faith and trust make miracles.*

CHAPTER 10

C lara cleared away the supper dishes from in front of
Emanuel and Irma. Irma had been staying with her
since she'd returned to the village, and each night
they ate beneath a cloud of unspoken words. Clara knew
Emanuel was trying to leave the solution of her dilemma up
to Irma, but Clara dearly wished they would just speak of
what was at the forefront of both their minds. Perhaps then
the perpetual fog of tension thick enough to be sliced like a
pound cake would dissipate from her little kitchen.

"A very special person will be arriving in the village
soon, Clara. I want her to stay with you." Emanuel's voice
followed her into the pantry as she retrieved a tin of coffee.

"Oh?" she said, coming back into the warm, cozy
room. "And am I to know who this special person is?"

A gentle smile creased his lips. "Do you ever?"

She chuckled. "No."

"I have no doubt you will see to her comfort and in-
struction until she can assume her place in the village."

Clara paused in her preparations of the coffee pot and

glanced at him. "Then she'll be staying?"

This was odd. There always existed the possibility that an Assignment would chose to remain in the village, and was attested to by her presence and that of the other villagers, but no one since Meghan had elected to stay on. That someone was coming into their midst with the express purpose of remaining put her curious mind to work churning out an answer as to why. Try as she might, however, none came.

Emanuel nodded, and turned to study Irma, who had remained silent through much of the meal. Clara prolonged her absence from the table, in hopes that they would start talking.

Carefully, she scraped bits of leftover food from each plate into a bucket and stacked them beside the sink. Still nothing but stiff silence came from the two people at the table. Taking a freshly baked apple pie from the pie safe, she sliced it into eight equal pieces and then transferred three of the pieces to porcelain plates covered in soft pink, moss roses. Beside each slice she laid a silver fork. Unable to drag the task out any longer, she turned to the table, a plate in each hand.

As she made her way toward them, she silently pleaded with Emanuel to speak the words that had been hovering on his lips throughout the meal.

As if reading her mind, which wouldn't have been anything out of the ordinary, Emanuel said, "You've been here for a while, Irma. Have you spoken with Meghan yet?"

Clara knew that if Irma had spoken to Meghan Emanuel would have sensed it. When Emanuel finally broached the subject, it brought a sigh of welcome relief from Clara. She hated the signs of tension that had etched his handsome face since Meghan's nightmares had begun.

Proceeding to the table, Clara set a piece of apple pie before each of them, then returned to the other side of the room to fetch coffee. As unobtrusively as possible, she cocked an ear toward the conversation.

Irma glanced at him, and then shook her head. "I haven't found the right time yet."

"There will never be a *right* time for this," he said gently. "It will be just as troublesome tomorrow as today. There is no easy time." He leaned a forearm on the table, picked up his fork and toyed with the piecrust. "For Meghan to find her destiny, she must hear what you have held back from her all these years. Neither your ghosts nor hers can be conquered from behind a wall of secrets." He gazed out the window into the gathering twilight. "The Transition will be coming soon. Steve will be leaving, and she must know before then."

Clara set filled cups before each of them. Not wishing to intrude, she went back to the other side of the room to complete her chores, but kept an ear turned toward them. The tiny voice of her conscience reprimanded her for eavesdropping. Such a nasty word. She quieted the whispers by deciding it was only interest in a fellow villager.

Irma glanced up sharply from adding cream and sugar to her cup. "The Transition? How soon?"

He smiled. "You know I can't give you an hour or a day. The human mind has a pace of its own. But I can sense that the doctor grows stronger each day."

"They're in love, you know," Irma said so softly Clara had to strain to hear.

A sigh escaped Emanuel, and he laid his fork aside, his pie uneaten. "Yes, I know. It was expected. It's why I assigned Steve to Meghan. Their love will make them strong."

Irma stood and walked to the window that overlooked the small town square. She glanced toward Meghan's cottage. "Strong enough?"

"Time will tell," Emanuel said, frowning.

Clara's heart twisted painfully. She knew Emanuel was once more regretting the decisions he'd made years ago. For that matter so was she and had been for all these years. But that didn't make this chore any easier to face.

He smiled at her and gave his head an infinitesimal shake. "Regret is the barrier of progress."

❋ ❋ ❋

Later that night a shrill scream awakened Steve from a deep sleep. Beside him, Meghan thrashed and moaned, fighting the bedcovers, and in the process, hopelessly imprisoning her legs and further intensifying her struggle.

He reached for her, but she fought his touch, cringing from him in a way that tore at his heart. "Meghan. Please, sweetheart. Wake up. You're dreaming."

"No! Don't!" she screamed and pushed at his hands. "Please don't."

He grabbed her shoulders and shook her. "Wake up, Meghan. It's me, Steve."

Finally, her eyes fluttered open, and, for a moment, she stared at him. Naked fear filled the blue depths of her eyes, as if she was looking at a stranger who meant her harm. He stroked her face and kissed her lightly to assure her he had only love to give her. She shuddered and blinked. The fear evaporated, and recognition took its place. She threw herself into his arms. Tears rolled silently down her face.

He gathered her close and allowed her to cry out her anguish against him. Long moments passed while her sobs subsided, then her even breathing told him she had gone back to sleep.

Long after the room lay in silence, Steve remained awake. The sky outside was brightening with the coming day, and he continued to wonder what could have caused such terror to invade Meghan's dreams.

* * *

In the days following their first love making session,

Meghan's dreams came again and again, and Steve held her through the night. Though he asked repeatedly, she avoided talking about them. During her waking hours, her energy seemed boundless, and her interest in making love increased with each day. Steve wondered if it was because she spent the daylight hours trying to outrun the visions that came to her in the night.

Josiah and Steve had finished the planting and now, they had only to water the fledgling seedlings and wait for them to mature into producing plants. When Steve wasn't working with Josiah, he stayed as close to Meghan as possible, not wanting to miss a moment together and not wanting to be far from her should her night demons come to call during the day.

Sometimes, he thought his need to be near her was not as much his need to protect her as it was because he was afraid their moments together would soon end. Then he would shake himself free of such doubts with a reminder that he wasn't going anywhere, and they had forever together. Still the unreasonable and unfounded fear of being separated from her rode at the back of his mind daily.

Since Timothy spent more and more time with Josiah, it left Steve and Meghan free to do as they pleased, and what they pleased was spending every waking and sleeping moment together learning about each other. But what pleased them even more was loving each other into exhaustion.

After one particularly spectacular afternoon of making love, they lay in the bed, sated and entwined in each other's arms. Over her bare shoulder, which he'd been nibbling playfully while complaining about not having eaten lunch, he spotted the lantern on the night table. The mist inside swirled lazily.

He released her and reached for it. "What's this for?" he asked, recalling the face it had revealed to him the first night he and Meghan had made love.

Meghan took the lantern from him. "Lots of things," she said, perching it on her bare stomach.

She never thought the day would come when she would be comfortable sitting naked in front of another human being. But with Steve, it seemed the most natural thing in the world.

"I can see the beginning of a Transition in it. I can also keep track of *escaping* Assignments."

She threw Steve a playful glance, then laughed lightly, the kind of laugh that warmed Steve to his toes and made him want to kiss her senseless.

"So that's how you knew where I went that first night," he said, nuzzling her neck, then sitting a little straighter.

She grinned. "Yes."

He picked up the lantern and looked into the mist. He saw nothing except a faint glow beginning to form at the core of the globe. "What's happening now? Why is it glowing like that?"

Meghan bolted upright and snatched the lantern from him. She stared into it for a long time. Her complexion paled. Abruptly, she set it aside. Quickly rising from the bed, she grabbed her clothes and swept from the room.

* * *

The following morning, when Steve awoke and wandered into the warm kitchen, Timothy was at the breakfast table.

"We're taking Timothy for a walk in the woods," Meghan announced, avoiding Steve's gaze.

"Sounds like fun," Steve said, smiling at Timothy, but guessing that this sudden need for togetherness was an evasion tactic so she wouldn't have to explain what she saw in the lantern. After she'd left the bedroom the afternoon before, she'd managed to find something to do that took her somewhere Steve had not been able to find her. When she came to bed last night, he'd already been asleep.

Her actions last night and her refusal to discuss it with him convinced Steve that whatever she saw couldn't have been good.

"Let's go," she said, handing Timothy his jacket and boots.

They left the cottage, wound their way past Clara's and into the woods above the river. Meghan held Timothy's hand, making any adult conversations impossible. Later, when Timothy started exploring on his own, Steve attempted to broach the subject, but every time he tried, Meghan found a way to evade the subject. Later, when Timothy rejoined them, she avoided conversation with Steve by showing Timothy a snow bunting perched on the swaying limbs of a tree, then a pine cone that had been picked clean by the birds foraging for winter food, a deer track in the snow, and a boat pushing up the river to Albany.

By the time they'd walked to the cliffs overlooking the river, she had managed to sidestep him with all the dexterity of a wild animal evading a hunter. But the hunter may or may not be victorious in his quest. Steve, on the other hand, would not give up until he got answers.

Timothy ran ahead of them, jumped a small snow bank, then threw himself on his back in the snow. His arms and legs seesawed on either side of his body. When he stood and surveyed his handiwork, he'd made a snow angel. He looked at the adults and pointed at the indentation.

Meghan clapped her hands. "Well done."

A second later, he was running off through the towering pine trees.

Meghan started after him, but Steve, seeing the opportunity he'd been waiting for all day, seized her arm to hold her back. "Let him go. We can see him. He'll be fine."

She glanced in Timothy's direction once more, then relaxed and matched her stride to Steve's. But by her constant scan of the trees ahead, he knew she was either worried about the boy's safety or searching for another way to avoid his questions.

"Meghan," Steve touched her hand. Instantly, she snatched it away and crammed it in the pocket of her jacket. "What did you see in the lantern?" He saw her stiffen.

"Nothing."

Stopping, he turned her toward him. "I don't believe you. *Nothing* doesn't cause a reaction like yours."

Keeping her eyes averted, she kicked at the snow with the toe of her shoe, then raised her head and looked to where Timothy busied himself making snowballs and pummeling an unsuspecting, innocent pine tree.

Steve glanced at the boy then back to her. "Is it something about him?"

She walked to a downed tree. Brushing the snow from the gnarled bark, she sat, tucking the folds of her dark green skirt around her legs for warmth.

Finally, she looked at Steve. "No, it's not about Timothy."

Quickly, he joined her. "What was it then?" She shivered, and he pulled the collar of her down coat around her reddened cheeks. "Please, tell me. I can see it's troubling you." He turned her face to him. Her blue eyes glittered with tears. "Let me help, Meghan."

She sighed heavily. How could she tell him what the lantern's globe had shown her? How could she tell him she'd seen him and Timothy leaving Renaissance together? How could she stand the pain of saying the words that would seal her isolation from him?

She should have realized they were living a dream, that neither he nor Timothy had a place here, that their lives lay beyond the village. From the very beginning she'd known that. She never should have allowed herself to believe otherwise.

Steve's hand touched her arm. "Meghan?"

She turned away from him and instantly sucked in her breath. She felt the blood drain from her face. Timothy was balancing himself precariously on a huge rock. Below him lay a drop of hundreds of feet to the frozen river.

She shot to her feet. "Oh, my God," she whispered. As if frozen in place, she couldn't seem to force her body to move. She could only stare at the child who stood three steps away from death.

Terror swelled inside her, but she tried not to show it for fear of frightening the child. He grinned at her and pointed at himself, as if to say, "Look at me!"

Swallowing hard, she smiled at Timothy. "I see you." Without taking her gaze off Timothy, she grabbed Steve's sleeve. "Steve, stop him," she whispered.

Steve, who had also spotted Timothy and stood, stepped around her and walked slowly toward the child. The crunch of snow beneath his feet filled the tense silence and battered her brittle nerves.

As Steve drew closer, Timothy peered over the edge. "That's a long way down, isn't it, buddy," Steve said in a totally controlled tone. "Maybe we should get you down from there before you fall."

He reached slowly for Timothy. The boy allowed himself to be lifted down. A heavy sigh of relief escaped her. Meghan could see by the look of longing Timothy threw toward the big rock that he wasn't happy about ending his adventure.

She forced her voice to sound normal. "I think it's about time we got back for supper." She took Timothy's hand and began the trek back to the village.

Steve hung back, watching them make their way down the snow capped ridge. As they disappeared behind a hillock of dense pines, his breathing slowly returned to normal and his nerves unwound. He dropped onto the downed tree. Glancing briefly at the rock, he propped his elbows on his knees, clasped his hands together, and rested his chin on them.

When he'd pulled the boy off the rock, a realization had bloomed inside him. If he and Meghan had not been there to prevent it, Timothy could have slipped off that rock and fallen to his death. While that frightened him immeasurably, what followed frightened him even more.

Timothy was just one child. As Steve gazed absently out over the frozen landscape, he wondered how many kids outside the village would die because he wasn't there to prevent it.

* * *

"I want Steve and Timothy to move in with Josiah." Meghan stood before Emanuel in Clara's cozy living room. A fire blazed in the hearth beneath a blackened iron kettle of water that hung from the cast iron crane. Behind them, Clara fussed with a bolt of red fabric.

When Meghan had gotten back to her cottage, she'd left Timothy with Steve and hurried out before he could ask any more questions. Now, with Emanuel's concerned gaze centered on her, she wished she'd thought this out before coming here.

From his rocker, Emanuel stroked his beard and continued his silent study of her. His sandaled feet thumped softly on the wide pine boards, generating the chair's continuing, monotonous motion. The flowing folds of his robe swayed with the unbroken cadence.

Finally, he spoke. "And exactly what has brought on this decision?"

"Last night, in the lantern, I saw them leaving. Since that means that the Transition will soon come, I need to distance myself. I need to break the bond." Meghan spoke quickly, trying to get it all out before she changed her mind.

"Why? You've never felt this need before."

Meghan hesitated to answer. In the conversation's lull, Clara could be heard bustling about the kitchen. China clanked against china as she dried her dishes and stowed them in the cabinets, the sound reverberating in Meghan's ears, increasing the growing throb in her temples. The click of the cabinet's latch grated on Meghan's already raw nerves. Still, Emanuel waited for her answer.

"I love them both," she blurted. "I'm afraid, if they stay with me, my love will have undue influence on them."

Again, Emanuel said nothing for a long time. "You could go with them," he said, breaking his silence.

"No." Meghan gaped at him, and then shook her head adamantly. "No. That's not possible. We both know that if I did, the memory of the love I hold for them, as well as any memory of Renaissance, would be wiped from my mind. I would rather live here where I am safe and can hold the memories close."

"Safe from what, Meghan?" Clara's voice came to her from the kitchen. "What lies out there that frightens you?"

Both she and Emanuel turned toward the older woman.

A flash of the nightmare flitted through Meghan's mind. Was it the unknown in the nightmare that she feared or the loss of Steve's love? Or both? "I . . . I don't know."

Meghan waited in strained silence while Emanuel studied her. Finally, he nodded, his decision made. "Very well. Tomorrow Steve and Timothy will move into Josiah's cottage, and Irma will move into yours."

Meghan issued a sigh of relief. One more night, then she would be free of Steve's questioning eyes. Maybe it was the coward's way out, but she could not bear living with him and knowing he would soon leave her. It was better this way. Better for all of them. The bond between her and Steve had been allowed to grow too strong, and it must be severed before it caused him to make a decision he'd live to regret—a decision they'd both regret.

Meghan thanked Emanuel, and then turned to say good night to Clara. But Clara was looking at Emanuel, smiling and nodding approval. Oddly, her expression bespoke intense relief.

CHAPTER 11

The alley reeked of rotting garbage, stagnant water, and human waste. Meghan wrapped her arms around her frail little body to ward off the cold biting at her exposed flesh. She hadn't eaten for days, and her empty stomach growled in protest. Ahead of her, a woman trudged along, darting in and out of the dense shadows.

She hurried to catch up, but her little legs lacked both the length and the power to close the growing gap between them. If she lost sight of the woman, she just knew that terrible things would happen. She ordered her legs to move faster, but to no avail. The woman disappeared into the darkness.

Cold, afraid, hungry, and so very, very tired, she gave up. With a plaintive sob, she sank down on a pile of smelly rags beside an overflowing dumpster. The sound of the woman's retreating footsteps faded into the night.

Alone and uncertain what to do, she pulled her shivering body into a fetal position and covered her legs with the thin material of her skirt. Hopeless tears rolled down her cheeks. The emptiness in her stomach had become a gnawing ache.

A shadow fell over her, blotting out the meager illumination from a street light at the far end of the alley. Thinking the woman had returned for her, she looked up and found a very tall man gazing down at her. Behind him, another man held the arms of the woman. Anguish showed in the woman's face, and though her mouth moved, no words came out.

Suddenly, the man seized Meghan's arm and hauled her to her feet. Pain radiated from where his bony fingers dug into her flesh. Fear overwhelmed her. She cried out and struggled against the strong, imprisoning fingers. His nails tore into her tender flesh, but she continued to struggle. He laughed and threw her to the ground. His weight pressing her into the hard asphalt made it hard to breathe.

"Let me go!"

* * *

Steve grasped Meghan's upper arms tighter. "Meghan. Wake up." He shook her. "You're having a nightmare again."

She fought him with a ferocity that made him use more of his strength than he would have liked to. Sweat beaded her brow. "Let me go!" Her fingers clawed toward his face.

He held her at arm's length to keep her from making

contact with his skin and ripping his face open with her nails. "Meghan, wake up." He gave her a strong shake. Finally, her eyelids fluttered open.

She stared up at him, her wide eyes reflecting the fear he felt coursing through her trembling body. Even in the moonlit bedroom, he could see the paleness of her face, feel the panic in her quaking body. Whatever she'd been dreaming about had terrified her. His heart tearing from his chest, he gathered her close.

"Tell me about it, Meghan. Let me help you." Didn't she know that he'd lay down his life to ease her pain? Didn't she understand that she could tell him anything and it would not change how he felt about her?

She shook her head against his chest. "No."

Her voice was so small, so plaintive, so helpless. How he wished he had the answers to bring her peace. Unfortunately, until she shared what the dreams were about, he could only hold her and love her until morning came and the sun banished the demons from her dreams.

❊ ❊ ❊

Steve awoke to find himself alone in the big bed. Quickly, he slipped out from under the warm quilt and dressed, then headed into the kitchen. At the table, Meghan and Irma sipped coffee. Timothy's cereal bowl sat untouched in front of an empty chair. He could have cut the tension in the room with a dull knife.

"Good morning," he said, offering both women a broad smile.

"Morning," Irma muttered, not looking up from her deep contemplation of the coffee she swirled in her half empty cup.

Meghan neither spoke nor returned his smile. She merely nodded, then rose and took bacon and eggs from the refrigerator.

"Just coffee for me," he said, looking from one to the other of the silent women. "Josiah is waiting for me. I haven't been there for a couple of days."

He sent a playful glance in the direction of the woman pulling a cup and saucer from an overhead cabinet. She ignored him.

Was she angry that he would be spending the day working in the garden? Though he would have loved nothing better than to remain close to Meghan after her traumatic night, he had promised Josiah that he'd help him do the fertilizing. He couldn't go back on his word to the old man.

He took the filled cup Meghan gave him, noting that she was careful not to allow their fingers to touch or their gazes to meet. Was she embarrassed about the night before? Somehow, he didn't think so. The tension emanating from both women told him it was not Meghan's dream throwing the silent gloom over the kitchen, nor his planned day away from her. This was something else. From the way both were fidgeting, neither of them wanted to be the one to talk about it.

Uncertain that he really wanted to know, but even more certain that someone had to start the ball rolling to defuse the tension before the room exploded, he pushed them to share.

"Is someone going to talk to me about what's going on, or are we just going to sit here avoiding each other?" The two women exchanged glances. "Well?" he prodded.

Meghan glanced at Irma one more time and took a seat at the table. She rested her forearms on the blue checked tablecloth and clutched her hands together, her fingers entwined so tightly the tips were turning white. Unease settled like a lead ball in Steve's stomach.

"You and Timothy will be moving in with Josiah today." The words rushed from Meghan, as if she had to say them before she lost her nerve.

Steve felt like someone had kicked him in the gut. "What? Why?"

Studying her clenched hands, Meghan remained silent for a time. "Because I want you to."

Her first announcement had only taken the wind out of Steve's sails; this one crushed his soul. He was speechless. Though he tried desperately, he could not find a reason for this sudden decision. Had he done something, said something?

"The Transition will soon begin, and it's customary for me to separate myself from my Assignments before that happens." She glanced at Steve, then back to her hands. "It makes things easier all around."

Steve dropped into the closest chair and lowered his cup back to the saucer without drinking. "Easier? For who?"

He couldn't believe what he was hearing. Had the last days they'd spent together meant nothing to her? Had their declared love been just a way to pass the time, a means to an end, a way to complete the healing she'd said had to take place before he could leave the village?

"Assignment? Is that how you see me?" He continued to stare at her. Out of the corner of his eye, he saw Irma slip unobtrusively from the room.

"It's how I *have* to see you. I never should have let it get too personal." She still didn't look at him.

"Too personal? Meghan, we love each other. It doesn't get much more personal than that and what we've shared over the past days. With all your mystical powers, you can't control that."

Standing, she walked to the other side of the room. She rolled up the sleeves of her green blouse and began filling the sink with hot water and soap. "I know that. But I can remove the temptation." Her movements stilled, and she leaned heavily on the edge of the counter, her hunter green, ankle-length skirt molding to her hips. "Please don't make this hard for me."

Steve pushed his chair back, the legs making nerve-wracking grinding noises as they scraped across the wooden floor, and went to stand behind her. He placed his hands on her shoulders, then leaned close to her ear. Her flower-scented hair brought back memories of long hours locked in each other's arms.

"There's no need to worry about making anything easier or harder," he whispered softly, "because I'm not going anywhere."

Without warning, she whirled out of his hold and quickly put the width of the room between them. Her blue-eyed gaze met his, and he nearly cried out at the pain he saw reflected there. "Yes, you are. You may not believe that now, but you will go back to your world. I think we both knew that from the start. We were foolish beyond words to ever let ourselves believe otherwise."

He remained silent. Though he wanted to, he couldn't deny he'd given it thought. He had only to recall yesterday, after he'd pulled Timothy from the rock, and how his thinking had veered to the children that might die because he wasn't there to prevent it.

He shook his head. They were just musings. He'd never intended to act on them. He was a doctor. Doctors naturally thought in terms of human life. But that didn't mean he was going anywhere.

"I love you," he said, hoping the declaration would break through the icy barrier she'd erected between them—that she would declare her love in return, and they could forget this nonsense about his moving out and leaving Renaissance. When she neither answered nor looked at him, he sighed. "Obviously, I'm the only one feeling that way."

He waited, hoping for her to deny his words or, at the very least, indicate in some way that he was wrong, that she did love him. The silence dragged out. Meghan continued to stare at her hands.

Barely able to control his frustration or the pain coursing through him, he stomped from the room and then the house.

Meghan looked toward the closed door. "I do love you," she whispered to the empty room. Unchecked tears trickled down her cheeks. Searing, unbearable pain flooded her. She sank, boneless, into a chair and buried her face in her hands. If she felt this bad now, how would she ever endure the pain after Steve had left the village for good?

A gentle hand touched hers. Meghan glanced up. Through her tears she could see Irma, her face revealing her concern. "Was it really necessary to send him away?"

Drying her tears on the corner of a dishtowel, Meghan nodded. "I had no choice."

But had she? She could have begged him to stay with her. He loved her enough that she could have convinced him. Then what about the children? Who would heal them, see to *their* pain? And what about later when he came to regret his decision?

And he would.

Unfortunately, there was only one answer to this dilemma they'd created for themselves. Steve's destiny lay outside the village. Meghan's lay here, with only the memory of their love to ease the yawning ache left by his absence.

✳ ✳ ✳

Irma entered Meghan's bedroom on tiptoe, hoping against hope that the girl would be asleep, and she would be granted a reprieve from telling her the secret that had been hidden in her heart for over twenty years. As Irma neared the bed, Meghan rolled to her back and gazed up at her.

"Hi," Irma said quietly, taking a seat on the edge of the bed. "Feeling better?"

Meghan nodded sleepily, but Irma could tell from the pain etched around Meghan's eyes that the separation from Steve still hurt.

She blinked against the sunlight and rubbed her eyes. "How long did I sleep?"

Not long enough, Irma thought, dreading what was to come. "About an hour."

She hated having to add to the burden Meghan carried on her heart already. But Emanuel was right. There would never be a good time for this. Truth be known, it was past time.

Meghan sat up. "I should be starting lunch for Timothy."

Irma laid a hand on her shoulder. "Timothy will be eating lunch with Josiah and Steve."

Meghan fell back against the pillows. She didn't say so, but Irma could read the relief in her eyes. "I could have cooked for him." Only she knew the depth of the pain that felt like a rock on her chest, squeezing the very life from her.

"I know, but . . ." Irma stared at her, drinking in the woman's face, framed by white-blond hair and still damp with tears. She'd grown into a real beauty. "I asked Josiah to keep them there so I could talk to you without being interrupted." There, she'd taken the first step. She was barely aware that she was pleating the beige material of her tailored dress between nervous fingers.

Sliding up, Meghan propped her pillows behind her. "What about?"

"You . . . me."

A frown furrowed Meghan's brow. "I don't understand."

Taking a deep breath, Irma stood, walked to the foot of the bed, and looked back at the woman waiting to hear what she had to say. Now, if she could just find the words. Suddenly, a voice whispered in her ear, *You can do this.* As if by magic, the words began to tumble from her lips.

"When I was twenty-six, I met a twenty-year-old man and fell in love. I had never experienced an emotion to equal that one in my entire life, nor had I ever been so happy."

Meghan waved a hand toward her. "If this is to make

me change my mind about Steve . . ."

"No, this is not about that." Taking her seat on the side of the bed, Irma continued. "Hear me out, please." Meghan nodded. "Unfortunately, his parents didn't agree with his choice of women."

"Why?"

"Well, to start with, I was six years older than him. Added to that, I was dirt poor, came from a foster home, and he'd met me in a soup kitchen." She laughed without humor. "When you're dealing with a family who gave away more money to charity in a year than I had seen in a lifetime, you couldn't have many more strikes against you than that."

Meghan reached across and took her hand.

"I can't hate them too much for their concern. Davis . . . that was his name . . . Davis had a heart condition, but he insisted on donating his time four days a week in the soup kitchen. His parents not only worried about his association with *those people*, they worried that the work would overtax his heart." She stopped and smiled at the memories. "But his kind and loving nature made him go against his parents' wishes to share what he had with those less fortunate." She blinked back the moisture in her eyes. "It was what I loved most about him.

"When we got married, he took me to live with his parents because he was too sickly to hold a job. Besides, I got pregnant shortly after, and he felt better about me being there, so, despite being treated like an outsider, I didn't object." She smiled. "Lord, we were so happy. We'd take the baby and go to the soup kitchen together. While we served the homeless, she was never at a loss for play-mates and babysitters. Everyone loved her."

This story had been bottled up inside her for so long. And now that she'd begun, she was finding it easier and easier to talk as time went on. Words tumbled through her memory and out into the light of day almost faster than she could voice them. "Then . . ." She swallowed hard, but when she continued, the unshed tears choked her voice. "Then his big heart just gave out one day. Right after the funeral, his parents threw me out of the house. But they wanted to keep my baby."

Meghan sat straighter. "How terrible!"

"I couldn't let that happen," she took a deep breath and went on as if Meghan had not spoken. "I took her and fled back to the only place I knew, the streets. From the first days, even though the people who had always showered her with love lived with us, the streets scared my daughter. I tried to shield her from anything that would frighten her, but in the streets, it seemed everything scared her.

"Then . . . I . . . Something terrible happened, and my sweet, little daughter bore witness to the entire incident. Soon after that, my in-laws found us, and I was forced into hiding even deeper in the maze of the homeless. One of them, Marion, whom I later learned was a Guide, realized that neither my baby nor I would heal from the terrible incident unless we escaped the streets. Somehow she found a way to send us to the mountains, to a cabin where we would be safe from my in-laws and where they would never find us. A place where we could get the love and care we needed."

"Renaissance?"

Irma nodded. "We fled the city, taking nothing with us but my never-ending grief for the loss of my beloved Davis and the . . . Well, the memory of that terrible incident. It didn't take long before we wandered into the woods and into the mist of Renaissance. In the village, I healed from the pain of my husband's death. I'd found somewhere my daughter could not be taken from me, a place where I was surrounded by the unwavering love I'd known only with my husband."

She stood and moved away from Meghan, hoping the distance would make it easier to continue her story. And it did, until she looked at Meghan's trusting blue eyes. She forced herself to go on with her story.

"With the healing came the time when we had to make a choice. Leave the village or stay forever. I wanted to stay, but I couldn't forget the troubled, starving, homeless I'd left behind. The people my beloved Davis had given his life for. I had to go back, to care for them as they'd cared for my daughter and me, just as Davis had cared for them, but I couldn't take her back there. Since she'd witnessed that incident, she'd been haunted by nightmares and her fear of the streets. Only after we'd come to the village had the child slept without waking engulfed in terrifying screams. And there was still the risk of my in-laws finding us again and, this time, achieving their goal–taking my baby.

"I begged Emanuel to keep her in Renaissance. Lovingly, he had assured me that he would make an exception, and I could leave her with them and he could erase the haunting memories from her mind and end her nightmares. But, there was a dear price to pay. In erasing the memory of that terrible incident, he'd also erase all memory of me from my daughter's mind. And, one day she would have to hear the truth. For the sake of my child's peace-of-mind and safety, I agreed."

Irma looked at Meghan and swallowed hard. This was the part she'd been dreading . . . the part that could drive Meghan away from her for good.

"I left her and returned to life in the streets, this time as a Guide who would send the needful to the tiny village to be healed as I had been. I visited her often. Although she had no idea who I was, it gave me great joy to see her grow up happy and healthy among people who loved her and to eventually become one of the village Healers." Irma stopped, stared at Meghan, and waited for her words to sink in.

"Healers? I don't understand. The only person young enough to be your . . ." Meghan broke off in the middle of her thought. Mouth open, she stared at Irma. Over and over she told herself that she had to be wrong. Silently, she implored Irma to deny what she was thinking, but the woman said nothing. "You're my . . . mother?"

Irma took a step forward, her hand extended in front of her. "Meghan. I . . ."

Meghan backed away, plastering her back against the bed's headboard. "No. Don't touch me." She was still trying to understand what she'd just heard. "You deserted me to go back to that horrible place? Me? Your own flesh and blood?"

"I had to. Try to understand. Those people took care of us, kept us safe."

"But I don't understand. When we got here we were safe. You could have stayed. You said Emanuel gave you that choice. But you didn't. You left me." Meghan shook her head trying to make sense of all this. "All these years, you never told me. Why?"

Irma drew back her hand and clasped both of them at her waist. Tears trickled down her cheeks. A plea for absolution filled her eyes.

"Once you'd grown and I saw how happy you were, I was afraid to tell you, afraid it would bring back those horrible nightmares. I was sure that by telling you the truth, I'd lose what little I had of my daughter."

"You never had any of me. You left me. And as for the nightmares, they're back anyway." And, finally, they were beginning to make sense. "How long did you think you could go on living a lie?"

"I don't know. I should have remembered that the village allows no one to escape destiny. Whatever troubles the people come to the village with, when they leave, the problem will be waiting for them to eventually face on the other side of the mist. The difference is that they are strong enough to face it triumphantly. I wasn't so sure about you"

"You could have given me that chance," Meghan said bitterly. Then suddenly, something Irma had said about facing one's problems in the outside world sank in. Cold, icy chills coursed over her, freezing her emotions. "Are you saying that I have to leave here?'

"Only if you chose to, but Emanuel will tell you that your destiny lies outside the village."

"No! I'll never leave here! Never!" She heard the panic filling her voice but was helpless to control it.

Wanting nothing more than to put distance between her and this woman who had just announced she was her mother, Meghan climbed from the bed, skirted Irma, and hurried into the kitchen. She never stopped running until she entered the living room, the place in this tiny house where she always knew the most peace. The smell of the pine assaulted her. It should have been pleasant, soothing, but it wasn't. Nothing seemed to be able to calm the chaotic confusion inside her.

One truth remained clear. She had escaped the

troubles of her childhood, but everything evolves, and she, too, must live the life she was given. She was sure Emanuel had warned Irma of that, but Meghan couldn't do that in Renaissance. No matter how much or how fervently she denied it, like Steve, her destiny lay beyond the misty walls of the village, where she would be cleansed of all memory of her life here and the man she loved.

While she would lose all recollection of the village, she knew from working with her Assignments that whatever memories she had from the outside world, she would retain on her re-entrance. Whatever haunted her dreams was out there . . . waiting for her to come back.

CHAPTER 12

S teve didn't go directly to Josiah's after leaving
Meghan's cottage. Instead he climbed the hill to
his favorite rock. There he gazed out over the seemingly empty glen and the frozen Hudson River. Though
he couldn't see the village, his heart told him it was there.
That Meghan was there. As he stared absently at the dor-
mant winter landscape, he tried to make sense of what had
just happened in Meghan's kitchen.

In the last days, his life had changed so radically that
he found it difficult to remember he'd had another life outside this sleepy little place. Since walking through that
veil of time into Renaissance, he'd found a woman he loved
beyond measure and a life so satisfying and undemanding
that he never wanted to leave it. Now, he had a sense that
both were in danger of slipping away from him and that
stopping it lay far beyond his control. The helplessness of
the situation weighed him down like a large rock.

Resting his elbows on his denim-covered thighs, he
pulled the collar of his plaid woolen coat higher around his

neck, then rubbed the tips of his cold fingers together and thought about Meghan. Closing his eyes, he could feel the texture of her silky skin, the caress of her hair as it fell over his naked body. He could smell the wildflower fragrance so unique to her.

While all that was appealing, her outward appearance made up only a small part of the person he'd come to love. Her gentle manner, her concern for Timothy, and her ability to see through the maze of confusion and chaos to the truth of any situation had endeared her to him more than any other human being he had ever met.

Leaving her would be like abandoning half of himself. It hurt immeasurably that she could even give credence to such a thing, that she could so easily give up what they had. Couldn't she see his anguish? Didn't she understand that no matter what Emanuel said or what strange visions she saw in that lantern . . .

That thought gave him pause. *The damned lantern.*

Is that where her crazy notion came from? Had she seen him leaving in that weird little crystal ball of hers? Is that what prompted her to run from the bedroom that night, then make this decision to remove him from her life? If she had, he knew, although he had some serious doubts as to its ability to predict the future, that she did. She looked at what she viewed in the lantern as Gospel.

He wracked his brain for a way to prove to her she was wrong, that no matter what mystical power told her otherwise, he loved her and would not leave her. Nothing came to mind, and he had to wonder if he'd ever be able to change her thinking. Did he have any power over this situation at all?

The village seemed to be ruled by destiny, and things happened here whether those affected thought it right or not. Though freewill was never infringed on, these loving people had a way of unobtrusively guiding a person in the right direction, illuminating the right path without pointing it out. It just seemed to happen.

He thought of Timothy and how the boy had always been near him, trusting him. Steve felt safe in assuming that Meghan had never told the boy he *had* to get close to Steve. The boy just seemed drawn to him. Their developing closeness had been the catalyst that started the intrusion of his outside life into his idyllic existence in Renaissance.

If—and that was a huge *if*—Meghan was right, and he would be leaving the village, could he go back to being a doctor again?

Hesitantly, he held his hands out in front of him and studied them. They hadn't changed, except for the few calluses he'd gotten from working with Josiah in the garden. They were the same hands that had administered to his small patients. The same hands that had comforted and soothed the children in his care. They were strong hands, and despite what his father thought, the hands of a healer. But was he a healer?

Unable to find any of the answers he sought, Steve stood, ran his fingers through his hair, then, out of the corner of his eye, he noticed the mist gathering in the glen. He was immediately reminded of the day he first saw it. The day he'd walked into another time and found the woman he loved. But he also recalled Meghan telling him that a mist would gather when it came time for him to leave the village.

Was this the beginning of his end? Panic stiffened his body, then tingled along every nerve endings. Was he being closed out? Was this the . . . ? He struggled to recall what Meghan called this event. *Transition*. Was this the Transition that would isolate him from her forever?

The thought of never seeing Meghan again mobilized him.

Dashing down the hill, he cursed himself for ever stepping outside the perimeter of the village. How could he have been so damned stupid? They'd probably just been waiting for this opportunity to close him out.

Though his starving lungs burned, he forced his legs to go faster. A root tripped him, and he plummeted forward, rolling down the hill like a snowball being pushed by a child making a snowman. Snow packed inside his collar. A rock bit into his back. Waves of physical and mental agony washed over him. The branch of a tree swished painfully across his cheek. He reached out a hand to grab something, anything to halt his forward movement, but his momentum made that impossible.

Finally, at the bottom of the hill, he came to rest against the base of a pine tree, his head slamming against the unforgiving trunk. Blackness threatened, but he fought it off and pushed himself to his feet, hitting the ground at a dead run toward the thickening mist.

As he approached it, the mist glowed from within as if a thousand candles had been trapped inside. Then the glow began to weaken, fading quickly. Fearing that the mist would dissipate and the village would vanish again, and Meghan would be lost to him forever, Steve dove headlong into the thick vapor.

Scrambling to his feet and clawing his way through it, he finally emerged into the clear air, relieved to see that before him lay the footbridge. Without hesitation and before he could be stopped, Steve dashed across it and into the village. Winded, but free from the fear that he'd be barred from re-entry, he leaned against the post at the end of the bridge.

He glanced up and could just make out Clara Webb, the village weaver, through the remaining remnants of the mist. She smiled at him, her expression reminding him of an angel he'd seen in a museum painting by Botticelli a long time ago. As the mist continued to dissipate, he could see her more clearly. Her dark skirt, white blouse and mobcap echoed Josiah's mode of dress from a bygone era. The bright sunlight glinting off her head turned the white hair peeking from beneath the cap to a silver halo.

Unable to catch his breath, Steve bent double to ease the excruciating stitch burning through his side.

"Dr. Cameron?"

"I thought . . . I thought . . ." He couldn't breathe and complete the sentence at the same time, and right now, air was the essential choice.

Clara was silent for a time. He could feel her studying him. "You thought you were being shut out," she said gently. "That's not our way, Dr. Cameron. When the time comes for you to leave, you'll know."

Not *if*, but *when*. *Why were they all so hell-bent on getting rid of him? Well, if they wanted him out of here, they'd have to carry him. He damned well wouldn't go easily or willingly.*

He looked up to tell her he wasn't going anywhere, his lungs still stinging from his marathon run, but the words wouldn't come. He tried to force himself to speak, but it turned to a coughing spasm.

Deep concern darkened her soft brown eyes. "Are you all right?"

He waved a hand at her. "Fine. I'm fine."

Then, as the mist cleared completely, he noticed the young woman at Clara's side. Gold curls cascaded in soft waves over the woman's shoulders left bare by the brief pink camisole top. In her hand she held what looked like a down jacket. Had the Transition been to admit her into the village? Was she a new Assignment?

She seemed too young to be looking for answers here. She couldn't have been more than nineteen, twenty at the very most, and should have been on the outside, living a full and exciting life, dating men, planning a family. She stared at him with alert blue eyes, her full mouth turned up in a smile.

Then something in her gaze, an inner peace, brought Steve upright. He'd seen that look before. But where?

"Hello, Dr. Steve."

That she knew his name didn't surprise him. He'd grown quite used to people here knowing things they shouldn't, couldn't know. But the way she said it, her soft voice . . .

Quite suddenly something began burning his leg through the pocket of his jeans, as if someone had dropped a lit match into it, but without the resulting pain. He reached in and found nothing but the keychain a dying little girl had given him six years earlier. As he wrapped his fingers around it, the heat vanished, leaving behind a comforting warmth.

Drawing it from his pocket, he stared down where it lay curled in his palm. The words engraved in the rectangular piece of plastic echoed in his head, as they had so many times before.

Faith and trust make miracles.

Comprehension came slow, but then, like a thunderbolt out of the clear azure sky, the possibility registered.

But it couldn't be. He had to be wrong. That little girl had died six years ago. But had she? He hadn't been there, hadn't heard her draw her last breath, hadn't signed her death certificate. He'd just assumed . . .

"Ellie?"

The woman smiled and nodded.

Her grin saturated him with untold elation. It spread through him like a summer sun, permeating the cold parts of him that had existed in the darkness of failure for so long.

His mind raced in a thousand directions. "But how?"

"How else?" Ellie stepped toward him and caressed his cheek with her smooth palm. "My Christmas miracle. I told you all you have to do is believe."

Then she hugged him, her slight body warm with the life pulsing through it. He still doubted that it had been a miracle, but he couldn't find another name to put to it at the moment. He was too busy enjoying the beat of her heart pounding against him, affirming that life did indeed exist inside the beautiful, young creature she'd become.

"How did you get here?" he asked, holding her at arm's length, afraid to let her go, lest he find he was dreaming all this.

"Hobbs brought her." Clara stepped forward and rested an arm around the woman's shoulders. "Ellie was here before."

A vision of Meghan's curio cabinet and the one-eyed

teddy bear among the other strange things there flashed through Steve's mind. "You came here to heal."

Though still happy at the woman's recovery from what he'd seen as certain death, he felt a stab of disappointment that it had been Renaissance that had ultimately brought her back from the threshold of death and not him.

"Not heal. She came here to prepare." Clara smiled lovingly at Ellie. "This time, she's come to stay, to fulfill her destiny, as we all must do eventually."

If the village didn't heal her, then how was it she was standing here before him, alive, vibrant, and healthy?

* * *

In the small cottage at the side of the square, Meghan held the lantern at eye level and gazed into the globe, which mirrored the scene in the square. She'd watched Steve race down off the hill as the mist gathered, knowing he thought the Transition he was seeing was meant for him. But this Transition had been entirely for Ellie.

Without any family and having been prepared to return to the mist, Ellie was ready to take her place among the permanent residents of Renaissance. Clara would train her to become a Healer, and Josiah and Alvin would build another cottage to house her.

Before long, Ellie would be as settled as the rest of them into the slow-paced life of the village that Meghan loved.

An ache formed deep inside her. Now that he'd seen that all his children didn't die, there would be only a couple more steps to Steve's healing before he'd be ready for his own Transition. He would step back into the life awaiting him beyond the mist.

Meghan would remain. Hopefully, by then she would have found a way to live with the agony of Steve leaving and the pain, indecision, and upheaval that had come with Irma's revelation. Right now, she ached physically and mentally from head to toe and she could see no cure in sight.

The swirling mist inside the globe obliterated the scene at the bridge. Meghan set the lantern on the table beside the winged chair. She knew Irma wanted forgiveness, but how could she forgive a mother who had deserted her for years and left her in the care of strangers, albeit loving ones? If the visions and nightmares hadn't started, would Irma ever have told her who she was?

She recalled all the lonely days she'd endured, wondering why she had no parents, why no one ever spoke of them and sidestepped any mention of them. She remembered all the times she'd secretly wished she had a mother to confide in. She also remembered when she'd stopped wondering and accepted the fact that whoever her parents had been, they must have simply decided they didn't want her.

Disdain for the woman who called herself her mother filled Meghan. Now, all those unanswered questions were swimming around in her head again. This time, she had the answers. Irma had not cared enough about her to stay with her or to take her with her. She'd been right all along. Her mother had simply not wanted her. Irma had cared more about the people in the streets than she had her own flesh and blood child. Oh, her reasons were honorable, but Meghan could not envision herself giving up her child for any reason.

All she'd learned since being in Renaissance came to the forefront—she should look in her heart for forgiveness, but, truth be known, Meghan was afraid there was no forgiveness to be found there for Irma. No forgiveness that would erase a lifetime of lonely hours.

* * *

Steve stared after the two women strolling toward Clara's thatched cottage, one bent slightly with time, the other preparing to embark on a life so different from that of any other woman her age that even he couldn't imagine what it would entail.

Before they disappeared inside the cottage, Ellie turned, smiled that beautiful smile he'd held in his memory for six years, and waved to him. He returned the wave, watched the door close behind them, and then set his footsteps toward Josiah's cottage.

Ellie was alive.

It seemed impossible, but he'd held her, felt the substance

of her, heard her breathing. Instead of elating him, he felt the weight of failure settle more firmly on his shoulders. He'd been so sure she wouldn't make it. What had changed her condition from terminal to . . . life? He'd even tried experimental treatments to save Ellie, but none of it had worked. Had Dr. Anderson found something he'd missed?

Still baffled and weighed down by a sense of failure he hadn't felt in some time, Steve rounded the corner of Josiah's cottage and headed toward the garden area, his mind an eddy of thoughts. As he neared the garden, he saw Josiah standing at the edge, his sightless gaze centered on the plants, his face solemn.

Tall rose bushes blocked Steve's view until he stepped around them and moved beside Josiah. He turned to look in the direction Josiah faced. His breath expelled in a sharp gasp.

Everything in the garden, with the exception of a few plants, was brown and dead and draped limply on their sides over the humps of dirt surrounding them.

Steve blinked, hoping his eyes were deceiving him, but when he opened them, the same devastation met his gaze. A terrible emptiness increased the weight of the guilt over Ellie's survival. "What happened?"

"Don't know," Josiah said with a sigh. "They been looking poorly for the last day. I fertilized them and watered them, did all the things I was supposed to do, same stuff I always do, but I guess it wasn't meant to be."

Steve gawked at him wide-eyed. While he felt hollowed out with a sense of intense loss, it didn't seem to bother the old man in the least that, after days of work and nurturing, almost their entire crop had died.

"Not all of them," Josiah said, unnerving Steve by reading his mind.

"But there are so few left." Steve scanned the garden and estimated a dozen plants had survived. "What good are any of them now. The ones that are okay will probably die, too."

"Not necessarily," Josiah said, sitting on an overturned bucket and lighting his pipe. He drew several times on the curved stem, and blew out a puff of gray smoke. The fragrance of cherry tobacco wreathed their heads. "The ones that lived will grow healthy and produce," he said in a matter-of-fact tone. "The ones that died will be plowed under for fertilizer. They'll help the next generation grow even stronger. That's just the way of things." He puffed again and exhaled another ring of smoke. "No matter how little, there's always a lesson to be learned in all that life throws our way, my boy."

Steve was listening to Josiah, but only half hearing what he said. He couldn't take his gaze off the rows and rows of dead plants. They were only plants, but he couldn't ignore the parallel between them and the children he'd lost. He'd nurtured both, and both had died. Despair engulfed him until it became a physical pain.

From the corner of his eye, he saw Josiah take a final puff on his pipe, then stand and shuffle toward his house. Though he tried, Steve could not remove his attention from the field of dead vegetables. It was as if something held him there, immobilizing him.

In the back of his mind, he replayed the theory Josiah had about the souls of the dead living on in the flowers before passing on to heaven. At the time it had seemed like the nonsensical musing of an old man. An explanation for something that had no explanation.

The sun danced over the field. Waves of heat rose in the air, blurring the garden. As Steve watched, the up-surge of light radiated out, thickening into a glassy veil that morphed and twisted, changing form and color. The sun glinted off the surface, the shimmering illumination nearly blinding Steve. He blinked his stinging eyes. Slowly, from each dead plant, shapes began to rise on the other side of the glistening wall, shapes of . . .

Children. Rows and rows of children. The children he had failed.

CHAPTER 13

Standing at the side of the garden, facing a field of ghostly children born of his tortured imagination, Steve felt the weight of the morning's events pressing him into the ground. How much more was he supposed to endure before he went mad? But were they really ghosts or just phantoms born of his doubt in his skills and his failure to save children who could not be saved?

A pain began to form in his chest. It grew and intensified until Steve could hardly stand it. He dropped to his knees, clutching at his chest. Was he having a heart attack? No. This was not a physical pain. Inside him the odd pain twisted and writhed until it was nearly beyond bearing. His entire body throbbed with it. He closed his eyes and prayed for it to go away. He clutched both sides of his head and pressed his palms against his pounding temples. But it remained to torture him until he lay on the ground curled into a fetal position. Only then did it ease until finally, as if flushed from his body, it disappeared as quickly as it had come.

For a long time, he lay there, breathing hard, trying to understand what had just occurred. It seemed that each day produced a new torment for him. What had happened to the peace he'd known since coming here? Maybe he never really had it. Maybe it was as insubstantial as the vaporous cloud that surrounded this damned place. Maybe it had gone the way of his common sense when he'd begun to accept all the crazy happenings he'd seen in this place.

Steve sat up and slowly regained his feet. He glanced at the rows of vegetables. The ghosts were gone. With no other explanation to turn to, Steve decided he must be going mad.

Blindly Steve turned from the reminders of his failure and fled Josiah's yard. He had no idea where he was going or how he would get there. He just knew he had to get away from the children. As if chased by a band of demons, he raced across Josiah's lawn and into the square. Once there, he looked frantically around him, searching for a place to go that he would afford him peace. His gaze was drawn to the small thatched cottage that lay just this side of the footbridge.

Meghan.

❋ ❋ ❋

Mesmerized by the scene in the lantern's globe, Meghan fought back the threatening tears. While she observed

Steve beside the garden, a kindred pain unlike any she had ever experienced knifed through her. It surprised her that she could feel his acute agony. Never before had she shared in an Assignment's awakening process. But then, from the very beginning, nothing with Steve had been as it usually was with Assignments. She'd always felt far too much of his inner turmoil.

Still, despite the pain, she touched the globe as if by doing so she could absorb more of his torment, but she couldn't. She knew in her heart that, though she would have gladly taken every bit of his pain into herself to free him of this suffering, this was his alone to bear. When the pain disappeared, and it would, Steve would be a new man on his way to leaving Renaissance for good. This was Steve's rebirth.

She wiped at the tears blurring her vision and saw him turn in her direction. He strode across the square, the sunlight dancing off his dark head, his muscles straining to eat up the distance between them.

Her heart started pounding excitedly. Quickly, Meghan set the lantern aside, rose, and went to the door. She opened it to find Steve, poised to knock, on the other side. Without speaking, she stepped aside to allow him to enter.

He dashed past her and stopped just inside. He stared at her, his eyes filled with pain and questions. "What's happening to me?"

"Life," she told him, leading him toward the living

room and the crackling fire. "When the soul experiences the re-birthing process, it can be as unpleasant as a baby entering the world."

He faced her, his handsome face distorted by his inner agony. "How do I stop it? How do I make it go away?"

"Accept it," she told him calmly. But she could see that the confusion and questions were making it impossible for him to sort through the recent events and see their true significance.

For a long moment they faced each other in silence. The rich odor of pine and cinnamon, the smell of Christmas, wrapped around them. The fire snapped, and the logs shifted in the fireplace. Sparks billowed up the chimney. The handless clock ticked away phantom minutes.

"I don't think I can," he finally said, his husky voice a tortured whisper.

Though she appeared composed and controlled, inside, Meghan was anything but calm. Intense misery ebbed from him to her until she could no longer stand to see him this way. She knew his soul writhed and twisted, awakening to a new state of being, but she also knew he had to experience the bottom of despair before he could climb back to the top. Even knowing all that, loving him as she did, she could not stand by and do nothing to ease his torment. Though she would suffer later, she had to help ease his pain, and she was certain if anything could do that, it would be her love.

Her decision made, her fate sealed, she slowly walked toward him. When she stood within inches of him, she slipped her arms around his neck, pulled him close, and spoke with her lips a mere breath from his. "Let me help you."

For a moment, he stared down at her, then as if he understood what she was telling him, he sighed and buried her mouth beneath his.

The tension began to ease from him. Meghan pressed closer, hungrily devouring the mouth that she had needed so badly since he'd walked from her house. Like a rose seeking sustenance from the blazing sun, her lips opened to receive him.

How could she have let him go, when she needed him so desperately to fill the empty corners of her heart?

Suddenly, he pulled back, leaving her starved for more. "Meghan, are you sure?"

She stared deep into his coal black eyes, eyes still haunted with the vision of the children, caressed his cheek, and smiled. "I need you as much as you need me." Not until she said it did she realize how important his love was to helping her close the open wounds left by Irma's confession.

He smiled, and her heart flipped over. "I love you, Meghan. I will never leave you."

"I love you, too, and I will not let you leave me." For the moment, she allowed herself to believe that.

❊ ❊ ❊

Meghan's bedroom was warm with the sun slanting through the window, leaving puddles of light all over the patchwork quilt covering the bed. She pushed him backwards until the mattress cut him at the knees, and he crumpled onto the bed.

Settling over him, Meghan straddled his hips then leaned forward and claimed his mouth. He sipped at her sweetness and drank of her love. God, how he'd missed her warmth, her smile, her soft skin, the way she curled around him like a vine seeking its life support.

Slowly, as she pressed her mouth to his, she slipped her hands down his sides, over his stomach and stopped when she reached the button at the waistband of his jeans. Obviously, Meghan was taking the lead, and he had no qualms about letting her. He just wanted to lay back and be loved senseless, to be swept up in her passion and freed from reality, if just for a little while.

Steve felt the button slip from the fastening, then heard the soft *whirr* of the zipper making its descent. As she lowered the zipper, she allowed her fingers to trail over him, sending sparks of blazing fire careening through his groin. He grabbed her hands.

"Easy, sweetheart," he groaned. "I want to remember every moment of this."

Why had he said that? Now that she knew he wasn't going anywhere, and she wasn't going to make him leave, there would be more times like this, more nights and days spent in each other's arms.

She slid his jeans from his thighs. Her warm, moist mouth caressed his stomach. Then all thinking ceased. He could only feel. He closed his eyes and moaned her name.

Meghan smiled, relishing the power she had to turn this big man to hot, pliable clay with just a touch of her lips. Wanting to test her new power again, she moved her head lower to kiss the bare skin of his lower stomach. He squirmed beneath her hands. Moans of pleasure came from him.

Grabbing her upper arms, he slid her back up his body, then took her mouth in a greedy kiss that sent fire shooting through her body. A familiar need began building inside her. She slid her hands beneath him and ground her hips against him in a silent plea for more.

"Not yet," he whispered, his hot breath sending shivers of desire down her spine.

"When?"

"Soon. Very soon." His breath came in short gasps.

His fingers buried in her hair and brought her mouth back to his. She opened her lips and welcomed him inside, her own tongue tentatively touching his, then becoming the aggressor. She pulled back and outlined his lips with the tip of her tongue, enjoying the way he strained against her, trying to recapture it.

Then his hands slid over her back and down to cup her

buttocks against his straining erection. She collapsed on top of him, loving the feel of his body beneath her.

Frantically, she ripped his T-shirt over his head. Their arms tangled while they struggled to remove the remaining items of clothing from each other. At last, they were skin to skin.

She arched her hips. Her nails dug into him. "I want you," she whispered against his chest. "Please."

Steve eased her onto her back, covered her, and very slowly slid into her. With gently measured movements, he began the dance of love. But very soon gentle was not enough for either of them. A kind of desperation took over their lovemaking. Their movements became fast and furious, as if this would be the last time for them, and they had to fill themselves with memories.

Their frenzied movements intensified, her hips rising high off the bed to allow him full penetration. Her hands played over him, memorizing every valley and muscle, storing it for the time when he would be beyond her touch.

Meghan sensed that Steve's climax was close to the surface. Her own heat had built to blast furnace proportions. She tried to hold back, to wait for him, but failed. She cried out seconds before Steve stiffened and moaned, depositing his seed deep inside her. Even then wave after wave of pleasure continued to rocket through her.

When the tumult of their lovemaking had subsided, they lay wrapped in each other's arms, their breathing labored and rapid, neither of them wanting to leave the euphoric cloud and face the reality of the world around them. But Meghan knew the time would come and could not be put off any longer.

"Are you going to talk to me about the garden?" She felt Steve stiffen against her.

"No." He kept his one word reply clipped and unemotional. He didn't want to think about the garden and what had happened there, much less talk about it. Meghan, however, was not so easily put off.

She pushed herself to a sitting position and looked down at him. "Not talking about it is not going to make it go away."

Sighing, he glanced up at her through sleepy eyes. "Can't we just take a nap and forget it?"

"No." She slipped from the bed, grabbed his clothes, and tossed them to him. Then she picked up hers and went into the bathroom. Just before the door closed behind her, she called back to him. "I expect you to be dressed when I come out, then we're going to have coffee in the kitchen, where it's safe, and talk."

❅ ❅ ❅

Twenty minutes later, Steve faced Meghan across the kitchen table. "Well?" she said expectantly.

He clasped his hands around the hot coffee mug, almost

enjoying the pain of it burning into his palms. Anything was better than returning to the pain of seeing all those kids in that field. "Meghan, I have never in my life experienced that kind of pain. What on earth would lead you to believe I want to talk about it?"

Meghan sipped her coffee, then set the cup down and reached for his hand. She curled her fingers around his and looked into his eyes. "The pain you felt was the return of life. It happens to all the Assignments."

"The pain I could stand. It was all the kids. . ." His voice broke.

"I know the visions were difficult, but trust me. They were necessary."

Steve pulled his hand away. "Why? What possible purpose could be served by reminding me of all those kids I lost, all those kids I couldn't help?"

She curled her empty fingers into a ball and shook her head. "You know I can't tell you. That's something you have to figure out for yourself. Otherwise, it *wouldn't* serve a purpose. It's part of the healing."

"Screw the healing!" He stood and paced to the window. Pulling the bright yellow curtain aside, he gazed out at the woods beyond the village. Her prodding had brought it all back and with it came the pain. "You people sure have a weird way of making a point."

"Not really. You'll come to realize exactly what all that meant, then you'll be ready to . . ."

He swung toward her, knowing what she was about to say but needing to hear it from her lips. "What? I'll be ready to what?"

She dropped her gaze to her fidgeting hands. "Leave Renaissance."

"Damn!" Steve strode back to the table, grabbed her by her upper arms, and pulled her from the chair and into his arms. "I don't care what you saw in that weird little lantern or read in your tea leaves or saw in the changing leaves or any other special divination device you have. I am not leaving. If you don't believe me, ask Irma. I told her that I'm staying. How can I make you believe that?"

He'd felt her stiffen slightly at the mention of Irma's name, but he didn't realize she was crying until he felt the moisture soak through his shirtfront. There was no need to ask her what she was crying about. He knew. Deep in his heart, he knew and had probably always known, no matter how much or how often he denied it. He would be leaving Renaissance. He wasn't at all sure that the pain of admitting that wasn't worse than seeing that field full of his kids. But somewhere deep inside, he'd held close the belief that if he didn't admit it out loud, they could both go on pretending it wasn't true.

However, even though he knew his leaving prompted her tears in part, he sensed that somehow the mention of Irma had helped provoke them, too.

After a few minutes, she drew back. Her cheeks bore

the stains of her tears.

"It's more than the question of me leaving, isn't it? What else is bothering you?"

She pushed her lips into a smile. "Nothing. I'm just being weepy." She stirred in his embrace. "Enough of this deep talk."

When she tried to pull away, he held her fast. "No. I know something is bothering you, and since you probed my psyche, I think it's only fair that I get to probe yours."

This time, when she pulled back, he let her go. She slumped into the chair and leaned heavily on the table. "Irma is my mother."

"Your mother? Irma?" It was Steve's turn to drop into a chair. Shock robbed him of speech. Nothing could have been farther from what he'd expected her to say. "I don't understand."

Briefly, she related the same story Irma had told her. When she'd finished, she looked pale, drained. "I wish she had never told me."

"What? How can you say that? You found your mother. That's a gift most people would give their right arm to have."

"I don't even really know who she is. She never cared enough to stay with me, to allow me to grow up with a mother. She just walked out because those people meant more to her than I did."

He recalled how Irma had told him that the kids in the

park were beautiful and the sadness he'd seen in her eyes. Now, he was sure she'd been thinking of her own child. At that moment, if he couldn't figure out anything else that had happened today, he knew that Irma loved her and had only left her because she felt it had been the right thing to do. "That's not true. Irma loves kids."

He could see that his words had no effect on Meghan. But he could also see by the way she avoided looking at him that there was more.

"What aren't you telling me?"

She started to cry again. This time she made no attempt to hide her tears from him. She turned worried eyes to him. "She told me my destiny lies outside the village."

Hope welled up in him. If he had to leave, if the choice was taken out of his hands, then this meant they could go together. He wouldn't lose her after all. Before he could say anything, her face crumbled.

"But I can't leave the village. It's been my life for too long. Besides, if a Healer leaves Renaissance, their memory is wiped clean of anything that happened here. They don't even remember the village."

Steve leaned toward her, feeling their chance at happiness together slipping through his fingers and trying desperately to hold on. "Surely in your case Emanuel would make an exception." Even as he said it, he knew it was futile hope. Her next words confirmed it.

She shook her head. "There are no exceptions. I won't

remember anything about being here—Timothy, Emanuel, none of it." A fresh rain of tears streaked down her cheeks. "I won't remember you or our love."

Frustration surged through him. He slammed his fist on the table. "They get you coming and going, don't they? They keep saying they want you to be happy, to enjoy life, to live it to the fullest, then they snatch away anything that will make that possible." Anger such as he'd never before experienced boiled through him. Every time he found a grain of hope to hang onto, something or someone snatched it away.

Meghan rose and came around to his side of the table and sat on his lap, then wrapped her arms around his neck and rested her head on his shoulder. "There's nothing we can do to change things, so please, let's enjoy the time we have left."

Steve wanted to cry out, to punch someone, but he did neither. Meghan was right. If he were truly going to leave, and he hadn't totally decided he would, or could, leave her behind, why waste the time left to them?

She straightened and smiled a watery smile. "I have a Christmas gift for you." Before he could say anything, she moved off his lap and headed for the living room.

He followed her. He'd forgotten it was almost Christmas. With the spring weather in the village and all that had been happening recently, things like that just seemed far beyond them. "I'm afraid I don't have anything to give you."

"You gave me your love and, with it, the happiest days of my life." She stood on tiptoe and kissed him, then continued toward the living room.

Steve followed, his heart heavier than one of the barges that plied the river. It would take every ounce of strength he had to walk away from Meghan, but as the days passed, he was coming to believe that Emanuel had made that decision for him. But that didn't mean he had to go. He'd fight the man with every breath in him to stay with Meghan.

Meghan walked to the corner of the room where the blue spruce stood decked out in its Christmas finery. He hadn't even noticed that it now had several gaily-wrapped packages at its feet. Meghan shuffled through the gifts and extracted a long slender package wrapped in bright green paper and sporting a large gold bow. She handed it to Steve.

"Merry Christmas."

He kissed her, and then they sat side-by-side on the hearth while he unwrapped it, revealing a white box. Carefully, he removed the lid. On top of the tissue lay a folded, blue lined handkerchief with the initial "S" embroidered in one corner. He knew from seeing Irma's that Guides carried these. With a sinking heart, he remembered one other fact. Guides were not allowed to remain in the village.

Laying the handkerchief aside and trying not to think

of what the piece of material symbolized, he folded back the tissue paper.

He stared at the cold metal. With his forefinger he traced the long, rubbery loops of the stethoscope much like the one he'd left lying on his desk back at St. Francis Memorial Hospital the day he'd walked out for his mountain vacation. "It's . . . nice? I'm sure it would come in handy if I were going back to work."

She smiled. "It's not for *work*. It's for you. Take a moment everyday to listen to your own heart for a change. Take a moment to remember that *you're* still alive." She took his hand and kissed the fingers one by one. "Remember you have a purpose, and that these hands hold the skill to heal." She looked deep into his eyes. "And don't ever be afraid to remember the children. They're who you are. Without them, you lose the meaning to your very existence."

As much as he wanted to tell her she was wrong, he couldn't. He had no idea why, but from the first time he treated a child, he'd known they were going to be his life's work. The gifts she'd given him confirmed what they both knew deep inside. He *would* leave, it was just a matter of time. But the doubts about himself remained. Could he go back? Could he face losing another child?

She stood and reached for his hand. "Timothy is with Josiah, and Irma will be spending the night with Clara so she can help with Ellie's instructions. That leaves us totally alone. Help me make dinner, and we'll have a picnic in bed."

He looked into her eyes and saw a silent plea for him to share this gift of time. Steve didn't need a second invitation to spend a few more precious hours with her, but first he had to do something.

The mention of Ellie reminded him that he did have something to give Meghan. He reached into his pocket and pulled out the keychain. "I've read those words a million times and still don't believe in miracles. I guess if there truly is such a thing, miracles just don't happen for some people. Maybe it will work for you."

He placed it in her palm. She stared down at it for a long time, but said nothing. When she walked to the cabinet and laid it among her other mementoes of past Assignments, Steve stood behind her, his hands on her shoulders. A ray of sunlight shafted through the window and fell on the lone tear lying atop the small plastic rectangle.

* * *

That night, the nightmares came back with a vengeance.

CHAPTER 14

T he semi-darkness of the alley surrounded Meghan. The stench of garbage and the unwashed body of the man holding her made her gag. A scream rent the air. It was the lady. The other men were doing something to her. She screamed again, loud, long and bone chilling. It hurt Meghan's ears. She turned toward Meghan.

"Mommy!" A young voice cried out. It sounded like . . . But it couldn't be. It came again. "Mommy!"

Meghan suddenly realized the identity of the voice. It was hers—and the lady was her mother.

"Meghan, baby, don't look," she pleaded. "Turn away."

But she couldn't. The two men were tearing off her mother's clothes and throwing her to the ground. She whimpered. They were hurting her.

"Don't hurt my mommy!" Meghan cried and struggled against the rough hands biting into her thin arms. She kicked out at the man's shins. "Leave her alone!" Meghan's pitiful strength was no match for the big man towering over her. He laughed at her struggles.

"Please, baby, don't look." Her mother's voice was weak and choked with tears.

"Shut up, bitch," a rough voice said, then the man holding her mother down slapped her hard across the face. The sound echoed around the alley, bouncing off the brick buildings surrounding them.

"Hurry up, Jake," the man standing over them ordered as he unzipped his pants.

"She won't stop squirming," the man called Jake spat.

He slapped her mother again. This time, her head lolled to the side. Blood seeped from the corner of her mouth. She didn't move anymore.

"Mommy!" The scream tore from Meghan's throat. She twisted and flailed, trying in vain to get loose.

* * *

"Meghan! Wake up."

Steve's voice yanked her from the alley and back to the safe haven of his arms. She snuggled against him, held onto him as if she would never let go, and sobbed for the woman in the alley and for the little girl.

Repetitive visions of her horrendous nightmare played through her mind. She could hear the screams, the curses, the desperation in her mother's voice. She could see the savage expressions on the men's faces, the blood seeping from her mother's battered mouth, feel the bite of the man's fingers digging into her arm.

Could it have been just a bad dream? It had been so real, so vivid. Meghan rubbed her upper arm and was surprised at the tenderness she found there, just as if someone had held her in a vise-like grip.

With a certainty she felt from the very bottom of her soul, Meghan knew the nightmare had shown her a replay of a true event. Her mother had been brutally raped, and she'd seen it.

Irma had said that, as a child, Meghan had witnessed something that caused her to have nightmares. Was that why she had brought Meghan to the village? To forget seeing her mother violated in the worst possible way?

No wonder Irma hadn't wanted her to remember or be exposed to that brutality again. The animosity she'd been feeling toward Irma drained away, and the wall she'd erected between herself and her mother crumbled.

Just the idea that Irma had been forced to live with this unspeakable burden for all these years broke Meghan's heart. At least Irma had seen to it that she'd been granted the blessing of oblivion. She'd left Meghan in Renaissance to protect her—not because she didn't love her, but because she loved her too much to let her live with the memories.

Fresh sobs emanated from deep within Meghan, but they were for a totally different reason. She no longer cried for the terror she'd seen in her dreams or for the deserted child, but for the woman who had borne so much for a child she loved enough to bear the heartbreak of separation.

She clung to Steve and tried to block the horror of her nightmare from her mind.

Steve held her close, stroked her trembling body, kissed her head, and murmured soothing words. Very slowly, his calming ministrations took hold, and, though she continued to cling to him with surprising strength, very gradually, her body relaxed against him.

"Wanna tell me about it?" he whispered against her hair.

She hiccupped softly and shook her head. Knowing instinctively that she needed to come to terms with what she'd experienced, he didn't push her. Instead, he settled her more comfortably against his chest, then closed his eyes and waited for her to go back to sleep. But even then, he wished she'd tell him what the dreams that terrorized her so much were about.

He had nearly dozed off when Meghan sat up. She pulled her knees against her chest and wrapped her arms around them.

"What is it?" he asked sleepily.

"She was raped."

Steve came alert instantly. "Who?"

"Irm . . . my mother. Two men in an alley raped her when I was just a child. I saw it." She began to rock her body. "I saw it all."

Reaching out and grabbing her arm, he stopped her

movements. "What do you mean you saw it? How?"

She turned and stared at him, her features illuminated by the moonlight coming through the window. Fear shone brightly from her eyes. "I saw it . . . in my nightmare. I saw everything. There were three men. One held me down while the other two . . ." Shaking her head, she looked away.

Steve sat up and eased her against him. "It was a nightmare, sweetie. That's all. Just a bad dream."

Vehemently, she shook her head again and pulled away. "No! It was real. I know it."

By the look of sheer agony on her face, Steve could tell she really believed what she was saying. He couldn't stand seeing her like this. This had to end . . . soon. And there was no better time to do it than right now.

"Well, there's one way to settle it." He swung his legs over the side of the bed and grabbed his jeans. Standing, he began to slide into them. "Get dressed."

"Why?"

"We're going to ask Irma." He picked up her robe and handed it to her. "Put this on and meet me in the kitchen." Before he walked out the door, he threw a concerned look over his shoulder at Meghan.

Meghan sat very still until she heard the front door close and realized he was serious. Slowly, she slipped on the robe and padded to the kitchen. Purposefully, she pushed her nightmares to the back of her mind, unwilling to contend with them until Steve was back here. She needed his strength to lean on for the short time she had left with him.

More to keep her mind busy than because she wanted it, she made coffee, then set three cups and the sugar bowl on the table. Taking a ceramic pitcher from a cabinet, she filled it with milk and set it next to the sugar.

Dropping into one of the chairs, she waited for Steve to come back. She wasn't sure if talking to Irma was a good idea, but she knew she had to. But what if Steve was right, and it was just a crazy dream?

But it wasn't. Deep down inside where her fear lived, she knew what she'd seen was a replay of the "terrible event" that Irma had referred to the day Meghan found out Irma was her mother. She wrapped her robe tighter around her shivering body and stared at the dark windowpane.

That Emanuel had been able to wipe the memories from her mind for so long amazed Meghan. She knew as well as the other villagers that Emanuel possessed powers none of them could even fathom, but this went beyond that.

If his powers had been strong enough to hold the memories at bay for over twenty years, why now had they come back? What had prompted them to start? It hadn't been Irma's story. When the visions had started, Meghan had yet to learn the story. So, why now? The answers eluded her.

By the time she heard Steve and Irma coming through the door, the coffee had finished brewing, and she'd filled all three cups.

Irma looked dazed. Her hair was messy, and her eyes still held remnants of sleep. The robe she'd hastily grabbed was tied tightly around her waist. Her hands were buried in the pockets. Her complexion was pale, and she chewed nervously on her bottom lip.

Meghan grabbed Steve's hand for support. *Thank you*, she mouthed at him. He nodded and squeezed her hand.

"Sit down," Steve said gently, pulling out a chair for Irma.

She sat without question, her gaze never leaving Meghan's troubled face. Steve took the other seat and looked from one to the other, waiting for one of them to start talking. They both stared into their cups.

"Meghan?" he finally said, deciding neither of them was going to take the initiative.

She glanced at him, then to her mother. "I know," was all she said. The two words embodied more pain that one person should have had to bear.

Irma remained silent, but, to Steve, she again looked as old as the bag lady in the park. Her features twisted in pain, and she dropped her gaze back to the table.

Meghan slid her hand over Irma's. "They raped you. Why didn't you tell me? Why did you let me believe you deserted me? That you didn't love me?"

"I . . . I was ashamed and mortified that because I had kept you with me instead of letting Davis' parents take you, I had exposed you to that terrible night, and that you'd hate me for it." Irma's voice, the voice Steve recalled as being strong, confident, and forceful, emerged almost timid, afraid. "I couldn't have endured that." Silent tears cascaded down her cheeks. "I've always loved you, perhaps too much."

Steve recalled the acute sadness he'd seen in Irma's eyes in the park when she talked about the children and realized that she was thinking of the love she held for the daughter she'd had to give up. Her eyes had not been glazed with age. They'd been glazed with a loneliness that had grown throughout the years.

Slowly, Meghan left her chair and walked to stand beside Irma. She squatted down, then took Irma's face between her hands. "You have always been very special to me, but I never thought it was for any other reason than because you're a good person." She smiled, tears beginning to shine in her eyes. "Now I know, it *is* because you're a good person, but it's mostly because I love you, Momma, and nothing can change that."

Irma sucked in her breath, then pulled her daughter to her and sobbed against her shoulder.

Quietly, Steve rose and left the room, leaving mother and daughter to re-discover each other. Perhaps now, Meghan's nightmares would stop. He hoped so because he wasn't sure how much longer he'd be here to hold her and chase away her fears.

❊ ❊ ❊

"You know?" Emanuel said, taking a seat on the grass beside Meghan.

The talk she and her mother had had long into the night was still fresh in her mind, so Meghan didn't have to ask what Emanuel was talking about.

She snuggled the last of the daisies Josiah had left on her doorstep that morning into the flowerbed outside the front door of her cottage. Then, after admiring the new splash of color in the already profusely blooming flowerbed, she turned to the village Elder.

"Yes, I know. We talked last night."

"And, you're all right with it?"

Meghan smiled. It went without saying that his empathic abilities had already told him so without her verification. She breathed deeply of the smell of freshly turned earth and the perfume of the flowers. Today, it was almost possible to ignore the shadow of Steve's leaving that hung over her happiness—almost.

She turned to Emanuel and confirmed what he already knew. "I hate that such a thing happened to her, but it certainly wasn't her fault. So, yes, I'm fine, better than fine. I have my mother back."

She stretched out her curled legs to relieve the cramps that had begun to form from sitting on them for too long. Propping her hands behind her to support herself, she looked up at the clear blue sky and raised her face to the sun. The sunshine warmed her inside and out.

Ever since she and her mother had talked, she'd felt a lightness invade her soul that she hadn't even realized she'd been missing.

"And Steve?"

Emanuel's question stole a bit of the sunshine from her heart. "He's staying in the village," she said, not believing her own words, but terrified to admit otherwise.

Emanuel leaned forward to get a clear view of her face. "Do you really believe that?"

She looked at him and knew there was no point in lying. "No, but I can't let myself or him believe anything else."

He patted her arm, his touch almost as warm and reassuring as the sun. "I know, child, but you must. It's not Steve's destiny to remain here."

The joy she had been feeling moments earlier evaporated. The sun, once brilliant and friendly, seemed to have hidden behind a cloud of despair. She sat forward and concentrated on her nervous fingers as they pleated and unpleated the material of her blue skirt. There was no sense arguing the point. She'd known all along that he wouldn't stay, but she allowed herself to hope. Now, once Emanuel had put it into words, even the hope was gone.

By the time she raised her gaze, Emanuel was gone. Questions played over and over through her mind.

How will I bear the pain of losing Steve?

Will just his memory be enough to fill my heart during the empty days stretching into an endless future?

"May I join you?"

Meghan jumped and looked up to find her mother standing beside her. She smiled broadly.

She patted the grass and said, "Of course. Pull up a piece of lawn and sit down."

Irma tucked the skirt of her navy dress beneath her and sat. She looked at the flowers and sniffed the air. "They're beautiful."

"Yes, they are, but I can't take the credit. Josiah grows them, then gives them to me to plant. Their beauty is entirely his doing."

Meghan watched her mother closely. She glanced around, as if searching for anything to say except what brought her here. Another few moments passed with Irma remaining silent.

Obviously Irma was finding it difficult to say whatever she had to say, so Meghan spoke up. "You didn't come here to admire my flowers, did you, Momma?"

At the sound of the word *Momma*, Irma's head swung toward Meghan, a bright smile painting her lips, but the smile faded almost as quickly as it had been given birth. "No. I'm afraid I didn't." She broke eye contact and looked instead toward the other side of the square. "Emanuel sent me."

Dread gathered in a heavy ball at the pit of Meghan's

stomach. It was hard to believe that when she came out here to plant the daisies that her mood had been so light and happy.

"He wants you to know that you must leave the village." She paused.

Meghan felt the blood drain from her face. "But I don't want to leave here. I don't want to go out there where the violence that befell you exists." She didn't say that she had to remain here because it was the only way she could hold onto Steve. "This is my home, the only home I remember."

"When I left you here, I promised Emanuel that, when the time came, you would leave here and go back into the world. Besides, you can't hide from your destiny, Meghan. Your life lies beyond the village."

Meghan bolted to her feet. "No!"

Slowly, Irma rose. She took Meghan gently by the shoulders. "They arrested the men who attacked me. They aren't there anymore."

"But there are others. Aren't there?" She studied her mother's face, sure she would lie to get Meghan to leave Renaissance. But she didn't.

"Yes, but there are also good people. People who love and care for each other. People like your father."

Frantically, Meghan sought for a reason that would keep her here. "But the village has always had four Healers. If I go, that will leave only Josiah, Clara, and Sarah."

Irma smiled. "Clara is training Ellie to replace you. It was always Ellie's destiny to come back here and take your place. So you see, you have no choice. You must leave."

Meghan looked across the square to where Josiah and Steve were deep in conversation.

She drank her fill of his good looks and gentle smile. He was growing more and more confident of himself every day. There would be one more lesson for him, then the Transition would come. She knew that as surely as she knew that what her mother said was true.

The answers she had so fervently sought last night before Irma came were clear to her now. The dream had started because it had marked for her the beginning of her departure from Renaissance, something she'd never dreamed she'd have to do. It was time for her to fulfill her destiny, just as it would very soon be time for Steve to fulfill his.

It seemed that no matter what either of them did, she would lose him forever.

CHAPTER 15

S teve glanced across the square to where Irma and Meghan were talking. They were smiling at each other, then suddenly, Meghan's smile vanished, and she bolted to her feet. Even from here, he could see the distress on her face.

"No!" The sound of her voice carried clearly across the square, but, when she turned away from him, the rest of what she said was lost.

He continued to study the animated conversation of the two women. What in hell was going on? They'd seemed quite amiable last night and this morning. So what was going on now?

Irma leaned toward Meghan and said something. A moment more passed, then Meghan raised her head and glanced toward him. The look of intense distress on her face tore at his insides. He took a step toward her and felt a hand on his arm.

Josiah's softly accented voice came from behind him. "Let them settle this between them. It's not your concern, my boy. We have work to do. Come."

Steve knew Josiah was right, but to see Meghan so upset made him want to run to her.

Josiah started around the cottage but paused when Steve made no move to follow. "Steve, leave them to it. Come."

Taking a deep breath, Steve followed Josiah. Whatever it was that had perpetuated the exchange between Irma and Meghan, *they* had to settle it. After all, despite having seen and talked to each other during Irma's periodic visits to the village, they were actually just getting acquainted as mother and daughter and, no doubt, there would be a few rough spots for them to get past.

As he rounded the corner of the cottage, Steve glanced over his shoulder. Irma had taken Meghan into her embrace. He sighed in relief. Whatever the problem had been, it appeared to have passed. He turned away and continued to follow Josiah to the garden.

What he saw there stopped him dead in his tracks. The entire garden was a profusion of mature, green plants, their stems thick and healthy and laden with vegetables.

"How . . ."

Josiah chuckled low in his throat. "Figured you'd be a bit surprised."

"A bit surprised is an understatement. Two days ago this garden was full of dead plants."

"It's just the way of things, my boy. When it comes to fate, you can't give up, because you never know what's waiting around the corner." He patted Steve's shoulder. "Fate may be fickle, but it has a mind of its own, and if we take the time to let things happen, we come to realize they're usually for a good reason."

Shaking his head, Steve had to agree. If he hadn't learned anything else during his stay in the village, he'd learned that nothing happened here without a purpose. There was a lesson in this phenomenal occurrence. He turned to ask Josiah what it was, but the old man had disappeared, leaving Steve to mull over the significance of dead plants coming back to life all by himself, which he wasn't at all sure hadn't been Josiah's plan all along.

He walked through the rows of flourishing vegetation, thinking. The plants had died. He'd helped Josiah plow them under and plant the new crop. Now, it was as if the disaster had never happened.

Suddenly, he remembered the faces of the children he'd seen floating in the sun's heat rays over the field of dead plants, faces of the children he'd lost. Had all those tragic deaths paved the way for other children to live? Was that the lesson? Had their sacrifice not been in vain? Would the children who died lead the way toward new treatments, new ways to conquer the demon that stole them from their loved ones, new ways to preserve other young lives?

As an oncologist, he should have known that, but the deaths had become so blinding, so overpowering, the grief so intense, that all he'd been able to see was his failure to save the children.

Steve felt his spirits lift. The burden he'd been carrying for so long diminished. But a new concern replaced it. If he'd missed that, how many other things had he missed by being too blinded by death to see the facts?

Before he could analyze that, a movement at the far end of the garden caught his attention. He turned in time to see the tail of Emanuel's robes disappear around the corner of Josiah's cottage.

* * *

Meghan sat on the grass where Irma had left her. She heard the approach of someone and looked up to the silhouette of a large, robed figure. Emanuel.

She knew he'd come. Being privy to Steve's reason for coming into the mist, she'd sensed the moment he had started understanding what Josiah had been teaching him. It was only a matter of time before Emanuel showed up to announce the start of Steve's Transition. Still, she held onto the fragile hope that she'd been wrong.

She had no desire to hear the words that would confirm her worst fears, but something drove her to it. "Is it true?" she said softly, her voice quaking with the pain that coursed through her.

Emanuel sat beside her. "Yes. He's healing, and very soon the Transition will come." He gazed thoughtfully into the distance. "It has to be this way. You know that. There are children waiting for him, children who will not die, children who must go on with their lives and do great things." He waved his hand across the horizon. "Somewhere, there's a child who, because of Steve, will live to grow into a future policeman, who will stop a crime that would leave a child orphaned; or a teacher, who will educate a future President of the United States; or a nurse, who will comfort a patient in pain; or perhaps a peacemaker, who will find a way for men to live in harmony. They all need to realize their destinies and men like Steve must make that possible."

Her heart sank. She'd known that to be the way of things. Steve had a destiny waiting for him, just as she did. The bitter pain of that admission rested on Meghan's heart like a huge boulder.

"How soon?"

"Before the sun sets."

Acceptance of their separate fates was a hard pill to swallow, one that tore through her like a March wind, cold and cutting to the bone. But accept it she must.

"And me? When am I to leave?"

"Emanuel! Meghan!"

Both of them looked toward the frantic voice. Ellie raced across the square, her face red and twisted with concern, her blond hair flying out behind her.

"Timothy . . ." she choked out, stopping before them and

struggling to catch her breath. "He's gone . . . disappeared."

From the other side of the square, Steve emerged from behind Josiah's cottage. He took one look at the small group on Meghan's lawn and hurried to join them.

"What is it?" he asked, seeing the look of total horror on Meghan's face.

"Ellie says Timothy has disappeared." Meghan was wringing her hands.

Steve knew the boy had planned on spending the day with Ellie in the woods. He also knew how prone Timothy was to taking off on his own. What frightened him most was if the boy was in trouble, he couldn't even yell for help.

Taking Ellie's arm, he tried to calm her down. "Slow down, catch your breath, and tell us what happened."

Ellie looked at him with anguished eyes. "Walking . . . through the woods . . . I turned . . . to watch a bird. When I . . . looked back . . . he was gone. I searched . . . couldn't find him." She bent over.

Steve waited, hoping she'd be able to tell them more once she'd controlled her breathing.

"Where were you?" Meghan's voice clearly reflected her anxiety.

Ellie pointed toward the hills above the river.

Steve looked at the village Elder. Emanuel nodded. Knowing what he must do, Steve started forward, then turned to Meghan. "Get Alvin. He knows these woods well. Then get blankets and hot chocolate ready. He'll be cold when I get him back here."

"No! Ellie can do that. I'm coming with you."

Before she could take a step, Emanuel grasped her arm and shook his head slightly. "Some lessons must be learned alone," he said in a voice so quiet she barely heard him

"Find Alvin. Send him after me as quickly as you can." Every moment Timothy was out there, beyond the village's spring temperatures, he was in danger of freezing—especially in his condition. "We have to work fast," he yelled back to Meghan, then darted off at a dead run toward the woods.

Sprinting across the square and over the footbridge proved easy going. When he had cleared the perimeter of the village and left the spring-like temperatures of Renaissance behind, the winter air hit him in the face, momentarily stealing his breath and sending shivers over his coatless body.

He pushed forward. The snow, more than knee-deep in some spots, hampered his progress and slowed him to a snail's pace. Nevertheless, Steve continued to force his legs to keep moving.

As he trudged on, his mind raced with the symptoms he hadn't allowed himself to even think about since meeting the boy—excessive fatigue, lack of appetite, easy bruising. All signs of serious illness. Tests were needed, but Steve's years of experience told him that Timothy had acute lymphoblastic leukemia and needed medical attention soon, if he was to beat it. And he could beat it.

Huge progress had been made in curing A.L.L. in children. Recently, in an article out of St. Jude's Hospital, he'd read that the cure rate had risen yearly. But even the rising cure rate would not help Timothy if he froze to death out in these woods before they could start treatment.

Upon reaching the cliffs Ellie had said they were on when Timothy disappeared, Steve slowed his pace and began scanning the snow for footprints. The chill winter air cut through his thin shirt sleeves. He rubbed his arms to warm them, and shoved his hands in his pockets to absorb the warmth of his body. He'd circled the area several times before he noticed a set of small prints that headed into the woods above the cliffs.

Steve followed the prints until he came to a spot where evidently Ellie had crossed their path, walked in ever widening circles, and annihilated them totally. He moved to the outside edge of the crushed snow and searched once more for the boy's prints and the direction in which he'd gone.

Ten minutes later, he found them. They headed to the spot where Timothy had climbed on the rock the day he and Meghan had taken the boy for a walk. He sprinted in that direction, traveling close beside the trail Timothy had left.

"Timothy!"

He listened, knowing the boy couldn't answer him

in words, but also aware that Timothy was a smart young man. Steve kept praying he'd find a way to signal where he was. Nothing. He strode on for a few more yards and repeated his call.

"Timothy!"

He'd walked only a few more feet when he heard what sounded like a piece of wood being beaten against a tree. Holding his breath and listening intently, he followed the noise. He searched for any sight of the boy. Then the noise abruptly stopped.

"Timothy!"

The sound came again, from above his head. He looked up to see a woodpecker hammering on the dead trunk of a tree. Damn it! Where was he? Panic began to seep into him.

To quell the fear, he started repeating a litany of hope. "He's okay. I'll find him." Over and over he repeated the words until the panic slipped away.

Again, he called the boy's name, then waited. Very faintly, he could make out the sound of sobbing. Trying to make as little noise as possible, he moved toward it. As he got closer to the edge of the cliffs, the sobbing grew louder. When he could go no farther without plunging over the side, he stopped. The sobbing was coming from below him.

Stretching out on his stomach, Steve eased himself far enough forward to see over the cliff's side. Below, on a ledge barely large enough to hold him, was Timothy.

"Timothy," he said quietly, so as not to frighten him into making a sudden move. Timothy glanced up, his eyes red and large in his pale face. "Hi, Buddy. I've come to bring you home."

Timothy nodded eagerly. He was shivering, and his lips were slightly blue. His hands, devoid of mittens, were turning red from the cold.

"This is some fix you've gotten yourself into, buddy." Steve forced a smile.

He offered Steve a weak smile and stretched out his hand in a silent plea for rescue.

"I know, buddy. Hang in there. I'm going to get you out of this, I just have to figure out how."

Steve looked around. The drop to Timothy's perch was steep and covered with snow-coated rocks. If Steve wasn't careful, he could end up in the river himself. He checked his surroundings for something he could use and spotted a wild grape vine clinging to the branches of a leafless oak tree.

"I'll be right back. I'm not leaving without you," he told the boy before moving slowly back from the edge, then getting to his feet.

It took several yanks on the vine before it finally let loose and dropped to the ground. Steve took the end and bent it back and forth to assure himself it wasn't too dry or too rotten for the job. As the bark split, he could see green wood below it.

He wedged one end of the vine in the crotch of a young maple tree then secured it around the trunk. Giving it several experimental yanks, he assured himself it would hold. Arranging his features so the intense fear he was feeling did not show, he walked toward the cliff. Once more, he eased himself to the edge of the cliff and looked down.

A sinking feeling invaded his stomach. Below he could see the steady flow of the icy cold Hudson River. If either of them fell to the river, they wouldn't have a chance in the strong current and cold water. They'd die in minutes from hypothermia.

Carefully, he lowered the vine over the side to Timothy, praying as he did so that Timothy had enough strength for what he would need to do. "Grab hold of this and wrap it around your hands and hang on. I'll pull you up," he told the child as he fed the last of the vine over the cliff's edge.

Timothy nodded and did as he was instructed.

"Good boy. Now, hang on."

Steve slid back, then stood and began to pull. The vine came up an inch at a time, then suddenly stopped. No matter how hard he tugged, it wouldn't move. Wrapping it around his leg so he wouldn't lose the progress they'd made, he crept near the edge again.

As he peered over the edge, he could see Timothy's arms were stretched above his head, his hands still holding the vine.

Deliberately keeping his tone light, Steve called down to him. "What's the problem, buddy?"

Timothy pointed at his right leg. By pushing himself forward as far as he dared, Steve could see the child's foot was wedged between two rocks. In a way, it was good that it had happened, otherwise Timothy might have tried to save himself and ended up plunging into the river. It had more than likely been the thing that had saved his life. However, it made rescuing him harder for Steve.

"Okay, let go of the vine. I have to figure out how to get you unstuck before I can bring you up here." The vine instantly went slack.

Steve unwound it from his leg. He'd have to lower himself down to Timothy, but he wasn't sure the vine was secured enough around the tree to hold his weight. What he could use was someone to hold it while he went over the edge. He scanned the woods for any sign of Alvin Tripp. He was nowhere in sight. Steve was on his own.

He ran his fingers through his hair, sat back, and considered his options. He could go back to the village for help and hope that Timothy stayed where he was and didn't freeze to death in the dropping temperatures. Or, he could find a way to get down there and bring the boy up.

Going back was out of the question. He'd have to do this alone. His decision made, Steve began to plan his strategy. He would have to lower himself down to Timothy, free him, then pull both of them back up the cliff face. The boy was light enough that his weight didn't concern Steve. What did concern him were the ice-covered rocks and his own freezing cold hands.

He glanced at the black clouds scuttling across the darkening sky and realized that it was not evening that was approaching, but a storm. Steve surveyed the horizon. The distant mountains had already disappeared behind a wall of blinding snow. It wasn't just a storm; it was a blizzard.

Temperatures had already dropped several degrees, and his hands were freezing cold. He hoped he could hang onto the rope to complete the rescue. He blew on his hands, rubbed them together and tucked them in his armpits to warm them. Several moments later, the tingle told him that blood was flowing freely through them again.

Taking up the vine, he tied it around his waist and twisted the end around his fist. Backing up slowly, he worked his way to the edge.

"Here I come, buddy. Make sure you stay to one side so I don't land on you."

Checking to see where Timothy was, Steve started over the side. Slowly, he lowered himself. A stiff wind rose and buffeted him, turning his exposed hands almost as cold as they had been before his warming process. The tail of his shirt escaped his jeans and cold air climbed up his back. He ignored all of it and concentrated on his descent.

A bald eagle screeched and skimmed the water below in search of supper. Timothy cringed against the rocks.

"It's okay. He's not going to hurt you. He's looking for something to eat, and little boys aren't his favorite," he told the boy, talking as much to ease his own nerves as Timothy's. Steve moved his foot and cautiously placed it on what looked like a rock sticking out from the cliff. "Besides, you're too big for him to carry home in his beak. He needs something small like a mouse or a fish."

He glanced over his shoulder and saw Timothy relax, although he kept a wary eye on the bird until it disappeared from sight behind a large pine tree jutting out from the cliff.

"Bald eagles aren't really bald, you know," Steve went one, his voice beginning to quiver from the cold. "They only look that way because their heads are white."

He continued his impromptu nature lesson while, at the same time, he eased down the rock face. Soon, he felt Timothy's cold hand touch his leg. Moments later his feet touch the narrow shelf on which the boy stood.

He eased his hands to his side and carefully turned to face Timothy. The boy wrapped his arms around Steve's legs. "Yes, I'm glad to see you, too, buddy. But we've got to get you out of here before you catch pneumonia." Or we both fall over the edge, he added silently.

Carefully, Steve squatted and looked at where Timothy's foot was caught between two rocks. After a quick inspection, Steve decided that it was the heavy sole of Timothy's hiking boot that was allowing the rocks to hold him prisoner. If he removed Timothy's boot, he could pull his foot free.

With his fingers close to numb, Steve began unlacing the boot. Timothy put his hand on Steve's bent head. He could feel the cold seeping into his scalp. He tried to work faster, but his fingers refused to cooperate. Finally, the last of the lacing came free. Grabbing Timothy's ankle, Steve eased his foot from the boot.

"Okay, buddy. Put your arms around my neck and hang on. We're outta here."

The boy fastened his arms tightly around Steve's neck and buried his face in his hair. Trust emanated from him, and despite the chill coming off the child's body, Steve could feel new warmth invade his soul. He had to fight doubling over with the pain of the moment. It felt as if someone had torn his soul from his body and stuffed it back in.

It took some careful maneuvering and slow going, but a few minutes later, Steve eased them both to safety at the top of the precipice. They both fell to the ground in a tangle of legs and arms. After some squirming, Steve managed to sit up with Timothy on his lap.

Steve gave a huge sigh. He hadn't failed. He'd done what seemed to be the impossible and had been success-ful. The complete elation from what he'd just done made him close his eyes and smile. Adrenaline pumped through him at an alarming rate, making him extremely aware of the life he'd just saved and the life in him that had found new meaning.

Timothy's arms snaked around Steve's neck. He buried his face close to Steve's ear. "I knew you could do it, Dr. Steve."

CHAPTER 16

Meghan sensed them before she saw them come through the trees and into the square. Timothy straddled Steve's shoulders. An ear-to-ear grin split Steve's face. Without bidding them to, Steve's emotions flooded into her. His heart overflowed with happiness. She could feel his intense joy more clearly than she had ever been able to feel the emotions of any Assignment.

While that should have pleased her, the reason for his elation, beyond Timothy's safety, wrenched her already bruised heart. Steve, even if he didn't realize it, had made a decision that would leave her lonely and heartsick.

Everyone had gathered in the square to wait for Steve's return, and, now, the small group of villagers flowed past her to greet the returning males. Steve walked past everyone and stopped only when he was face-to-face with Meghan. Timothy smiled down at her from Steve's shoulders.

"His name is Timothy Kendall. He's five years old, and he lives in Westchester with his parents, Mary and Louis Kendall," Steve said, his smile growing in proportion to his blossoming happiness.

Stunned by this information, Meghan gasped. "How do you know?"

Steve lifted Timothy to the ground and looked down at him.

"I told him," Timothy said, his voice clear and sure.

A gasp went up from everyone. Everyone except Emanuel, who just smiled and moved to the outer perimeter of the crowd.

Robbed of the power of speech, Meghan put her hands over her mouth. Tears burned her eyes. She dropped to her knees and hugged Timothy close. She'd never felt anything as satisfying as the sound of that little voice.

Then she recalled the vision in the lantern of Steve and Timothy walking out of the village hand-in-hand. It was all falling into place, just as she'd seen it. Now that he could speak, Timothy would be leaving the village with Steve. She was about to lose both of them. Her embrace tightened.

She glanced up at Steve over Timothy's head. He turned away, but not before she saw the moisture filling his eyes, too.

"You're squeezing me to death," Timothy complained, squirming in her arms. She released him and leaned back to look into his dear face. Using the tips of his chilly fingers, he gently wiped away the tears from her cheeks. "Don't cry."

Meghan smiled through the tears that refused to stop

gathering. "It's okay. They're happy tears because I'm just so glad you're okay and that you can finally talk to us. Aren't you happy that you can speak again?"

Vigorously, he nodded his head, his hair falling in soft waves over his eyes. Impatiently, he pushed it away. "Can I go home now?"

She looked at Emanuel. He nodded. Meghan's heart tore in half. She knew that it would never stop aching for this small boy. "Of course you can."

Emanuel stepped forward and leaned down to speak to Timothy. "Before we begin your preparations to leave us, I think Clara has some of those oatmeal cookies you're so fond of at her cottage. Would you like to come with me and have a few?"

Timothy nodded vigorously. "Hot chocolate, too?"

"I think that can be arranged," the elder said with a smile. The other villagers began to disperse. Emanuel led Timothy away by the hand. The old man had only gone a few steps when he stopped and looked from beneath his bushy eyebrows at Steve to Meghan and winked. "We should return in an hour's time. I'm confident that the two of you can find something to . . . occupy you in the meantime."

Steve smiled at him. While the thought of even another moment with Meghan thrilled him, the reason brought new pain to his heart. Emanuel was giving them an hour to say their goodbyes. "We'll try." He turned to Meghan. "What do you think? Can we find something to do for an hour?"

She gazed up at him and bathed him with that smile that filled every corner of his aching heart. Silently, she took his hand and led him from the square to her cottage. They entered together, hands clasped, and went straight through the house, never pausing until they'd stepped into Meghan's bedroom. Steve's gaze went to the lantern sitting on the night table. It was clear for the first time. No mist filled the globe, no images. Nothing. Even Meghan was being denied the right to see what was to come.

He turned to face each her. There was so much Steve wanted to say, but when he opened his mouth to speak, she laid her finger on his lips. "I want no promises that neither of us can keep. I don't know what will happen when we leave here. I can't predict it. I do know that somehow you will always remain a part of my heart."

He kissed her softly. "This will be the last time we're together," he said, emotion choking his voice.

She shook her head. "I will not allow myself to believe that. I can't. There would be no reason to face another day if that were true."

He could read in her eyes what he already knew in his heart. He was right. They had no tomorrows. Steve didn't try to dissuade her.

Instead, he used his fingertips to outline her features—those startling blue eyes, her full mouth, turned-up nose and rosy cheeks. He closed his eyes and repeated the process, consigning each detail to memory, so that later, down the long tunnel of time, he would have this picture of her to pull out and remember a magical time in his life when he'd found love.

As if reading his thoughts, Meghan's finger began tracing his features. He stood very still, drinking in the feel of her skin skimming over his, memorizing, storing his features in her mind. When she reached his mouth, he opened his lips and sucked her fingertip inside. She gasped. Her eyes widened. The birth of desire flushed her face.

"I need to see you, all of you," he whispered.

Sliding the fingers of one hand beneath the hem of her blouse, he inched the gauzy material up her body. As he did, the other hand trailed in its wake, caressing her naked skin. When his hand slid over her breast, and he gathered its fullness in his palm, she sighed and laid her forehead against his chest.

Gently, he raised her chin and looked into her eyes. A fine sheen of moisture had gathered there. "Don't cry, Meghan. We have known a love such as few will ever experience. A love that both of us will carry in our hearts until they cease to beat."

She blinked and a tear escaped down her cheek. He wiped it away with the pad of his thumb and then gathered her close to his body.

Against her hair he whispered, "You have walked in

my soul, and I will never be the same man I was when I first arrived here."

Meghan wrapped her arms around his neck, raised herself on tiptoe and held on tight. "Nor I," she whispered into the crook of his neck.

Her warm breath flowing over his skin made his breath catch in his throat. His body cried out for more, but he denied it. This time would have to see both of them through an eternity, and he would not rush it. He would savor and absorb every second, and he would see to it that Meghan did as well.

Leading her to the bed, he lowered her on the edge and knelt at her feet. With his gaze locked to hers, he began the slow process of undressing her. First the blouse skimmed up her body and over her head to be discarded somewhere beside them. She wore no bra to cover the lush swell of her breasts. His hungry eyes feasted on their beauty.

Then he stood, drawing her up with him. He fumbled with nerveless fingers at the waist of her skirt, unfastening the button and lowering the zipper. With a soft *whoosh* the skirt puddled around her feet. Her undergarments quickly followed, and she stood before him as exposed to his eyes as she had always been to his heart.

Steve's breath snagged on a rush of emotion so strong it made his head light. Sunlight shafted through the window turning her body the color of a statue cast in gold. Almost afraid to touch her, he ran a fingertip down the valley between her breasts.

She gasped and covered his hand with hers. Hot chills followed the progression of his hand, and she knew if she didn't stop him, she would surrender to the emotions buffeting her.

"No. I want to see you, too."

He dropped his hand and stood before her in silent acquiescence. Meghan grasped the hem of his T-shirt and peeled it up and over his head. She dropped it as nonchalantly as he'd dropped her clothes, all the while never losing eye contact with him.

She smiled faintly when she saw the rapid rise of his chest as he anticipated her next move. For having known each other such a short period of time, it continued to amaze her that he could read her so well.

Trailing her fingertips over his skin, barely touching him, she teased his flesh and gloried in the way his breath caught as she grazed the tips of his nipples on her way to his waistband.

Her fingers had just closed over the cold metal of his belt buckle, when he grabbed them, stopping their hurried movements. "Be careful, my love."

Meghan smiled, knowing he was telling her that too much and this love making would reach its conclusion long before either of them wanted it to. Keeping that in mind, she slid his belt from the buckle and opened the fastening at the waist of his jeans. The soft *whirr* of the zipper blended with their increased breathing.

She slid her hands under the waistband of both his jeans and his shorts and eased them over his hips. They hit the floor with a muffled *thunk*, and he stepped out of them.

Her gaze released his and moved to inspect the entirety of the man before her. Coherent thought deserted her. Steve Cameron was magnificent, the epitome of a Greek god come to earth. Muscles rippled over his legs and arms. The sunlight painted the hills and valleys of his body, accentuating the evidence of his full arousal.

Meghan grasped his hands in hers. Carefully, she explored them, remembering their ability to bring her to the heights of passion as well as console her when her spirits had been battered by life's intrusion. She kissed each finger and then turned them to repeat the gesture on each palm.

Then she laid them against her beasts. "Love me, Steve. Love me as if it will be the last time."

Knowing in his heart that this *would* be the last time, but as unwilling to say the words as she was, he lowered her gently to the bed and laid down bedside her. He pulled her naked body against him and allowed his hands to roam the contours of her back.

"I love you, Meghan. No matter what tomorrow brings, that will never change."

"Show me," she whispered into his mouth.

Unable to stop himself, Steve took her offered lips with a fierceness that had never entered their love making before. Desperation rode low in his belly, pushing him to get closer, to taste more of her, to know every microscopic part of Meghan.

Hungrily, he pried her lips apart and probed the sweetness within with his tongue, swirling and tasting. She met him with equal fervor, dueling with him in a kind of driven need to fill herself with him. Desperate for a breath, Steve pulled back, but immediately recaptured her mouth.

Their entwined bodies thrashed about the bed, twisting this way and that, trying to find the closeness each sought. Finally, they came to rest with Meghan atop him, her legs straddling his hips, her wet warmth caressing his arousal.

"Now, Steve. Now."

"No, not yet." He didn't want to end this and if he did what she begged him to, it would end.

"But time. . ."

"Time is irrelevant, remember," he said, his hands cupping her bottom, pulling her closer.

Meghan pulled away, her body going still, her eyes once more moist with unshed tears. "Not anymore."

Steve pulled her to him. For a long moment, they lay quietly in each others arms. Then Steve eased her to her back and straddled her legs. Very slowly, he pushed into her.

Meghan's hips rose to meet him, her hands clutched his shoulders, her nails dug into his flesh. Sharp pain radiated from the indentations she made there, but Steve ignored it. He concentrated on the passion, the building quest for satisfaction, the love that bubbled up and filled every part of him, the movements of the woman beneath him.

No time they'd made love could Meghan remember feeling this way. She craved the blossoming climax and at the same time dreaded it. Once the pinnacle had been reached, the downward slide would begin, and she knew that the landing this time would been anything but pleasant. Despite that, she drove her body to meet Steve's, longing for more, hoping for the miracle that would keep him in her arms forever.

Then all coherent thought ceased, leaving behind only awareness of their bodies straining against each other, driving toward the end that they both wanted to never come. But come it did and with an explosion that rocked them to their roots. No stars, no floating above the earth, waiting for the plunge downward. This time the world exploded in a shower of light and sensation so intense, it took their breath away.

When it was over, they lay so close that their sweat-slick bodies resembled one being. Neither of them attempted speech. What was the sense? Everything had been said.

Steve stared at the ceiling, his arms tight around Meghan, his mind busy trying to assess why there were no miracles for them. Basically, and, in all the ways that really should count, they were good people who tried to do right by their fellow human beings. What more could be asked of them?

Meghan stirred, rolling to her side. She stared at the lantern. A white mist had begun to fill the glass globe.

"We have to go. The Transition is beginning." Her voice revealed the tears that Steve had felt falling on his chest. She sat up and began gathering her clothes.

Steve sat up, watching her graceful movements as she slipped into her skirt and blouse. "What if I just refuse to leave?"

She turned to face him. "You don't have that option anymore. When Timothy spoke, the decision was taken out of your hands."

He stared at her. "You knew that, didn't you?"

"Not for sure, but I suspected. Timothy can't find his way back to the cabin without guidance."

"Someone else can take him." Steve's brow furrowed. "Alvin can take him. He travels outside the village all the time."

Meghan's movements stilled. She kept her back to him. "No, Alvin can't. It's part of what you must do, Steve. An Assignment heals inside the village, but he or she must face what lies outside, the thing that drove them here to begin with. Timothy is part of your healing process. I don't know how or why, I just know that he is. Only Emanuel understands that. It's why Emanuel didn't send Alvin to help you save Timothy. You *had* to do it. You *had* to be the one."

Where a small light of hope had resided inside Steve,

the gloom of despair took over. Slowly, he dressed and left the room to gather his few belongings.

＊ ＊ ＊

Steve and Meghan walked into the square together, no longer touching, no longer looking at each other. Meghan was sure if she looked at him her heart would break into even smaller pieces than it already had.

Emanuel and Timothy awaited them.

"Can I go home now?" Timothy looked at her with pleading eyes.

Meghan glanced at Emanuel. He nodded.

"Yes, you can go home now." Her voice emerged barely above a whisper. She took his hand. "Let's go get you ready." As she and Timothy headed toward her cottage, she glanced at Steve and knew she would never think of him without her heart bleeding.

Steve watched them until they disappeared inside the house and the door closed behind them. A warm hand came to rest on his shoulder.

"You must prepare to leave as well, my son." Emanuel stood beside him, his face a mixture of understanding and concern. "The Transition has begun." He nodded toward the fine mist that had just begun seeping up from the ground.

"But I'm not going back," Steve protested in one last desperate attempt to remain behind with the woman he loved.

Emanuel raised an eyebrow. A faint smile played around his mouth. "Aren't you?"

Steve avoided the elder's probing gaze. He knew Emanuel sensed what Steve knew deep in his heart. He *was* leaving the village, but to admit it would be severing his last tie to Meghan, and he'd rather slit his wrists than do that.

"We all must face the inevitability of our destiny."

Much to his sorrow, Steve had done just that during the walk back with Timothy. He'd had plenty of time to put together all that had happened since coming over that small footbridge into this remarkable place.

Heartsick, Steve had come to the realization that he couldn't hide from life in this misty village. He had to leave and face it head-on. Despite what Meghan had told him when he got here, he never really had a choice. From the very beginning, everything that had happened here had been aiming him toward that end.

His life lay in the outside world, in the children's wing of St. Francis Memorial Hospital . . . with the kids.

Out there were children who needed him, children like Timothy. Because of Meghan and Renaissance, Steve understood what he'd always known—while some children will die despite him and his skills, many will live because of them. He couldn't hide here from the inevitability of death. Just like the plants in Josiah's garden, death was not an end but a new beginning. Finally understanding that everyone chooses their own destiny, he'd also come to understand that it was up to them to fulfill it. Most importantly, he knew now that none of this had ever been about the kids or even his ability to heal. It had always been about him and his faith in himself as a man, and, in finding that, he'd found peace within himself

He'd leave and take Timothy with him. It would break his heart to leave Meghan, but he must return to his life.

At that very moment it came to him that although he'd found himself and a renewed confidence in his skills as a doctor and a man in the village, the one thing he'd been looking for had still eluded him . . . that one lousy miracle.

He raised his head and met the blue-eyed gaze of Ellie Stanton. Then again, maybe he had seen at least one miracle. But even with the evidence before him, he had to know exactly how Ellie had lived when he was certain she wouldn't.

He walked to where Ellie lingered on the outer edge of the group of villagers who seemed to have appeared from nowhere.

"Are you going to tell me now?" he said quietly.

She inclined her head a little. A cascade of bright yellow hair fell over her shoulders in soft waves. "It was the experimental drug you gave me. It just took longer to work than everyone expected. By the time it kicked in, you were gone. No one knew where you were." She touched his hand, her skin warm on his. "So you did save me after all."

Pleased, but a bit annoyed at her silence, Steve frowned. "Why didn't you tell me before?"

"Because you had to learn your self-worth before I could. You had to see it with your own eyes, feel it in here." She laid her hand over his heart.

Steve relaxed. She was so very much like Meghan. He smiled. "You're going to be a wonderful Healer."

"As are you," she said, and turned toward Clara's cottage.

※ ※ ※

Meghan finished dressing Timothy in the clothes that he'd worn when he'd arrived in Renaissance. When that was done, she had only to take him to the square to meet Steve for their journey back to the cabin.

She tried to clear the advent of Steve's departure from her mind, but the pain that twisted in her heart reminded her with every breath. Methodically, she allowed the images of his time there to pass through her thoughts, savoring every detail and storing each of them carefully for a time when he would not be there.

In the future, she wanted to be able to close her eyes and feel his hands skimming over her body, the gentleness of his lips on hers, the beat of his heart against her breasts. She wanted to be able to hear the sound of his voice whispering love words in her ear and the caress of his breath on her face.

And, if she had to leave Renaissance, as Irma and Emanuel said she did, she hoped that the memories would be strong enough to sustain themselves so that she would have them on the outside.

"Are we going now?"

Timothy's excited question brought Meghan out of her daydreams.

"Yes, sweetie, we're going just as soon as I get one more thing."

She went into the living room and from beneath the Christmas tree she took the long box that held the stethoscope she'd given Steve. Then she went to the curio cabinet, and pulling the keychain from her skirt pocket where she had placed it when she first realized without a doubt that Steve would leave her, she put it beside the one-eyed teddy bear. Placing the memento in the cabinet was always the last thing she did before bidding goodbye to an Assignment.

On her way back to where Timothy waited for her by the front door, she spotted the lantern on the table. The bottom of the clear globe was filling with swirling mist. Her soul cried out in protest of its meaning, but for Timothy's sake, she swallowed, drew herself up, and took a deep breath.

"Okay, let's go." Taking his hand, she led him out of the house and back to the square.

Outside the cottage, the mist thickened and rose

slowly, covering the ground in a glittering veil of crystalline white fog. The Transition was nearly complete, and, soon, the two people she loved would be gone from her life, from her world.

She glanced at Irma. Tears rolled freely down her mother's cheeks. She knew what it was like to lose those she loved. Meghan could only hope and pray that it would be her good fortune to be reunited with them as she had been with Irma. But, in truth, she held out little hope. Smiling weakly at her mother, Meghan turned to Steve.

He had on the red plaid jacket she remembered from when she first saw him entering the village. Steve stepped forward, blinking several times to remove the gathering moisture in his eyes. He cupped her cheek in his hand. Closing her eyes, she nestled her face into his palm. Tears trickled from beneath her closed eyelids and fell onto his skin.

"I'll always be with you," he said, softly, his heart hurting more than it ever had in his life. "Right here." He tapped the left side of her chest.

She opened her eyes, pressed her hand over his, then released it, and stood on tiptoe to kiss him. Her lips felt cool and silky. She tasted of her salty tears.

For a moment he entertained the insane idea of picking her up and making a mad dash for the bridge before they could stop them. Surely if he hugged her close enough, her memory would stay with her, her love would follow her.

She stepped back. Her eyes told him his thoughts had

found their way to her, and she shook her head. "As much as I want that, it's not going to work. I will have to leave here eventually, but not now and not with you."

The anguish in his heart reached into his soul and lacerated it until it bled.

"When you leave here, if you don't remember me, I'll find you and help you remember. I'll teach you to love me again."

She searched his face as if looking for the answer that would make what he'd promised come to pass. "I want to believe that."

He gripped her shoulders. "Then believe it with all your heart. We can make it happen."

Her watery smile told him he was chasing rainbows. Miracles just didn't happen for him and evidently, they didn't happen for Meghan either. For the first time, Steve knew how Irma must have felt when she had to leave Meghan behind.

"Can we go?" Timothy tugged on Steve's pants leg.

Steve grabbed Meghan. Oblivious to the villagers standing around them, he kissed her hard, savoring her taste, her smell, the feel of her body against him. He tore his mouth from hers and cradled her face in his hands. "I love you. How can I leave you?" The anguished question came from deep in his soul, torn from his heart and flung into the cosmos.

Meghan took his hands from her face and stepped

back. Tears rolled freely down her cheeks. "I love you, too." She handed him the box with the stethoscope and the handkerchief. "Go, now, while I can still let you."

Steve hadn't noticed until then that the mist had risen like an impenetrable wall around the village until, like the day he'd arrived here, it obscured the outside world completely. With a sinking heart he took the box and cast one last longing look at the woman he loved, grabbed Timothy's hand, and stepped onto the footbridge.

He could hear the villagers calling their farewells. He knew if he turned to wave goodbye, he might not be able to resist the temptation of going back for Meghan. Rather than turning around, he waved over his shoulder. Their voices slowly died away, as if muffled by a great pillow.

In seconds, the mist had closed around them.

Moments later Steve and Timothy stood atop the hill for a long time, looking down at the misty valley. Slowly the swirling mist cleared, leaving behind a glen filled with trees and bushes and snow. It was as if the village had never existed, but Steve knew better. In his heart it would always exist. Just as Meghan would always be his love.

He took the blue handkerchief from the box and rubbed the soft linen over his cheek. It smelled of Meghan—fresh, clean, and scented lightly with the perfume of wildflowers. Tucking it inside his shirt pocket, he took Timothy by the hand.

"Let's go, buddy. There's nothing here for us anymore."

The sad truth of his statement shattered his heart.

* * *

The Hudson Highlands—the day before Christmas—the gateway cabin

As Steve and Timothy emerged from the trees surrounding the cabin, through the thickly falling snow, Steve could see three people on the porch, two men and a woman. The woman gestured wildly and pointed toward the woods from which he and Timothy had just emerged. One of the men had an arm around her shoulder and was trying to calm her. The second man, listening patiently, was Durward Hobbs.

Long ago, Steve had decided that not one thing that had happened to him, from the day he'd first met Irma in Central Park up to this very moment, could be chalked up to coincidence. Neither could it be explained with pure logic, a strange assertion for man who had always had to see proof of everything in life. Therefore, iHt came as no surprise to him then that he knew the frantic couple talking to Hobbs had to be Timothy's parents. He soon had his answer.

The woman spotted them and screamed. "Timmy! Thank God." She rushed to them, fell to her knees, and enveloped her son in a hug. "Thank you," she said to Steve over the boy's head.

Her husband, a middle-aged man, who, even in casual clothes, made Steve think of a banker, came to her side and hugged his son, then stood and grasped Steve's hand, pumping it several times. "Thank you. How can we ever repay you? Where did you find him?"

Steve waited for the barrage of questions to stop tumbling from the man before he even tried to answer. "I found him . . . in the woods."

"Mommy," Timothy said, extracting himself from his mother's smothering embrace and jumping up and down, "you should have seen. There was a lady, and she had a magic lantern, and she could see me and all kinds of things in it. The town was all covered in smoke and stuff and no one could see us, 'cept the people that was there and . . ."

"Whoa, sport. Slow down." His father smiled apologetically at Steve. "He's always had a very vivid imagination, very inquisitive, too. Gets him in trouble sometimes."

Tell me about it, Steve thought, recalling the climb down the cliff face.

"It's healthy for a boy to have an imagination," Hobbs offered, winking at Steve.

Meghan had said the children remembered the village, but the adults don't believe them. Too bad. Adults could learn a lot if they just listened to the kids more often. Steve recalled listening to tales of fairies and witches—and miracles—and dismissing them as a child's fertile imagination. He promised himself, from now on, he would pay closer attention to the tales his small patients told him.

His thoughts took him by surprise and he tried to recall when he'd actually made the conscious decision to return to the pediatric wing of St. Francis. As with most of the things that had happened to him in Renaissance, no specific time came to mind.

"Yes, well, sometimes Timmy goes too far afield." His mother smiled and wiped the tears from her eyes. "He has a habit of getting wrapped up in his fantasies and taking off somewhere. This isn't the first time he's gotten lost."

"Well, I think he may have learned a lesson this time." His father squatted down in front of the boy. "You can't go running off for hours like that. We worried about you. Besides, no telling what could have happened in the woods. Mommy was really upset this time."

"I was okay, Mommy. Meghan took real good care of me."

"Meghan?" His father frowned.

"Oh, Louis. It's just another of those imaginary playmates he invents."

Suddenly, something occurred to Steve. "Did you say he'd been missing for *hours*?"

The snow crunched loudly under his boots as Hobbs stepped closer to the group. He eyed Steve with an intensity that made Steve uncomfortable.

"Why, yes," Timothy's father said. "He took off almost as soon as we got out of the car to go look for a Christmas tree in the woods. Why?"

Hobbs cleared his throat and sent Steve a speaking look. "Sometimes it just feels longer than it is."

Timothy's mother nodded in agreement and ran a caressing hand over the boy's hair. "Especially when a child is missing."

Having gotten the silent message the old man had been sending him, Steve winked at Hobbs. "Well, time is relative after all, isn't it? What seems like days to some of us, seems like hours to others."

Hobbs winked back at him.

"Well, we have to be going," Mrs. Kendall said. "We have to get Timothy to bed early." She looked up at the sky, blinking against the snowflakes falling on her face. "I do hope this storm doesn't last. If it does, I hope it's the last we have this week." She glanced at her husband. "I really don't want Timmy to miss his doctor's appointment."

"Oh, for heaven's sake, Mary. You have a whole week to worry about getting to St. Francis for Timmy's appointment." He raised an eyebrow at Steve. "Women."

St. Francis? Steve's gaze darted to Hobbs.

The old man just smiled.

CHAPTER 17

C lara grasped Emanuel's hand in hers. "Please think about this. You can't just send Meghan out there to face her past alone. She's lived her entire life in the village. To send her out there with no one to lean on and with no recourse if she finds the outside world intolerable is . . . well, it's cruel."

Emanuel sighed thoughtfully and patted Clara's work-worn hand. "Perhaps you're right. What do you suggest?"

"Send Irma with her and then allow Meghan to come back here if it becomes too much for her."

Emanuel frowned and rose from the fireside chair to pace the room. Only his footsteps on the bare pine boards and the crackle of the flames devouring the logs in the hearth could be heard in the small room. "But the rules, Clara. What about the rules? When a resident of the village leaves, they are not allowed to return. That has always been the way of things here."

Clara folded the long piece of freshly woven cloth that was draped over her lap. She paused in her labors and looked at Emanuel. "You have always said that a rule that cannot be broken for a good cause should have never been made to begin with."

Emanuel stopped and stared into the leaping flames for a long time. He stroked his beard and looked toward the woman whose wisdom he had come to rely on more times than he could count. How subtle she was in her suggestions, making them sound as if they were his all along. Often, he was never sure who had actually devised the solution to a problem, him or Clara.

"Perhaps it is time to make an exception to the rule."

＊ ＊ ＊

Meghan walked toward Emanuel where he waited in the town square for her and Irma. Meghan's hand was enclosed tightly in her mother's.

On the surface, the day seemed like any other day in the peaceful village. Birds twittered high up in the trees. Flowers nodded their colorful heads beneath a warm afternoon sun. Josiah tended his garden. Neither the people nor nature were aware of the drama unfolding around them.

"You won't be needing that," Emanuel said, pointing at the suitcase Meghan clutched in her hand.

Meghan looked from her mother to the elder. "I don't understand."

"Because of the special circumstances involved here,

I have decided, with the help of my trusted advisor." He smiled at Clara who stood just to the side of the small gathering. "I have decided that you will return to the village once more before you make your final decision whether or not you will stay."

Meghan stared at him, her emotions a turmoil of confusion. She was not leaving for good. She felt a surge of elation. But he'd said nothing about her memory of her time here if she chose to leave.

"What of Steve? If I return and decide to leave, will I remember him, will I remember his love?"

Emanuel's expression turned to one of sympathy.

Meghan didn't need words to understand what that meant. She would return, but she would still be sentenced to life without Steve, without his love. If she chose to leave, she would do so without her memories of him. Nothing had changed except she was being allowed to leave long enough to face her demons, then return and make her final decision.

"Child," Clara said, coming to stand beside Meghan and encircling her shoulders with a comforting arm, "you must have faith." She smiled, but Meghan could see her expression held the same sympathy as Emanuel's did. Clara dropped her arm and stood back.

Resigned, Meghan looked at Emanuel. "I'm ready."

Emanuel nodded and glanced at Irma. "And you? Are you ready, too?"

"Me?" The surprise on Irma's face clearly meant she had no idea she would be accompanying Meghan.

"These demons of your past belong to both of you. You must face them together," Emanuel said.

As he said the last word a mist began to gather, but it was not the normal mist. Instead of being white and enclosing the perimeter of the village, this mist was golden, thick, and only appeared at Meghan's and Irma's feet. Slowly, it swelled and grew higher. Inch by inch Meghan and Irma were enveloped in the smoky wisps. Moments later, they could see nothing but the inside of the golden cone of fog.

* * *

Steve waved one more goodbye to Timothy and watched the small entourage disappear into the thick trees that surrounded the tiny cabin. Hobbs would guide the Kendalls back to their car, and they would head home to prepare for the next day's Christmas festivities. Timothy would no doubt regale them for many days to come with stories of his exploits in Renaissance, and they would shrug them off as the boy's vivid imagination run amuck.

And Steve would . . . What?

Sighing, he brushed the thick layer of snow from the cabin's top step and then sat. Resting his elbows on his knees, he gazed longingly toward the woods bordering the

Hudson River. Somewhere out there was the woman he loved, and he had no way of getting to her.

No, he would not accept that. There had to be a way. He'd just have to find it. He'd stay right here until he did.

He sighed. What the hell was he thinking? Staying here was senseless. Besides, he had responsibilities back in the city. Kids who needed him. Kids like Timothy. Meghan would not want him to forget the kids. Now that he knew that what he did for them was not pointless, not an exercise in futility, he didn't want to forget them, either.

He should be inside gathering his belongings to start back. Somehow, he could not bring himself to do it. He peered up at the gray sky. Snowflakes pelted his face.

Little lace doilies, each the same, yet each different. Meghan's words played through his head. He held out his hand and allowed one to land in his palm. For a very short instant, it remained there. Then just as suddenly as it had appeared, the delicate flake was gone, leaving behind a tiny dot of water. He closed his hand tightly and waited for the pain around his heart to subside. He had to get away from here before the memories drove him mad.

He glanced toward the driveway at his car. Nearly four inches of snow covered it. Hobbs had assured him it was fixed, but fixed or not, driving through a blizzard was not smart. He'd start out in the morning, he told himself. The notion of being here, close to Meghan, for just a little longer, took a fraction of the edge off leaving her for good.

Weighed down by despair and frustration, he remained sitting on the step and gazing into the woods. The snow continued to fall, as if a phantom hand sprinkled puffs of cotton from the sky, blanketing everything in a glittering robe of white silence.

He wasn't sure how long he'd been sitting there when the cold made itself known in the tingling of his fingertips and toes. He roused himself and looked down, then smiled. He looked like a snowman with the snow that had covered him. Standing, he shook it off, cast one more longing glance toward the woods, and then headed inside.

The fire Hobbs had started in the fireplace dispelled the darkness inside the cozy cabin. It had burned low, but still lent its warmth to the small interior. Steve threw a few more logs on the fire, watched while they caught and emitted long fingers of orange and red flames, then shed his jacket and threw himself into the only easy chair in the room. He closed his eyes, praying for the oblivion of sleep.

When he awoke in the same chair the next morning, disappointment flooded him. He had hoped that whatever unseen force had carried him back to Meghan's cottage the first night would have transported him back to the village, but it hadn't. He was still in the tiny cabin. Still without Meghan. Somehow that added a note of finality that hadn't been there before.

In the days that followed, Steve aimlessly walked the hills and meadows around the cabin. Inevitably, before the day ended, he would find himself back on the hilltop over-looking the glen where the village had been. Many times he told himself it was hopeless. Meghan would never come through the mist. He'd lost her forever. He should go back to the city, back to his job. But he always decided to wait one more day.

He had, in fact, packed up the car twice, driven down the driveway, and then turned around, pulled back by some unseen force. Each time, he'd raced to the hilltop only to find the glen as he'd left it the time before, devoid of any sign of Renaissance.

On the third day after his return to the outside world, he resolutely packed the car for the last time. He made one last trip to the hilltop, found it as he always had before, then headed for New York City with a heavy heart and an ache inside that he had no medicine to cure.

* * *

"I hear you've been added back on staff in the pediatric wing," Dr. Frank Donovan said, falling into step beside Steve as he made his way down the hall toward the elevators in St. Francis Hospital. "Welcome home!"

Steve knew that Frank was aware of his love for working with the kids. However, when Steve thought of *home*, the image that invariably appeared in his mind was a small, thatched-roof cottage on a flower bedecked square somewhere in the Hudson Highlands. "Yeah. It was time."

"I knew you couldn't stay away from those kids forever." Frank grinned in his usual good-natured, know-it-all style. "Didn't I tell you that the trip to that mountain cabin would do the trick?" He slapped Steve's back. "You look great!"

"Thanks." Steve didn't elaborate on the fact that he felt more lost and lonelier than he'd ever felt before, even after his mother died. His heart hurt constantly, and he felt as empty as a deserted church.

"Dr. Cameron, please report to your office," the loud-speaker blared.

"Busy morning. See you later?" he asked Frank, then hurried to grab the door to the open elevator.

"Lunch today. Haverty's Bar," Frank called after him.

"You got it," Steve said as the elevator door swished shut.

As the elevator rose to his floor, Steve wondered why he'd been called back to his office. Miss Holsted could normally handle most anything. He hoped it wasn't an emergency. He was due in surgery this afternoon and an emergency now would mean standing Frank up for lunch.

He'd only been back a couple of days, and already his schedule was bursting, leaving him little time for anything. Mostly, and gratefully, it left him little time to think about Meghan and how much he missed her, how empty his days were without a glimpse of her beautiful face, how . . .

Before he could sink into thoughts that would dog and

depress him for the rest of the day, the elevator stopped, and the doors swished open. He stepped out before the mass of people waiting to get on trapped him and then hurried toward his office at the end of the long hall.

"You called for me?" he asked the middle-aged, dark-haired woman behind the desk.

Her fingers continued to fly over the computer keyboard. "There's someone in your office to see you," she said, not taking her gaze from the screen. "No appointment," she added, her voice making it clear how much she disapproved of people who just popped into a doctor's office expecting to be seen.

Steve knew that overlooked detail did not make his organized, fastidious secretary happy. Anything that disrupted her well-oiled workplace infuriated her. Not being very organized himself, she had proven to be a godsend to him, and he tried very hard to do nothing to upset her; in return, she kept his work day running like a well-oiled clock. Keeping that information in mind, he wondered why Miss Holsted thought it important enough to summon him to see whoever it was without an appointment.

Without looking at him, she scooped up a stack of small pink sheets and handed them to him. "Your messages."

He took the sheets and shuffled through them as he moved toward the closed door. Opening it, he entered and without looking up, went straight to his desk. "I'm Dr. Cameron. What can I do for you?"

When his question was answered with silence, he looked up. Before him stood a somewhat handsome, but very distinguished-looking older man in a gray suit, white shirt and muted maroon tie. His hair was gray at the temples, but the rest remained free of the proof of approaching age. His chin showed the same small dimple that Steve's had and his eye color, though faded by age, reflected the color of Steve's. His tense expression mirrored his stiff posture.

"Dad?"

"Hello, son."

Steve's legs gave way. He dropped like a rock into his desk chair. If the devil himself stood in his office, Steve would be less surprised.

His father, a man who had strongly disapproved of Steve's becoming a pediatric oncologist, never came here. In fact, after their last blow-up, during which his father had expressed doubts about Steve's suitability for this field and Steve had walked out of the house for good, his father had never even talked to him about his profession. He'd have probably been happier if Steve had chosen to follow him into banking. As a result of their completely different viewpoints about Steve's chosen career, neither of them actively sought out the company of the other, not even on holidays. Their lives had shifted into different lanes and both liked it that way.

"Is something wrong?"

"Yes."

Fear rose up in Steve's throat. "What is it?"

"Me."

"You're sick?"

"No." Jason Cameron sat heavily in the chair on the opposite side of Steve's desk. "At least not with anything you can pull a pill out of your black bag to cure." He smiled without humor. "At least I don't think medical science has come up with a pill to cure stupidity yet."

This evasion was so out of character for his father that Steve was left wondering. Normally, Jason Cameron was so to the point and straightforward that he often left bodies in his wake. Confused, Steve frowned and waited for his father to explain.

"I know I have never supported you in your chosen career, and that was wrong of me. At least it was wrong of me never to explain why."

Steve held his breath. Was the old man dying of some terminal illness and feeling pressured to get this off his chest? As estranged as they'd been for most of Steve's life, he didn't want to see anything happen to his father.

Steve sat forward and leaned his forearms on the desk-top. "Why are you suddenly concerned with all this?"

Jason held up his hand. "Please, allow me to tell this my way, and, when I finish, I'll answer all your questions."

A dart of pain pierced Steve's tender heart. His father's last words brought a flash of Meghan walking away from him on that first day in the village and leaving him with a million unanswered questions. Odd how the strangest things brought back small snippets of memories to torture him.

"Are you okay?"

Steve jumped and looked at his father's concerned face. "Fine. Just a little heartburn," he explained. "So, you were going to explain why you're here."

Jason cleared his throat, fidgeted in his chair, a gesture totally unlike the man Steve knew. "I never made an effort to support your choice of careers, but I never told you why. When you were just a toddler, about two-and-a-half years old, your mother and I had another child."

"What?" Steve sat straighter. He could feel his eyes widen in shock. A sibling? He'd always thought he was an only child. This had to be the very last thing he'd expected to hear from his father.

"She was the most beautiful little girl anyone ever saw." His father's eyes misted, surprising Steve even more that his stern father could show so much emotion in such an open way. "I think you loved her more than even your mom and I did."

A sister? Steve plowed through his childhood memories for a sister, but came up empty. Then it occurred to Steve that his father was talking about her in past tense. "Loved?"

Swiping a hand over his face, Jason sighed. "She died at five months from SIDS."

"Why didn't you ever tell me?" He knew his father

could be cruel, but this went beyond even his range of hurt.

Jason took a deep breath. "After she died, you stopped talking to us and hid in obscure corners of the house. We'd find you snuggled up behind the couch or under the desk or hiding in the garden. You stopped playing with your toys. It took months of therapy with one of the best children's psychologists to get you past it. I'm not sure if you were too young to remember her, or if you chose not to, but you never talked about her after she died."

He straightened and leaned toward Steve. "When you decided to become a pediatric oncologist, all I could think of was how your sister's death had affected you, and how seeing children die day after day from something you had little power to control would affect you." He shook his head. "If your mother had been alive, I'm sure she would have handled it much better than I did." He smiled sheepishly. "Sensitivity has never been one of my strong points."

Steve was stunned into silence. In the past few minutes he'd learned he'd had a sister he couldn't remember and a father who actually had feelings and was not the cold-hearted bastard he'd always thought him to be. One thing that he did understand now was why the deaths of all those kids had thrown him for a loop.

He'd been sure when he left Renaissance that it had ended, but obviously it hadn't. So, there were still more pieces of this weird puzzle he called his life falling into place. He smiled and wondered how many more shoes had yet to drop.

"You find this amusing?"

Steve jumped. His father's face had assumed that stern, no-nonsense expression Steve knew so well. For a moment, he was snatched back to the days after his mother's death when Jason barely spoke to him unless it was in anger.

But he wasn't that small scared boy anymore. And the man before him was certainly not that unbending man. The wall that had separated them for almost thirty years began to crumble. "No. Absolutely not. Astounding, enlightening, and heartbreaking, but in no way amusing."

"But you laughed."

There was no point in explaining about Meghan or Emanuel or any of it. No one would believe him anyway. "Only because I find life an amusing carousel that changes with each passing hour, showing us aspects of the past that we had no idea helped shape us into who we are today. I'm learning slowly that each of us has a predetermined destiny, and that there is no such thing as coincidence."

At least not where Renaissance and its influence are concerned.

Feeling the ice around his heart thawing, Steve picked up a pencil. "You still haven't told me why you felt compelled to travel into the city and tell me all this."

Jason stood and paced the carpet in front of the desk. "Aside from binding up the wounds of our relationship, I have an ulterior motive." He stopped pacing and faced Steve. "My best friend's child is sick."

Steve came alert. "Oh?"

"I don't have a clue what's wrong with him, but I'm sure it's serious. I want you to see him."

"Why me?"

Jason frowned and cleared his throat nervously. "Because I'm told you are the finest in your field and this boy deserves nothing but the best and so do his parents." He paused and stared at Steve. "Will you see him?"

Steve couldn't believe what he had just heard come from his father's mouth. It was the seal of approval that Steve had waited for a long time. "By all means. Have his mom or dad call and make an appointment."

Jason smiled. "They already have. You'll be seeing him in a couple of days. His name is Timothy Kendall."

Steve nodded, only mildly surprised that the child turned out to be Timothy. *Another shoe drops. Emanuel, you are unbelievable,* he told the village elder silently, certain that somewhere out there in the mist the old man was nodding and smiling his approval.

* * *

When the golden mist began to dissipate, the fuzz that had enveloped Meghan's head also cleared. She and Irma were standing on a city sidewalk amidst garbage and squalor, staring into the yawning mouth of a dark, dank alley. The clamor of New York City street noises erupted around them, causing Meghan to cover her ears to block them out. The acrid odor of human waste and exhaust fumes made her nose curl in disgust. A cold wind whistled through the alley and swirled around them, chilling Meghan to the bone instantly. She hugged her bare arms to her.

She looked up at Irma and was shocked to find her mother had shed years and looked about twenty-five. Suddenly, it occurred to her that she'd never had to look *up* at her mother before.

A gray, mangy alley cat scooted past them, its wet tail brushing Meghan's bare legs. When she reached down to rub away the moisture, she saw the hands of small child. Her hands.

"What's happening?" She looked to Irma for an answer.

Irma, apparently as stunned as Meghan at their appearance, shook her head in wonder. "I don't know. Maybe we have to relive this to get past it."

"No!" Meghan recalled the images from her dreams and had no desire to see any of them again, much less watch her mother being defiled. "I can't do this. I can't go back there." Eyes wide, she backed away from the alley. Turning to run, she felt her mother's hand close around her upper arm.

"We may not have a choice, Meghan." Gently, she took Meghan's hand and walked slowly toward the alley entrance.

Meghan hung back. She couldn't do this. It was asking too much. She'd been fine in Renaissance. She could just go back there and forget all this. Emanuel said she could stay if she chose to. She could . . .

Faith and trust, Meghan. Faith and trust. Love knows a strength far beyond all human expectations.

Emanuel's voice came out of nowhere.

Meghan looked into her mother's eyes. Glowing there, she saw love, deep, abiding, and endless. But she saw something else as well. She saw a plea to help her mother rid herself of these terrible memories once and for all.

Meghan felt the fear drain from her. In her heart she knew that her mother would take care of her no matter what and that only by doing this together could they truly and finally lay the past to rest.

Out of nowhere strength began to seep into Meghan, strength unlike any she had ever known. "I love you, Momma."

Irma's hand grip tightened on hers. "Me, too, baby, me too."

Meghan knew instinctively that as long as she had Irma to take care of her, then she would make sure nothing happened to her mother. "Let's do it."

Together they stepped into the alley. Darkness closed in around them, the only light a pinpoint of brightness ahead and a small patch of sunlight framed by the towering buildings above. The rustle of rats scurrying through garbage broke the taut silence. In the distance a baby cried, but was quickly quieted. The screech of brakes and the rumble of traffic grew fainter with each step they took into the depths of the alley.

Then behind them they heard footsteps muted by the garbage the person walked through. Then another set of footsteps joined the first and then another. There were three of them, just like in her dream.

Her mother was right. They were about to relive the whole terrifying experience. How was putting her and her mother through this again going to solve anything? What if Emanuel was wrong? What if it happened all over again?

Trust, Meghan.

Meghan had always listened to Emanuel and she had no reason not to now, so she tightened her grip on Irma's hand and kept walking.

They had only gone a few more steps when the men sprang at them out of the darkness. Two of them grabbed Irma and wrestled her to the ground, tearing at her clothes. The other seized Meghan, imprisoning her small arms behind her. Frantically, she struggled against the iron grip preventing her from going to her mother's side. The man holding her laughed at her feeble attempts to free herself.

"Don't hurt my Mommy," she cried, her pitiful voice lost in the laughter of the man holding her. "Leave her alone."

"Don't look, baby, don't look."

The man cursed at Irma and Meghan heard the sharp sound of flesh on flesh as he slapped Irma across the face.

Meghan struck out at the man's shins with her feet, her sneakers making little impact. Her struggles increased, but to little avail. Her pitiful strength was no mach for her captor.

"Baby, I love you. Never forget that." Her mother's voice sounded weak.

The man standing over Irma was unzipping his pants. Meghan had to do something. She turned her head sideways and buried her teeth in her captor's forearm, biting down as hard as she could. The copper taste of blood invaded her mouth. She spit it out.

He let out a scream of pain, released her and doubled over, groaning and holding his bleeding arm. Meghan quickly looked around her and spotted a piece of a 2x4 nearby. She snatched it and swung it upward with all her might, catching the man in the face and sending him sprawling backward to lie motionless on the dirty alley floor.

His friends were thrown off guard by the commotion and turned to see the cause. When they did, Irma scrambled to her feet and pummeled the man nearest her with her fists. As the last one lunged at Meghan, she swung the board again and hit him in the jaw. He crumpled on top of his bleeding companion, blood gushing from a deep cut across his chin.

The last of them took stock of the situation and decided to make a run for it, right into the waiting arms of three police officers coming down the alley to investigate the noise.

Irma gathered Meghan close, her arms tight around her daughter. "We did it, Meghan. We did it."

Yes, you did, came Emanuel's' voice, *just as you did before.*

"Just as we did before?" Confusion colored Meghan's voice.

You never allowed yourselves to think beyond a certain point. It was necessary for you to come back here to relive that and to see that nothing happened that either of you should be ashamed of. Nothing. Your imagination gave birth to your unfoundedt fears.

"Why didn't you tell us that long ago? I could have had my mother if you had." Meghan was angrier than she could ever recall being.

"Because we wouldn't have believed him," Irma said quietly.

Meghan hugged her mother and in doing so realized she was once more full grown. For a long time, they just stood holding each other close, surrounded by their love and basking in their joint triumph.

Then a golden mist started seeping in, filling the dirty alley with a pure light and shutting out the dirt and grime of their surroundings.

* * *

An hour later, having made a date to have dinner with

his father, Steve hurried out of the hospital to meet Frank Donovan for lunch. He had a full afternoon of surgery so it would be a fast lunch, but he wanted to spend some time with his friend.

Haverty's Bar was a small, noisy, and friendly pub nestled between a dry cleaning shop and an Italian bakery. The owner, Ian Haverty, a robust Irishman straight from the Emerald Isle, served the best fish and chips in town with a side dish of Gaelic humor, and, on occasion, even a few verses of an Irish ballad.

Steve wound his way through the lunch crowd to the back of the noisy room where Frank had commandeered a table. He slipped into the chair and took a long drink from the glass of Irish ale Frank had ordered for him.

"I needed that. It's been one hell of a morning."

"A lot of appointments?" Frank stretched his arm above his head and signaled over the crowd for the red-haired waitress to come take their order.

"No. My father showed up in my office."

Once Frank had gotten his shock under control, Steve filled him in on what he'd been told. By the time he'd finished recounting the meeting with his father, the waitress had placed two overflowing platters of fish and chips in front of them and refilled their ale glasses.

"Holy shit! A sister?" Frank sprinkled vinegar liberally over the food, selected a golden brown fish fillet, and took a very large bite.

"You could have knocked me over with a feather." Steve took a bite of a crispy, brown French fry. He swallowed and paused. "Then there's Meghan."

"Meghan? Did you meet a woman up there?" Frank grinned at Steve, but the smile melted away. He stared at Steve for a long minute. "Hell, this is serious, isn't it?"

Steve nodded. "She's—"

"Hey, Haverty," Frank yelled to the bartender. "How about another round of beers for a couple of thirsty doctors?"

The flaming-haired Haverty shook his beefy fist at Frank in mock threat and laughed. Shortly thereafter the fresh drinks arrived. Frank sipped his without looking at Steve and then waved at a trio of men who had just arrived.

From the way he looked around the room, Steve sensed his friend didn't want to hear any more about Meghan. In fact, he was certain if he'd so much as spoken her name again, Frank would have found a way to change the subject. Steve never had time to try and work out what Frank's strange behavior meant.

Deep inside him, something strange was taking form. Awareness. But of what? It was the strangest sensation Steve had ever experienced. His heart beat faster. His soul glowed as if he'd just walked into the sunlight. That empty place deep inside him disappeared. Everything around him became sharper, clearer. Sounds were amplified. Smells grew more pungent. It was if he'd suddenly awakened from a long sleep.

For a moment he couldn't figure out what was happening to him and then suddenly, he knew.

CHAPTER 18

This time, when the mist cleared, Irma and Meghan were once more in the village, but now they were standing in her tiny cottage. In her heart Meghan knew there was nothing outside the village to scare her anymore and that the dreams would never come back to haunt her again, but now she had another, more difficult task to face.

"You must believe in your love for Steve as much as you believed in your love for me back in the alley." Irma cupped Meghan's cheek in her palm and then kissed her tenderly. "I'll be right behind you."

"It's time."

Meghan hadn't heard Emanuel enter the cottage, but she had heard Emanuel say those same words many times. Always before, with the exception of Steve's arrival, this announcement of an impending Transition had brought a sense of joy. This time, it felt like he had just pronounced her death sentence and took all the happiness out of Irma's and her recent victory in the alley.

Slowly, hands shaking, she gathered her belongings—her clothes and some personal items. She'd never needed much here. The mementos in the curio cabinet would remain behind to be guarded by her replacement, Ellie. All but the keychain Steve had given her. She'd carry that always to store her love for him and her memories within it so she'd have it when she got outside the village.

"There's nothing to be frightened of," Irma said, coming to put an arm around her. "You know now that there are a lot of good things beyond the village, things that you'll love: children wherever you look, playing, singing, laughing; people enjoying life; seasons that change, each as beautiful as the last in its own way; good people who care about each other."

And Steve, Meghan thought. "I'm not afraid of what lies outside anymore. I know you'll always be there with me," Meghan said. "I'm afraid of what doesn't lie outside." She turned to her mother. "Momma, I don't want to forget him. I don't want to not love him any more."

Irma gathered her daughter to her. "I know, baby. I know." She held her close for a time, then eased her away and tilted Meghan's chin up so they were eye-to-eye. "You must trust in destiny."

Destiny.

Meghan sighed. How many times had she heard that word and trusted in it, preached it to her Assignments? But it was a cruel destiny that had ripped her and Steve apart, a cruel destiny that had sentenced them to a life without each other. How could she believe in that kind of destiny? How could she accept it?

Even on the very slim chance that she would make it through the mist intact, the chances of seeing Steve again were so remote. She knew nothing of the city and how to navigate it. Added to that was the time difference. In here it had been weeks since Steve left. Out there, days had passed. Steve had probably returned to the city and his practice. How would he even know she was passing through the Transition?

Rather than believing in that nebulous destiny, she had to believe what he'd said before he left. He would find her. He would teach her to love him again.

But, what if he'd forgotten her? What if he no longer loved her? What if their love was just something that happened here and didn't exist beyond the boundaries of Renaissance?

"The Transition is beginning," Emanuel announced quietly.

Meghan glanced at the lantern for the last time. The bottom was filling with the churning mist. Soon, very soon, her memory would be wiped clean and none of it would matter.

As she stepped into the mist, Meghan let her heart speak for her. *Steve, I'm coming to you. Please be there. Please love me. Please help me to remember you.*

❋ ❋ ❋

Steve slammed on the brakes, and, after it slid several feet on the snowy driveway, his car came to a halt outside the cabin. Throwing open the door, he jumped out and, without closing it, raced toward the hilltop.

He was sure, when he got back, Frank Donovan would have him committed. Once Steve had figured out what the strange feeling inside him signaled, he'd jumped up from the table, thrown a handful of bills at Frank, told him to have his secretary cancel his appointments indefinitely, and then dashed to the parking garage to get his car. Midday traffic had been excruciatingly slow until he got out of the city, then he'd broken every speed limit getting here. Luckily, all the police seemed to have been busy in another part of the state.

The snow heading toward the hilltop was deep and made the going difficult and frustrating. He sank to his thighs at times and had to struggle to free himself. The icy crust on the snow cut painfully into his flesh. Tree limbs slashed across his cold cheeks leaving welts behind and the sting of broken skin. Still he pushed on, ignoring the cold and the pain and the snow. He had one goal before him— to be there when Meghan stepped from the mist. He could see the hilltop in the distance, but it seemed to take forever to get there.

Once on top, he looked down into the glen and saw . . . nothing.

For a long time, he stared at the landscape. Watching for the slightest hint of the mist, but nothing changed. The snow lay white, crisp, and unblemished, the sun glinting off it, the glare piercing his eyes like tiny arrows. Pine trees stirred marginally, nudged by a slight breeze off the river. A hawk squawked raucously at being chased from his perch high atop a barren oak tree by the clamor of Steve's rush toward the hilltop.

Despair washed over him. Steve sank to his knees in the snow and buried his face in his hands. "Meghan," he whispered. The ache inside him started in his toes and climbed up his body until he was consumed by it. Hopelessness washed over him in great suffocating waves.

He'd been so certain the unusual feelings he'd experienced in the pub had forecasted Meghan's emergence from Renaissance. How could he have misread that?

Faith and trust make miracles.

The voice of Ellie came from inside his head. He sneered at it. *Miracles.* There were no miracles for him and Meghan, only a lifetime of loneliness.

Faith and trust make miracles.

The insistent sound carried on the wind as it blew warm and soft against Steve's face, drying the tears he hadn't realized he'd shed until he touched his damp cheeks.

"Stop it," he muttered into his palms. "Stop it."

Faith and trust make miracles.

This time, he felt a small hand on his shoulder. He looked behind him only to find himself alone. As he turned back, his gaze stopped abruptly, fastening on a light dusting of white rising in the glen. At first, he thought it was loose snow blowing in the breeze, but then he realized it was the mist.

Vaulting up, he ran down the hill toward it, tripping and stumbling. He fell and rolled. Catching himself, he jumped to his feet and sped on, his gaze glued to the increasing mist. He had to get there before it disappeared, before he lost her again.

When he reached the glen, to his horror, the mist began to dissipate, drifting away on the breeze, as insubstantial as those damned miracles that everyone kept preaching to him about.

Faith and trust make miracles.

This time, it wasn't Ellie's voice, but the deep, booming command of Emanuel that rang in his ears.

Believe, Steve. Believe.

God, he wanted to, he really wanted to, but so far, he hadn't seen anything to make him believe. The thought had no sooner escaped his mind than he remembered what Ellie had told him. He had to believe it in his heart before she could tell him why she'd lived. He had to know it was he that did it. Maybe this worked the same way.

But how was he to start believing in something he

doubted, something so nebulous?

But you believe in Renaissance, don't you, Mr. C?

Irma? Yes, he believed in the village. He believed in its healing power and in the love he'd felt there and the rebirth it had given him. He believed in the man he had become and the strength it had imbued in him. He believed in the understanding of life and death it had taught him.

A few feet from him, a mist began to gather and swirl upward. As he watched, it spread, thickening and building. His heart soared. He stared at the milky fog as it double and tripled. If only she was inside it. If only she would come to him, intact. If only . . .

Then just as suddenly, it began to evaporate. Wisps of it broke off and glided into the air to vanish.

"No!" he cried, helpless to stop it, but knowing he must, somehow. But how?

As he watched, the mist continued to evaporate. Finally it was gone, and in the middle of the field stood Meghan. She stared at him, her brow furrowed in question.

"Meghan." He held out his hand to her, but she remained where she was. Wisps of mist swirled around her feet like a trailing gown.

"Who are you?"

He recognized the voice as the woman he loved, but her eyes were those of a stranger. Agony tore her name from his throat, but too late.

The mist had begun to gather again, swirling around

her, climbing up her body, obliterating her from his sight.

Panic filled him. "Noooo! Come back." He raced toward the column of mist. Just as he reached it, it began to glow with a blinding light. Ellie's voice came from nowhere.

Faith and trust. Faith and trust. Faith and trust.

Suddenly, the answer to the message that he'd sought for six years seeped into his mind. His love had brought Meghan to him, and only his unquestioning belief in their love could bring Meghan through the mist with her memory intact. If Steve believed in nothing else, the one thing he did believe in with an unshakable faith was their love for each other. All his doubts died away, to be replaced by a conviction so strong that not even the fates could ignore it. The answer had been there all the time. The miracle was love.

His heart bursting with love for Meghan, he stood back, waiting to witness his first miracle.

The mists seemed to stop swirling for a fraction of a second. Steve held his breath. Then from inside, just as it had the very first time he'd seen it, the foggy curtain began to glow. Only this time, the glow was so bright, so hot that he had to cover his eyes. The intense warmth burned into the back of his hand, yet there was no pain.

Moments later, he realized that the heat had cooled, and, without looking directly at it, he could see on the ground at his feet that the bright light had dimmed considerably. He raised his head.

Meghan stood before him. This time, the stranger within her gaze was gone. In her place was the woman he'd last seen in the village, her eyes filled with love.

"Steve."

One word, but all he needed to confirm the miracle. Deep inside, he knew with a certainty that surpassed anything that had come before or would come after today that the miracle he'd been waiting for all his life was Meghan's love. He opened his arms.

She ran into them, and he clasped her close, listening to the beat of their hearts combine. Unable to believe she was actually here, he held her away from him and traced her face with his fingertips. Then he kissed her as if he would never stop, until neither of them could breathe. Still he would not let go of her. As he whispered soft love words into her hair, he glimpsed Irma standing to the side, a broad smile curving her lips.

"I love you," he told Meghan. "I love you with every breath I take."

"You had to. It was the only thing that would have brought me to you. It's why I remember you and our love. If your love was not strong and pure, I would have been trapped in a loveless life without you."

* * *

Steve, Meghan, and Irma approached the cabin's front

steps, arms entwined. A breeze caressed the bare tree limbs above them, but this was not an ordinary winter breeze. Its warm breath brushed against them like a loving hand.

Floating on it came the laughter of a little girl with golden ringlets and a faith that could move mountains. They stopped walking and looked around.

"Ellie?" Steve said.

They waited and listened. The laughter came again, then died away, melting into the breeze.

Meghan laughed and turned to kiss Steve's cheek. "She'll make a good Healer."

"The best," he said.

They continued up the porch steps, but before they could go any farther, Steve stopped them. Sitting on the doorstep was Rags, the one-eyed teddy bear. Steve could have sworn he winked at them.

CHAPTER 19

New York City, Bowery Mission, four years later

Meghan and Steve finished the last of the dishes and stacked them on the shelf in the kitchen of the Bowery's homeless shelter. Steve stretched his arms above his head to ease the ache that had settled between his shoulder blades about an hour earlier. The hot room smelled of beef stew and biscuits.

"Tired?" Meghan asked, coming to encircle his waist with her arms.

"Hmm," he answered, stifling a yawn and pulling her more tightly against him.

Before coming here, he'd spent most of the afternoon with Timothy doing his annual checkup. The good news was there were no signs that his remission was reversing itself, and the boy's health just continued to improve.

Oddly enough, in the four years since Timothy had left Renaissance, his memories of the place had not diminished at all. However, he had confided to Steve that he didn't talk about it to anyone but Dr. Steve and Miss Meghan because neither one of them laughed at him. His parents continued to view Timothy's tales as a product of his vivid imagination and his friends, while fascinated with his stories of this magical place, looked at them as just that—stories.

"Hmm," Meghan said, smiling up at him. "Too bad you're tired. I had plans for later."

"But not too tired," Steve said smiling down at her and wiggling his eyebrows in what he knew was probably a very bad Groucho Marx imitation.

She giggled, then raised herself on tiptoes and kissed him soundly. "Thanks."

"You're welcome, but for what?"

"For helping out tonight."

"My pleasure, Mrs. Cameron." He kissed her back.

Steve found it amazing how Meghan, who had been terrified of the outside world and in particular this part of it, had settled into life outside the village with ease, and, in her new role as Guide, she'd even made it a point to accompany her mother on her many forays into the seedier sections of town.

"Well, I know it wasn't your plan to be dishing out stew and noodles on Christmas Eve, not to mention our fourth anniversary, but I know all the people who ate here tonight certainly appreciated it."

Still grinning, he leaned close to her ear. "How do you know what my plans were?"

She swatted at his arm playfully then winked. "Could they have been the same as mine?"

"Hmm, this sounds promising. Let's discuss it."

He sat in the nearest chair and pulled her into his lap. The well-used, somewhat rickety chair creaked ominously, but held their combined weight.

A homeless woman in shabby clothes and sporting a toothless grin wandered by. "You take good care of that girl, Dr. Steve. She's a very special lady."

"Oh, I know that, and I plan on taking extremely good care of her, Mrs. Jansen." Gently, he brushed long strands of golden hair off Meghan's face. "It doesn't bother you being in this part of the city? I mean with what happened to your mom and all?"

She grinned. "Not at all. My fear stemmed more from what I didn't know of the world outside the village than what I did and what I would lose by passing through the mist. My father was right. These are good people. Otherwise I never would trust them to watch over Faith."

They both turned to look at their golden-haired daughter sitting on her grandmother's lap and coloring with a lady who reminded Steve very much of a woman he'd spent many hours sharing coffee with in Central Park. The homeless woman laughed at something Faith said, then nodded obediently in response to the little girl's never ending chatter.

When Faith gave what looked to be directions to the

homeless lady, Irma laughed.

Though still active as a Guide, Irma had surprised everyone, when she emerged from the village four years earlier, by exchanging her ragged garb for the style she'd worn in the village. Tonight, her bright red dress matched her granddaughter's pinafore.

"She's beautiful," Steve said, still staring at his daughter, still unable to believe how complete his life was, "just like her mother. Do you have any idea how you two have completed my life?"

"Only because you make it a point to tell me daily." Meghan hugged him close, then glanced at the clock. "As much as I'm enjoying this outpouring of admiration, we have a long drive to the cabin," she said, standing and reaching for her coat on the hook near the door. "Frank will be there before we are if we don't hurry."

Steve stood and shrugged into his coat. Frank Donovan was Steve's closest friend, and he was looking forward to this evening. Ever since Faith's birth, Frank had been . . . different. Distant, as if coming too close to Steve's family would hurt him. It had started with him showing up late for dinner invitations, then making excuses so he didn't have to come at all.

Lately, he seemed to have gotten worse. His preoccupation with whatever was bothering him had escalated to the point of his having to be replaced in the middle of surgery last week. Finally, when Steve could not stand watching his friend being eaten up from the inside out, he'd cornered him and forced the problem into the open. He could still hear the sorrow and pain in Frank's voice as he related his story three days ago.

* * *

Haverty's was quiet at six o'clock and Frank was looking for some down time after a particularly rough day. Steve would have rather gone home to his wife and daughter, but Frank had always been there for him, and he couldn't desert him now.

After sitting at the table in silence for almost thirty minutes, Steve broached the subject of what had been troubling Frank since Faith's birth. "Listen, buddy, you have me worried. Why don't you get whatever's bothering you off your chest." He waited. Frank remained silent. "Is it because I'm married now? Do you feel left out of our lives because . . . well, you know?"

He'd never brought up the subject of the accident that had taken the lives of Frank's wife and unborn child, and he was loath to do so now. However, if it meant helping Frank, he was prepared to do that and more.

Frank shook his head and fumbled with his glass of dark ale. His shoulders were slumped more than they had been in days. Whatever it was, the burden was obviously becoming far too heavy for him to carry alone.

"Come on. Spit it out. You'll feel better if someone else helps you share the load."

"You never asked me about what happened the night of the car accident. Why?" Frank didn't look at him. Instead he kept his gaze fixed on the nearly empty glass.

Steve shrugged. "Never felt it was my business. I figured that you'd talk about when you were ready."

Frank glanced at him and smiled weakly. "Thanks."

Steve said nothing. He'd known for a long time that Frank was carrying something dark on his soul, and, now that he'd started to open up, Steve was not about to stop him because, in his opinion, the only way Frank would find relief was to get it out.

"I think it's time." Frank took a long swallow of ale. "I screwed up again in surgery today, and they had to call in Dr. Sampson to finish." He ran his fingers through his hair. "Jesus, Steve, that's twice in two weeks. What the hell is wrong with me?"

Three business men entered Haverty's, and Steve watched them as they chose a table in a corner in the front of the bar. He sighed in relief, knowing if they'd sat closer Frank might have shut down again.

"My guess? You need to get whatever's bothering you out in the open where you can look at it objectively."

For a long time, Frank said nothing. He spun the glass in the puddle of condensation on the table and stared blankly into the tan foam coating the bottom. Steve signaled the waitress for another round and remained silent until it had been delivered and she moved away, out of ear shot.

"Frank, does this have to do with the accident?"

Frank nodded, but never looked up or said anything.

Progress, Steve thought.

"That day in Haverty's when you started to talk about Meghan, I had to cut you off. The idea that you'd found someone to love and I had lost the only woman who had ever meant anything to me just about tore my insides out. After that, on order to handle it, I just avoided any mention. It was working, I thought, until you and Meghan got married, but even then I was still able to hold on by a thread, but Faith came along and the thread broke." He took a long drink.

Silence reigned over the table. Steve was afraid that speaking would stop Frank and now that he'd started, Steve was eager for him to cleanse himself.

He raised his gaze to the tin covered ceiling. "God, I thought I had it all: a beautiful wife that I loved more than I ever thought I could love anyone, a good job that more than provided for us and left Sandy free to stay home, and a home that could have fallen out of the pages of *Better Homes and Gardens*."

Frank reached for his glass and Steve noticed his hands were shaking. No wonder they'd thrown him out of surgery. Delicate heart operations demanded steady, sure hands.

"Then Sandy told me she was pregnant." Frank laughed

320

nervously. "Man, my world was complete." He shifted in his chair and the legs scratched loudly over the wood floor. "That day we'd been arguing in the house and we'd kept it going out to the car. I can't even remember what the fight was about. Something stupid and senseless." He reached for the glass, but Steve placed his hand over his friend's.

"That's not going to make anything go away."

Frank laughed again, a pain-filled sound lacking in humor. "Nope, but it sure takes the edges off." He reached for the glass again, then glanced at Steve and pushed it away. "Anyway, I pulled out of the driveway and started down the mountain road. We made a turn, and there it was. A big old sixteen-wheeler headed straight at us on our side of the road." Pain swallowed up Frank's words. He bowed his head.

Steve felt a pain slice through him. He grabbed Frank's shoulders in a firm grasp. "And you've been blaming yourself for something that wasn't your fault ever since, right?"

"I tried to tell myself that and so did my clergy, my in-laws, and my parents, but it just didn't wash. Truth is, I should have been watching closer, paying more attention to my driving and less to our stupid argument."

"And that truck driver should have been on his own side of the road," Steve pointed out, to no avail.

They continued to sit for a few more hours, Steve trying to make Frank see sense, and Frank drowning his guilt in a sea of ale.

"Ready?" Meghan's voice roused Steve from his memories, but the pain he'd seen in his friend that day remained.

Meghan stared at him, as if reading the worry plaguing his mind. "After tonight Frank will be okay. We have to get going. It's a long drive to the cabin."

Nodding, Steve took heart in the fact that soon his friend would have made peace with the loss of his wife and child. Steve followed her out the kitchen door and into the Mission's large gathering room. The room was emptying quickly now that the meal had been served and eaten. A few stragglers remained behind to help clean up.

Steve looked at his beautiful wife, then where Faith sat coloring with her grandmother and another woman. His wife and daughter made up the core of his very existence, and he didn't even want to think about losing them.

"You two about ready to head for the cabin?" Irma asked, handing Faith a bright green crayon.

"Yes," Meghan said, brushing a blond curl off Faith's forehead.

"Well, don't worry about us. We'll be fine." She smiled down at her granddaughter who had returned the bright green crayon to the pile in favor of a dark purple one.

Irma had offered to keep Faith for the night and bring her to the cabin first thing in the morning, to give them time to send Frank on the most fantastic vacation he'd ever take.

They stood at the table where Faith was still coloring pictures of Santa and candy canes in imaginative purple and dark blue.

Scooping his daughter off her grandmother's lap, Steve snuggled her neck, inhaling the smell of powder and a trace of the chocolate candy Irma had given her after dinner. "We'll see you in the morning, sweetie." Steve hugged her and kissed both of her rosy cheeks.

He held her out to Meghan, who kissed her daughter and smoothed her hair away from her face. "By the time you get home, all your gifts from Santa will be waiting for you."

"Don't let Daddy open them." Faith's little face was as serious as a traffic jam on the FDR.

"I promise, I won't let him touch one of them." Meghan frowned at Steve. "I told you you can't tease her like that."

He placed Faith back on her grandmother's lap and chucked her playfully under the chin. "I was just teasing you, sweet stuff. I promise to wait for you."

Faith stared at him for a long moment, as if assessing his honesty. Having decided to believe him, she grinned and nodded. "Love you, Daddy and Mommy."

"Love you, too," they said in unison.

Steve ruffled her curls, then took Meghan's arm and led her to the car.

* * *

Frank wasn't there when they got to the cabin, as Meghan had predicted he would be and Steve was certain he wouldn't.

Soon after their arrival, a knock sounded on the door. Steve went to answer it. When he swung the door open, he was surprised to find Frank standing there.

"I thought you wouldn't make it."

Frank leaned against the door frame and stared at him. "I almost didn't. I still don't see what all this is going to accomplish. This cabin may have been the thing that brought you back to life, but I think I'm beyond resurrecting."

Meghan smiled. "Faith and trust, Frank, that's all you need."

Steve had to smile at that. Meghan and he had only recently been made Guides. Already she sounded like Emanuel and Irma. But his delight in his wife's eagerness to do well was short-lived when he saw Frank's doubtful expression.

He looked as if the weight of the world was balanced squarely on his slumped shoulders. Steve had never seen his friend looking this bad. If it was possible, he looked even worse than he had that day in Haverty's when he'd finally let it all out. Lines etched his handsome face, and his mouth drooped. His hair looked as if he'd been combing his fingers through it repeatedly.

Steve took comfort in the fact that in a very little while, his friend would be facing life with a whole new joy, a joy that Steve had found and that he continued to find in his love for Meghan and Faith. Frank didn't know it, but he was about to receive the most precious gift he would ever get. A miracle that would change his life forever.

Without another word, Steve grabbed Frank's coat sleeve and pulled him inside and closed the door behind him. When he would have removed his coat, Steve stopped him. "We're going out again in a minute, so you may as well leave it on."

"Out? Where? I thought I was supposed to spend Christmas Eve here with you."

Meghan smiled at Steve, then at Frank, but said nothing.

Moments later, Meghan, Steve, and Frank trudged through the snow to the top of the hill. Waiting for them was Emanuel. It was, Steve knew, highly unusual for him to come outside the village to meet a new Assignment, but he'd made an exception this time, knowing that Frank would need special handling.

"Who in hell is that?" Franks asked, pointing at the man in the long white robe and beard.

Steve laid a hand on his friend's shoulder. "This is Emanuel. He'll be taking you with him."

"Taking me where?" Frank back away, but Steve held firm to his shoulder.

"To a place the likes of which you have never seen before," Meghan said.

Releasing Frank to pull his wife into his embrace, Steve grinned. "It's where I found Meghan, where my life turned around and I became a whole man again." He kissed her cheek. "I promise if you go with Emanuel, when you return, your troubles will be gone. Isn't it worth trusting him for that?"

Frank hesitated. It was not hard to see that the same logic that had held Steve back from accepting his stay in Renaissance was warring within his friend.

"What about my patients, my job?"

"I've seen to it that Dr. Carlson will take over until you come back." He waited for Frank to think about it. "You have always trusted me as your friend before. Please take my word for it that you will not regret going with Emanuel."

Frank glanced at the robed man and then at Steve and Meghan.

"The choice has to be yours, my boy," Emanuel said softly.

"What the hell? I can't feel any worse than I do now."

Emanuel smiled and ushered a dumfounded, but accepting, Frank into the glen where a thick fog had begun to gather. Meghan and Steve stood locked in each other's arms on the hilltop until the mist swallowed the two men up, and slowly dissipated.

Back at the renovated cabin, Meghan curled into Steve's embrace as they snuggled on the couch before a blazing fire. Soft strains of Christmas music drifted from the stereo, and the smell of pine, along with the smell of apple pies and sugar cookies baking in the oven, and orange and cinnamon potpourri simmering on the mantel filled the house. The tall, redolent spruce in the corner glittered brightly with shiny ornaments and multi-colored lights, its base obliterated behind the stacks of gaily wrapped presents awaiting Faith.

"Will the pies be done by the time Frank gets back?" Steve asked, blowing softly into Meghan's ear.

"Yes."

"How much time do you suppose we have before that happens?" He blew again, this time following it with a kiss.

She grinned up at him. "Time is relative."

Steve rose and took her hand and guided her toward one of the three bedrooms they'd added to the cabin when they took over last year as the Gateway Keepers for Durward.

On the mantel, the interior of a small, green lantern began to fill with a fine white mist, evidence that another miracle had just taken place within the mystical village called Renaissance.

Eye of the Dream

ELIZABETH SINCLAIR

ISBN#1932815686

Jewel Imprint: Amethyst

Paranormal Romance

$6.99

August 2006

little big heart

dolores j. wilson

today . . .

Widowed neurologist Dr. Daniel Lucas has a comatose Jane Doe patient. The only thing he knows about her is that she was badly beaten by someone and left for dead. And that he is strangely, inexplicably drawn to her. So drawn, he allows his young son to sit by the woman's bedside and relate stories of the old west once told to him by his deceased mother.

yesterday . . .

The abandoned wife of an abusive husband, Cassie struggles to maintain the small Montana ranch she and her young son call home. When drifter Daniel Lucas comes by she hires him on, grateful for both his physical labor and the support he lends against a greedy neighbor who wants her land. And although she is still legally bound to the man who deserted her and her son, Cassie finds a   transcendent passion. A doomed passion.

today . . .

Dr. Lucas' skill finally brings his Jane Doe back into the world of the living, and her secrets are revealed. Along with a brutal ex-husband who is coming back to finish the job he started. Is Cassie doomed to suffer the same fate twice? Or is love indeed strong enough to transcend time?

ISBN#1932815414
Jewel Imprint: Amethyst
$6.99
Time-Travel
December 2005

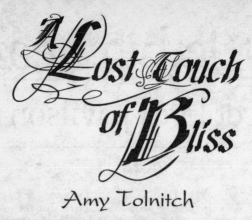

A Lost Touch of Bliss

Amy Tolnitch

Five years ago, Cain Veuxfort, Earl of Hawksdown, followed duty and broke Amice de Monceaux's heart. But now he needs her. Desperately.

For Amice has a very special talent. She is a Spirit Goddess, able to help restless souls move on. And Cain has a very restless ghost he wishes fervently would leave his castle. Anxious to regain order in his chaotic life, Cain offers Amice the one thing he's sure she can't resist; an Italian villa on the sea in exchange for her unique services.

Although Amice's wound is deep, and as fresh and painful as ever, she agrees to help her former lover. Life on the Italian coast will be the start of a new life for her. Perhaps then she will finally be able to put the past behind her as well as an importunate Highland lord who wants nothing less that her hand in marriage. But there is more going on at Castle Falcon's Craig than a simple haunting, and more than one tragic tale of unrequited love. Yet to set things right, for both the living and the dead, Cain must find the courage to shed his mask of indifference, Amice must move beyond her pain to forgive . . . and long dead, star-crossed lovers must lead them all on the path to . . . A Lost Touch of Bliss.

ISBN#1932815260
Jewel Imprint: Amethyst
$6.99
Available Now

R. GARLAND GRAY
PREDESTINED

IN AN ANCIENT REALM OF MAGIC, LOVE HAS A DESTINY OF ITS OWN

Abandoned at birth on the shores of a sacred loch, Bryna never knew her family or true heritage. She exists as a slave in the fortress of a Roman invader, her only friend an ancient, blind Druidess, Derina. Her life is bleak and without hope. And then Derina tells her she must rescue the prisoner in the dungeon.

Tynan lies naked, chained to a cold, stone slab, both body and mind tortured by the Sorcerer, evil ally of the Roman lord. The Sorcerer's purpose? To discover if this one, at last, might by the Dark Chieftain, the fulfiller of prophecy.

Even deeper in the dungeon, trapped by magical enchantment, are the faeries. They await their liberator, the one who has been prophesied.

And the Dark Chieftain awaits a destiny of his own . . . mating with the territorial goddess . . . a union that will set the land, and many lives, aright. First, however, he must gain his freedom and find her . And Bryna is on her way to the dungeon . . .

ISBN#193281552X
Jewel Imprint: Amethyst
$6.99
Available Now